THE LAST SPECIAL THING

ALYSSA K. BURNS

ISBN: 979-8-9940132-0-5

Burns Books Corp

Book Cover by @ tcdesign271 on Instagram

Editing by Meg Rosenthal

Formatting by Sabrina Grimaldi

To my mom for her relentless support and unwavering belief that you should always take the leap of faith.

To the readers, you're the special thing.

CONTENT WARNINGS

- Swearing
- Consensual sex
- Conversation around incarceration
- Illegal drug use in minors
- Underage drinking

CHAPTER ONE

"We did it!" a chorus of private high school graduates shouted, plastic red cups raised high in the air, liquor sloshing along the rims. They gathered in the guest house of someone's mansion, tucked in the hills of San Diego. The parents who purchased the alcohol for the minors were no doubt sipping from their own coupe glasses in the main house. The tennis court that separated the two residences gave a nice illusion of privacy. These were the types of parties that parents felt secure in their decision to fuel teenage intoxication because *they were safe in a house.*

Safe was such a subjective word. Amelia had heard of parties that seemed safe until someone grabbed their keys and wrapped their car around a tree. Or until two classmates who couldn't *really* consent got tangled in each other during the night, then couldn't articulate their choices in the morning. These were all stories exchanged in hushed voices during Monday morning homeroom. Amelia was never at those parties; she was focused on her future.

Whatever misguided intentions other parents had for providing alcohol to their darlings worked in Amelia's favor. Her parents would never support teenage drinking, which left her experience at the mercy of someone else handing her something. Like the animal shelter fundraiser her parents dragged her to, where a young bartender slid her Long Island Iced Teas instead of unsweetened tea. Or when her ex-boyfriend snuck a joint into the movie theater, and they watched the animated film of the year.

Amelia wobbled toward the crystal bowl and ladle on the antique foyer table, which was becoming covered with light rings of condensation. Clearly, her peers didn't know the value of the furniture. Or, equally as likely, they didn't care.

She scooped another helping of the mysterious, peach-colored concoction. While she didn't know what was in it, it worked to dull her senses. In particular, her taste buds. She raised the cup to her raspberry-painted lips. While she had to practically gag the first cup down, far too sugary for her taste, this one went down smooth.

She scanned the room of her peers. None of them would she have considered her friends. However, now that high school was over and her admission to UCLA was secured, she was determined to have a summer full of adventure, and an unsupervised graduation party was the place to start.

She was aware of her sheltered and privileged life. Her dad worked in finance, and her mom occupied her time teaching Pilates. Her older sister, Georgina, was studying abroad in Europe. As for Amelia, she had spent her entire life in dance, singing, and acting classes to prepare for the University of California, Los Angeles School of Theater, Film, and Television. First came L.A., and after would come an Oscar win. With college only a few months away, she could relax. Everything had gone according to plan.

Well, everything except for Weston.

She felt his eyes on the back of her head. The reek of pot tangled with his Dior cologne.

"You sure you need that?" he asked, his voice dripping with judgment.

Amelia twisted her mouth into a devilish smile as she turned around and met the eyes of her ex. He was her height, with blond hair meticulously styled and parted to the left. He wore an ironed navy-blue shirt, paired with straight-leg jeans that had been dry-cleaned. Amelia and Weston had come to the party together, but immediately separated.

"Need?" She swirled the peach liquid in her red cup. "No, definitely not."

Through her fake eyelashes, she looked up at him with a sweet smile. He didn't respond, and she took a large gulp to spite him.

His mouth was straight as his eyes washed over her. He was checking her out, or maybe evaluating her state of intoxication. She was never entirely sure of what he was thinking.

Amelia had carefully selected her outfit: wedge boots, black jeans, and a white blouse with lace trim. Her style was casual, but classy. The goal was always to resemble the display mannequins at Nordstrom.

Today, her dirty blonde hair had been curled, and her makeup had been professionally applied. The extra effort was a decision she would make again — photos from today would hang on the family wall for generations, after all. It was also the reason she was the last to slip into the graduation lineup, taking the final spot.

With hers and Weston's last names as Cox and Collins, respectively, they should have stood next to each other as they had since elementary school. While it was better to be fashionably late than not look perfect, it wasn't the only motivator in her decision. She had walked up to the line and seen Weston's face, scanning the crowd of seniors, fingers tapping against his jeans. She wanted him to wait on her, to wonder where she was. To prove she was somebody he still thought about even after the breakup. When his eyes found her, he scowled, and a satisfied smile had snuck across her lips.

"You're going to hate yourself in the morning." He eyed her manicured hand that gripped her cup.

"Perhaps." She shrugged. "What's it to you?" Her words were sharp like his, but underneath the bite, she was curious how much he still cared.

He had broken up with her three months ago, but they continued to spend time together. Post breakup, he escorted her to prom. He matched his blue tie to her dress. They slow danced, politely mingled, and in the limo on the way home, they disassembled their carefully curated appearance as they fucked on the back seat.

Weston didn't answer the question. Instead, he said, "I'm going to go smoke." It was his vice of choice. A boring one to her. Weston was rigid most of the time, and smoking pot was how he took the edge off. For her, whenever she had indulged with him, she ended up rotting on whatever coach or bed they were in as time slipped by. She preferred to be outside, particularly at the beach, clinging to every moment.

"Enjoy." She took another sip. "I have plenty of other people to celebrate the night with." She smiled mischievously.

He let out a deep sigh. *Good.* She took pleasure in disappointing him. He was the one who decided they should break up before they went to college. She planned for them to be high school sweethearts, as her parents had been. They would do long-distance for a few years, then find a mutually agreed-upon big city to start their post-grad lives together. She would become a famous actress, and he would be the dependable spouse who supported them. At some point, there would be kids —two girls and a boy —and a vacation house on a deep blue lake.

He cut their plans short by fifty years, saying the distance between their schools was *impractical*. He had accepted admission to Cambridge, Massachusetts, across the country.

While Weston initiated the breakup without so much as a tear or a hint of struggle in the decision, he still lingered in her life. In response, Amelia swayed between acting as if they were still together and being so angry about his indifference that she pushed him to feel *something*. Maybe she couldn't make him feel love or regret (she tried), but she worked to evoke the emotions that she could. She found little ways to make him feel jealous, angry, judgmental, or disappointed, as she did tonight. Weston wasn't an emotional person; eliciting a reaction was her way to punish him for the breakup.

Amelia sipped, letting the alcohol burn down her throat and coil in her stomach as he walked down the hallway. As he opened a door to the left, a thin layer of smoke snaked out along with girls giggling.

She turned back to the drinking crowd. It would be her to make him jealous, not the other way around.

Amelia wandered around the party. Other graduates approached her and talked about their college plans. She barely paid attention. The more she drank, the less she could focus.

After another refill, Amelia was chatting with the wide receiver on the football team when she spotted Weston approaching from the corner of the room. She moved her hand up the footballer's bicep, tilted her head back, and laughed. He eyed her with a curious slant to his smile, then spotted Weston.

"Of course." His smile fell, and he removed her hand before stalking away.

Everyone at their small high school knew they had dated for

two years, and no one wanted to get involved in their post-breakup nonsense. She knew staying friends was unorthodox.

"We're going," Weston directed, turning for her to follow.

She crossed her arms over her chest. "I don't want to."

He shifted back to her. "You can find another ride then." He shrugged with indifference, but his reddened, stoned eyes still hung on her, expecting her to obey.

She narrowed her eyes, trying to determine what options she had. After a few seconds, she softened her gaze. While she didn't want Weston to be in control, she also didn't want to be there. Amelia had been starving for excitement, but this party was about as fulfilling as one of her mom's chalky protein bars. They had come together, and they might as well leave together, just like prom.

"Whatever. Take me home," she said curtly. They lived a block apart, which was another reason it was easy for them to remain in a state of limbo.

They Irish goodbyed the party, and Amelia led him to her car. She wordlessly palmed him her keys. Weston's preference to smoke pot instead of drink deemed him the one more fit to drive.

In the passenger seat, she turned on an alternative band, and Weston winced as the screaming blared from the speakers.

"I don't know how you listen to this," he mumbled.

She relaxed into the seat and smiled, pleased at his annoyance. He used the blinker longer than necessary and kept his hands aligned at ten and two. Four songs later, played at an octave only Amelia felt necessary, Weston pulled up into the extended driveway of her house.

As he parked next to the rose bushes, she unbuckled and then pulled the car handle, simultaneously shoving her shoulder against the car door. She stepped out and momentarily lost her footing. She recovered with a practiced curtsey and a Cheshire cat grin.

Weston didn't acknowledge her performance. Her smile fell as he merely locked her car and handed her the keys.

"I loved you," she huffed. That little fact should have been enough to make her forever interesting to him.

"I know." His voice was flat.

She didn't say anything else. Weston had almost no feelings. He had never once told her that he loved her back.

She, on the other hand, had too many, and they often spun in conflicting directions. Especially when alcohol was involved, another reason she rarely drank.

She turned and led the way to the ivy-adorned steel gate that separated the side lawn from her expansive backyard. As she reached up to open the latch, Weston's hand caught hers. He brought a finger to his full lips to shush her, and she gave a slight nod. The last thing she needed was her parents catching her drunk. While they may have assumed she would drink at a graduation party, it wasn't the sort of indiscretion they would address. Problems in the Cox household were swept under the rug, where they were to remain until the end of time.

Weston slid in front of her and carefully pulled it open. He led them along the kitchen pass-through window and around the S-shaped pool, the main feature in the backyard oasis. At the end of the yard sat the granny flat where she lived. She had demanded that her parents let her move into it and out of the main house on her eighteenth birthday back in March. They didn't so much as blink. Just as she struggled to elicit a reaction from Weston, the same was true with her parents. She got what she wanted as long as she stayed on track for UCLA and didn't embarrass them in the community.

She tugged open the sliding door, and they slipped inside. Weston stepped over the pink lacey bra sprawled on the floor, and she wondered if he was recalling the same memory: he had stood behind her and unclasped that bra on the night he had been named valedictorian. It was also the bra she wore when he broke up with her the next day.

Amelia took a seat on the edge of her unmade bed and hunched over. She unzipped her boots and tossed them across the room. At the shift, her bag tumbled to the floor. A tube of strawberry lipstick and her phone spilled onto the pink frayed rug.

As much as she kept up appearances out of the house, her room was the one place she could let her guard down. She burrowed under the king-sized covers, fully clothed.

Weston took a deep breath, set her purse on the dresser, and plugged her phone into the charger on her nightstand.

Exhaustion from the long day of graduation activities marked by shallow smiles and forced conversations, overtook her. The spiked punch didn't do her any favors. She wanted to be comforted with warm arms wrapped around her. Her eyes found Weston.

Her voice was soft. "Can you lie with me?"

His lips twitched upward. It was the first inkling of a smile he had all night. Things were easier when she didn't make him out to be the enemy, but she couldn't help it. She was used to getting her way, and Weston put a wrinkle in that. It was hard to forgive.

Amelia watched him through her heavy eyelids, lashes fluttering open and closed. He diligently unbuttoned his shirt and untied his shoes. He slouched out of his dark jeans and folded them, carefully stacking all of his items on the cream lounge chair in the corner of her room. She tried to stay awake during his seven-step routine for getting ready for bed. In his boxers, he made his way into her bathroom and washed his face, then patted his skin dry with her microfiber towel. After he folded it into a square, he stretched his arms high and then touched his toes. Her eyes closed, but she could still hear the rest of it. He rustled next to her chair to make sure his clothes were stacked perfectly. The quick flick of his fingers texting his mom goodnight. A soft murmur of his mantras that he credited as the reason he was accepted to MIT.

When she finally felt him climb into bed and wrap his arms around her, she didn't even open an eye. Nuzzling against his bare chest, sleep claimed her before she could decide if she got what she wanted or if she would regret letting him stay.

CHAPTER TWO

Amelia opened one eye at a time as the sunlight poured in through her sheer curtains. She was curled on her side, her thick hair covering half her face. She rolled over, a groan escaping her lips as she swatted the space beside her. Empty and cold. Weston must have left and returned home. She wasn't surprised. Sometimes he would stay until she woke. More often, he wouldn't.

She slid her tongue across the cracks of her lips. With a sigh, she pulled back the comforter and slid out of bed. She stripped out of last night's clothes, cursing herself for not changing before she tucked in. Although she mocked Weston about his routines, she was envious of the discipline.

Dragging herself into the bathroom, she sighed at the reflection in the diamond-encrusted mirror in critique. She ran her thumb across her cheek. The powder suffocating her pores would cause a breakout in a few days. She was going to need to form better habits regardless of whether she was drunk or not.

Peeling off the fake eyelashes and setting them aside on the marble countertop, she stole another look in the mirror, wondering how much of her beauty was real and how much was manufactured. She pulled at the edge of her eyebrow, freshly waxed every twelve weeks. The hair on her legs had been lasered off when she was sixteen. Botox was only a few years away.

Turning on the sink, she cupped a handful of cool water and drank, easing the sandpaper feeling in her throat. She needed to start drinking a glass of water before bed. When the water warmed, she splashed it on her face, removing the last remnants of graduation.

There was a knock on the slider, and Amelia turned her head as Lauren walked in. Lauren looked around, and her eyes caught Amelia in the mirror. She did a once-over, lips pursed. She wasn't wrong for it. Amelia looked like shit.

"You drank last night." The disappointment was so heavy in her voice that Amelia's shoulders sagged under the weight.

"Like one cup. I'll be at college in a few months anyway. What do you think I'll be doing there?" She hated that she cared what her parents thought at all. Their praise and critique centered on her appearance and on maintaining their social standing, not who she was as a person.

"We're taking the boat out in an hour. You think you can pull yourself together for that?"

Just as Lauren ignored her comment about going away to college, she ignored the jab.

"Yeah, let me call Madisson and see if she wants to come." Amelia turned off the faucet.

If she were nursing a hangover for the better part of the afternoon, she wanted her best friend to be there as well.

"Great," Lauren said, her eyes sweeping over the room covered in discarded clothes one last time, before she left Amelia to get ready.

———

AT NOON ON THE DOT, Amelia and Madisson laughed in the back of her parents' pontoon boat. The breeze was enough to keep the hangover nausea at bay, and the girls traded stories about what happened after graduation.

"I can't believe you went to Chris' party," Madisson said, eyes wide. "I heard his parents are super weird."

Amelia glanced at her parents on the other side of the boat. Her dad was driving, wearing black sunglasses as he navigated the bay around other vessels. Her mom was skewering mozzarella balls and Roma tomatoes in a crocheted swimsuit cover-up.

Confident they weren't listening, Amelia lowered her voice. "I didn't even notice them. I think they came out once to refill the punch." Then she asked, "What did you and Max do?" She hoped the words came out neutral.

"We drank, probably too much," she giggled. "We mostly just hung out. He had a few friends over. He'll be moving into his own apartment this week." Madisson reached for the tanning sunscreen and squirted a dollop into her palm.

Max was a couple of years older than they were, but it never seemed like it. He hadn't gone to college, lived off his parents, and was content to orbit his life around Madisson. Amelia assumed that his parents paid for the new apartment.

Amelia thought they would break up when Madisson was accepted to college. But instead of going to NYU, as she had always dreamed about, Madisson chose San Diego State University. She said Max was only one of the factors that tipped the scales in SDSU's favor, but Amelia knew he was the determining factor. SDSU kept her in San Diego close to him.

She sighed, a quiet layer of jealousy that Madisson and Max were continuing their relationship when Weston had abandoned her.

"Weston was there?" Madisson asked.

"Always." Amelia reached for the sunscreen. "He was the one to take me home."

"Are you sure that was a good idea?

"What choice did I have? I either stay at the party as people get more drunk and obnoxious, or I go home with my ex. I made the best out of the bad choices." Amelia forced a laugh out.

The boat hit a small wave, and she put a hand against the tan leather backrest to steady herself. "Plus, we didn't even hook up this time."

"Are you over the breakup?" Madisson's words were tentative. She had been there every step of the way as Amelia processed it. She denied it, of course. Weston had a lot of pressure on him, and committing to long distance was hard, apparently. When two weeks passed, and he didn't come crawling back to her, she was so angry she dumped a box of his belongings in his front yard. He texted her later, saying he wanted them to be "civil" and he was "sorry." After that, she cried in Madisson's arms about the future he had ripped from her. Madisson stroked her hair in a way her mother never did and listened.

That was a few months ago.

"I'm over the breakup, but I still like being around him. Is that wrong?"

Madisson shook her head. "No. If you feel okay, then it's okay. I'm just making sure you're not getting hurt."

The girls pulled their designer sunglasses over their eyes and basked like lizards under the warmth of the sun rays. Lying next to Madisson, the boat rocking beneath them, Amelia was ready to savor every bit of the summer.

CHAPTER THREE

A few days after graduation, Amelia, Weston, and Madisson were outside the freshly painted white door of Max's new apartment. The location was unbeatable, right on the main strip of Pacific Beach and five blocks from the water. If this were her place, she'd never be home. She felt a calling to water; it's why she loved being out on her parents' boat. The crash of the waves, the tang of the salt in the air. She resonated with the unpredictability of nature. One moment, the waters would be calm. Next, it would tear down sandcastles. It was beautiful and destructive, and no one judged it for that. It was the same draw that brought her to acting: to remain the same person yet be viewed in a million different ways.

Her feelings about nature were one of the many differences between her and Weston. For their one-month anniversary, she had suggested a beach picnic. He had agreed to it, then spent the entire time complaining about the sand being messy and continually brushing off his pants. By the end of the date, he suggested that they should eat by her pool next time.

Weston liked things to be controlled and orderly. Amelia had told Madisson over the course of their relationship that Weston was the yin to her yang. Sometimes, though, if she was being truly honest, she found he could be a bore. Who doesn't feel the magic of the beach?

Despite their differences, breaking up with him had never crossed her mind. He was well off, and MIT would guarantee him a life of success. He would be the type of man who would take his wife to Tuscany on a Tuesday. She wanted that life, and Weston would be the man who could provide it for her.

She didn't vocalize these thoughts, though, similar to how Madisson never said Max was the reason she gave up New York. The girls had an understanding. They didn't need to say the ugly parts out loud.

"Hey, Babe!" Madisson bounded into the apartment and greeted Max with a long kiss. Weston moved around their embrace in the living room and took a seat on the blue-grey couch. Amelia followed and sat next to him, leaving inches between them. Madisson pulled back from Max after another minute and skipped over to the recliner. She plopped down cross-legged and put her chin on her fist.

"Can Weston get a G, please?" Madisson cooed to Max.

"Yeah, Babe."

Max's eyes were glazed, and his blond hair was buzzed. Tattoos stretched up his pale arms; fresh ones appeared every time Amelia saw him. He bragged about how cheap they were. He got inked in the garage of a friend of a friend. His ears were gauged, and a ring pinched his nose. He was the type of thin associated with self-neglect. Amelia could probably kick his ass in the gym. She smirked.

Madisson was his opposite. Her black hair hung to her belly button in mermaid-like waves. She was short and curvy, with brown doe eyes, long lashes, and smooth lips. Men wanted to help her: pay for her coffee, open her door, give her answers to a midterm. Once, a stranger riding a tandem bike offered her a ride, which she accepted on a whim. Madisson had pride about her assumed helplessness; it was a game to her to see how far men would go for her. Amelia admired her.

In the kitchen, Max scooped marijuana out of a jar, weighed it, then dumped the fuzzy green clumps into a ziplock bag. Max returned to the living room and exchanged the baggie for Weston's twenty-dollar bill.

"Thanks, man." Weston shoved the bag into his jacket pocket.

Madisson reached for the remote and turned on a crime show rerun as Max ducked back into the kitchen.

"Oh! I've seen this one!" Madisson said, clapping her hands together. A smug smile crept up her face as she turned to Weston and Amelia. "You'll never guess who the killer is."

A few minutes later, Max returned with a blue and purple swirl pipe packed with weed.

"Here you go." Madisson leaned out of the recliner to hand Max a Hello Kitty lighter.

"Thanks, Babe."

Amelia tried not to roll her eyes at the incessant "babe" ing, wishing Max would go to college just to add another word to his vocabulary.

Max circled the top of the weed in the pipe, burning it methodically. He pressed his mouth to the hole in the pipe and inhaled, his chest expanding. Puff, puff, then with stoner etiquette, he passed it to Madisson. She inhaled, closed her eyes, then released the skunk smell as if the exhale relaxed her.

Quiet dread wrapped around Amelia, knowing it would be her turn soon.

Amelia had smoked weed on occasion, always with Weston. It wasn't something she understood. Everyone else would crack up laughing at the stupidest things, and she was never in on the joke.

For that reason, when Weston handed her the pipe, she sucked quickly to get it over with. The pipe glowed faintly, but when she opened her mouth, nothing came out. She handed it back to Max, feeling like a fool.

"Only ash left." He looked at her quizzically, and she averted her gaze.

She scooted to Weston, removing the space between them. Resting her cheek against his shirt, she sought an ounce of comfort from him.

Weston neither leaned in nor pushed her off. Instead, his attention drifted to a poster on the wall, a vintage-looking print of a woman in a yellow bodysuit.

"Is that Uma Thurman?" Amelia asked, following his gaze.

"Yep." Max returned with the pipe filled again, and a knot formed in the pit of her stomach. She started planning out her excuse to skip the next round.

"How'd you know that?" Weston tilted his head down toward Amelia. They had never enjoyed the same taste in films.

"Fall Out Boy wrote a song about her, so I looked her up."

"Of course," Weston remarked, deflated. He patted her leg. They also didn't have the same taste in music.

"So, I got a roommate," Max said between hits, his eyes glazed. He let out another mouthful of smoke and then handed the pipe to Madisson.

Amelia evaluated the apartment. There was the couch she and Weston occupied, and the recliner where Madisson was curled. The flat-screen TV dominated nearly the entire wall, perched above an entertainment center cluttered with a few game center consoles. An ashtray that Madisson had made for Max in her ceramics class sat on the coffee table.

Behind them was a compact kitchen, but Max didn't strike

Amelia as the cooking type anyway. There was a bedroom door on either side of the living room, but she had assumed Max would use it as storage. He'd also taken up two bedrooms in his parents' house.

"Who's the roommate?" Amelia asked.

"I found him on social media. We've texted a couple of times." Max grabbed back the pipe from Madisson as she coughed into her elbow.

"Found him how?" Her brows furrowed as she lifted her head from Weston.

"I follow the local pizza shop's Instagram account, and he commented below one of their posts that he wants to move here and can't wait to try a slice." Max shrugged. "Figured I might as well ask if he already had a place. His account looks normal."

She laughed, but Madisson didn't meet her eyes.

"You're not serious?" Amelia asked.

"Why wouldn't I be serious?"

Tension spread across the room as noticeable as the growing stench of weed. She didn't say anything else. Lauren had warned her about killers who met their victims online under the guise of selling a toaster. Even Weston had the decency to look appalled at the admission. Madisson, always quick to diffuse anything uncomfortable, spoke next.

"How about a round of Mario Kart, hmm?" she asked with a tight smile.

"Great idea, Babe." Max moved to the entertainment center and powered on the game system.

When Max's back was turned, Amelia widened her eyes to convey her horror to Madisson. She must have already known about the new roommate's origin. Madisson kept her small smile but gave an incremental shake of her head, warning Amelia to drop it. She would have to ask her about it later.

Max grumbled as he untangled the controllers on the floor.

Amelia hadn't meant to tick him off; it was an honest question. But she and Max found themselves in a push-and-pull dynamic, which affected Madisson more than either of them. Moving in a stranger from the internet, though? He might as well have left Madisson out on the street to befriend the homeless.

Max held a game controller up. Amelia removed herself from Weston, who hadn't embraced her the way she had wanted anyway. Apparently, today would not be one of those days that they pretended like they were still together.

Max untangled the remaining controllers, and Amelia distributed them. Green for Madisson, red for Weston, and she kept the blue one for herself. Once everyone was ready, Max chose the course, and the group started the game.

They played round after round. As the person closest to sober, Amelia won a fair amount. However, Max, even stoned, was undoubtedly the best. The entire afternoon was filled with Nintendo characters racing around in outdated graphics, talking about aliens, and hitting the pipe during breaks.

When the sun finally descended through the living room window, Amelia's chest fell in disappointment. She vowed then and there that she wouldn't let her whole summer be this mundane.

CHAPTER FOUR

Days passed, and Amelia felt no closer to her goal of an incredible summer. Madisson had been holed up at Max's, and as much as Amelia hadn't felt enthralled by her visit there, she missed her friend.

They had spent all four high school years together in at least three classes each semester. They saw each other in every school play. Amelia was on the stage, and Madisson built the sets. Amelia once told Madisson she was too pretty to be behind the scenes. Madisson had taken offense. She shared that there was more to life than beauty alone and was proud to learn *real* skills. They didn't talk for two weeks after that. Finally, they were brought together by mutual apologies over a tub of sherbet ice cream. Besides that incident, which they both worked to forget, this felt like the longest time Amelia had gone without Madisson at her side. This was supposed to be their summer together. Max could have Madisson all to himself after Amelia left for UCLA.

Which is how she found herself back at the apartment that housed her best friend's boyfriend and, apparently, a pizza enthusiast stranger. Weston knocked, with Amelia standing behind. They waited for Madisson's drawn-out "Come in!" before entering.

Amelia's nose crinkled at the state of the apartment. It had only been a few days, but styrofoam take-out containers littered the countertops, and a stack of crusted dishes sat in the sink. She tried not to be judgmental. In fact, her intent for the new year was to stop giving a fuck what other people did. Six months into the year, and she still hadn't mastered the control and emotional peace that letting people do whatever they wanted was supposed to provide her.

Amelia stopped her surveying and instead admired her freshly manicured nails. During her last appointment, she opted for red with glitter tips in celebration of Independence Day, coming later in the week. Amelia loved dressing up, on and off stage.

"Hey, honey." Madisson rushed over and hugged Amelia.

Amelia draped her arms around her friend. "I was thinking we could go have a girls' mission for burritos?"

"I'm down," Max called from the kitchen. At her five-foot stature, Madisson looked up at Amelia. Her arms were still around Amelia's waist, and she squeezed tighter as Amelia sighed. Madisson smiled with her doe eyes. "It'll be fun if we all go, right?"

Amelia pursed her lips but agreed. Like everyone else, she also found it hard to say no to Madisson.

HER PLAN TO bring Weston along turned out to be a good one. It gave the girls a chance to have time to themselves on their walk to get burritos, while Weston and Max strolled a few paces behind them. The guys were deep in conversation about cars, passing a joint Max had brought, their laughter rising between puffs of smoke.

Amelia and Madisson linked arms as they strolled down the sidewalk. Amelia updated Madisson on her sister Georgina, who was supposed to spend only the school year abroad but was extending it to bounce around Europe in the summer.

"I thought she would want to come back and spend the summer with me before I left for college." Amelia rolled her eyes. "But I guess not."

"Well, maybe you'll overlap?" Madisson chirped.

Amelia shrugged and kicked a loose pebble out of her way. It was unlikely. Georgina had never been the stereotypical big sister who gave her guy advice or would listen to her complaints about their parents. With their four-year age gap, Amelia often had the door slammed in her face when she tried to hang out with Georgina and was relentlessly teased for her taste in music.

The group single-filed under the sun-bleached red awning of Valerie's Taco Shop. Max reached the door first and gave it a loud, squeaky push. The familiar sound of sizzling and upbeat Mexican music greeted them. A San Diego perk was that, being only a short distance from the border, all Mexican restaurants were authentic.

At the counter, they each ordered an oversized burrito, and Weston pulled out his card. They never kept track of who paid, or rather, whose parents paid. Weston's parents were the most well-off, but everyone in the group threw a card down occasionally. Between themselves, Madisson and Amelia had worked out what purchases their parents cared about more. Amelia could spend as much as she wanted on her nails, hair, the gym, smoothies, and anything else considered self-enhancement. Madisson's parents preferred that their daughter have cultural experiences, so activities like zoo dates and art exhibits were on her.

Madisson grabbed a handful of red and green salsa while Weston pocketed a fistful of napkins. Walking back to the apartment, Madisson poured a generous amount of red salsa on her carne asada and french fry burrito combo. Amelia unwrapped her Pollo Asada burrito and took a couple of bites, enjoying the beach breeze.

"What the fuck am I going to do when you start class a month before me?" Amelia asked. She wasn't ready for them to be apart.

"Shack up in the dorms with me for a month." Madisson wiped salsa from her lip.

"Yeah, right, Babe. You'll never be at the dorms. You'll be staying with me," Max chimed in from behind them with a stoned smile. He half-jogged up and put his arm around Madisson's shoulder possessively. She leaned into his chest but didn't respond. Amelia knew Madisson had been looking forward to the traditional college experience: sneaking in beers, microwaving quesadillas, and making new friends. None of which included being on a boyfriend's short leash.

Madisson shifted the conversation to Weston. "When do you leave?"

"Also August," he said after he'd finished his next bite.

"So fucking dumb," Amelia scoffed. She was the one itching to leave, and she was the one who would spend another month doing nothing in town. UCLA was the only one out of their colleges that didn't start until September. She didn't want her friends to begin their new lives while hers was on pause.

When they returned to the apartment, Max opened the unlocked door. A guy lounged on the couch playing the Nintendo console. Max had really moved in a roommate based on a social media comment about pizza. She wasn't concerned about Max, but his blatant carelessness irked her. Amelia couldn't wait for Madisson to be at the dorms. It had to be safer than this.

Max reached his fist out. "Glad you're up, man."

The pizza dude from the internet stopped the game and stood to bump Max's fist. He looked at Weston and Amelia.

"I'm Art." He leaned forward and extended a hand. "Art Anderson."

Weston shook it. "Hey, man."

While Weston circled to take a seat at the opposite end of the couch, Amelia couldn't help but stare.

Art had a smile that extended to the edges of his face. His hair was dark brown with sun-kissed ends, hanging a few inches past his shoulders. The band shirt he wore was identical to the one crumpled at the bottom of her dresser.

Turquoise blue eyes, outlined in Navy, held her gaze. It reminded her of the ocean, deep and mesmerizing. While she saw eye to eye with most men, including Weston, Art had at least six inches on her. Her breath caught as she was forced to look up at him, wading into those eyes.

"What's your name?" His voice was gentle.

She swallowed. "Amelia."

"Amelia," he repeated back. She didn't think his smile could grow any wider, but for her, it did.

He reached for her hand and cupped it, his thumb rolling over her knuckles. "It's nice to meet you." Shivers sprinted down her spine.

"You guys want to play something?" Max called from the kitchen. He could have been on another planet as far as Amelia was concerned. In fact, Amelia would prefer him there.

Art let go of her hand, and her shoulders relaxed.

"Yeah, let's play Smash Bros," Art replied to Max. His entire demeanor shifted from electric back to casual. He tucked a strand of hair behind his ear, and Amelia took a seat on the carpet, reclining against the couch.

Her eyes met his again as he distributed the controllers to Max and Weston. He was friendly and good-looking. But so was Ted Bundy.

"I'm going to sit this one out," Madisson announced to no one in particular and curled up on the recliner.

"We'll trade off the next time," Amelia promised Madisson. Madisson waved her off, unbothered.

As Art lowered next to Amelia, her heart jumped.

"Ready to play?" he asked, handing her a controller.

She willed her voice to hold steady. "I'm ready."

His top lip lifted to say more as their knuckles brushed.

"Art, you're first player. You have to pick the course, man," Max cut in, spoiling another moment. She could kill him.

As Art turned his attention to the courses, Amelia wiggled her fingers and then clenched the controller.

When all the characters had been populated onto the video game battlefield, she found her rhythm. As her fingers flicked between the face and shoulder buttons, Yoshi dominated the game.

"Wow," Art said after Amelia landed a combo that sent him flying off the edge of the stage to his virtual death.

"Pretty good for a girl?" Her eyes were trained on the game, but as he shifted beside her, his shoe tapped into hers, and her chest warmed. Neither moved.

"Wasn't going to say that," he chuckled.

The group rotated, taking turns sitting out for the next hour. They laughed and trash-talked until the sun set.

"We should go," Weston said after another loss.

Amelia bit her lip but nodded. She opened the space

between her shoe and Art's and pushed herself up from the floor.

She looked down at him and smiled. He returned it, but remained glued to the carpet.

It wasn't until Weston and Amelia had reached the front door that he found his voice. "Wait."

As he stood, hope swelled in her chest.

"Can I talk to you for a second?" Art asked her.

Weston raised an eyebrow.

"Meet you at the car," she dismissed him with a soft smile.

Once they were outside, Art pushed his hands into the pockets of his cargo shorts. "Are you with that guy?" He nodded toward where Weston had disappeared around the corner.

"No." It was true, and for the first time, it felt good to say.

He stood straighter at her response. "I'd like to see you again."

"I'm Madisson's best friend. You'll see me again." While the words were nonchalant, her heart beat quickened.

"Can I get your number? You know, in case of an emergency."

She held out her hand. He handed her a phone with a crack running down the middle.

She input her number and her name as "Amelia ICE."

He squinted. "ICE?"

"In Case of Emergency," she explained, then caveated. "Although, hopefully, no one finds you passed out somewhere and thinks I'd be the one to help."

"Oh, if I were passed out somewhere," he dipped his head, his voice lower, "you'd definitely be the one I'd want to see."

She swallowed and let the words hang in the night. She had no idea where things went from here, how they had gotten here to begin with. She wanted to kiss him, but that was crazy; she didn't know him. With the adrenaline pumping through her, she had to leave before she did something reckless.

"See you soon," she said.

Then she pivoted before he could respond. Before he could see through her calm, practiced disposition. The intoxicating energy ribboning through them was unlike anything she had known before. Walking away, she felt his gaze, but she didn't look back. You never look back.

CHAPTER FIVE

"Are you sure you don't want to come out on the boat with us today?" Lauren asked, dumping a packet of raw sugar into her coffee.

"No, Madisson has other plans for the 4th of July for us. We're going to the beach, though." Amelia slouched on the stool at the walnut countertop in front of her breakfast. Behind Lauren, the morning sun broke through the kitchen window, casting a light yellow across the original wooden floor.

James strolled into the room, holding an empty coffee cup. "Good morning, ladies."

"Morning, Dad." Amelia took a bite of avocado toast sprinkled with red pepper flakes.

"Amelia was telling me that she wouldn't be joining us today."

"Oh. Okay." He smiled at her and set his cup by the sink. "Lauren, honey, can you make sure to bring that cheese platter? The one with the little nuts?"

"Of course." Lauren rinsed his cup and placed it in the top row of the dishwasher.

Two knocks came in quick succession on the grand front door.

"Ugh," Amelia moaned. "Weston just come in!"

After two years, he still preferred to knock. Setting down her coffee, Lauren made her way to open the door before he could let himself in.

"Weston! So good to see you." Lauren pulled him into a hug.

"You as well, Mrs. Cox," he said, following Lauren into the kitchen.

James perked his head. "You didn't say you'd be with Weston today."

Amelia took another bite of her toast, remaining on the stool.

"Weston, my boy, how are you doing?" James extended his hand.

"Very well, and yourself?" Weston shook it. He moved toward Amelia and put his hand on the chair next to hers.

"Oh, we can't complain on a day like today, now can we?" James asked.

"Certainly not," Weston agreed. As he started to pull out his chair, Amelia shot up.

"We're ready, right?" she asked him through closed teeth. They didn't need to be here any longer for her parents to gush over the man who shattered her heart.

"Oh, yeah."

"Have fun today." Lauren was glowing at the sight of her and Weston. "Don't forget to apply sunscreen. You don't want to be wrinkled by twenty-five."

Amelia gave half a wave, then led Weston to her car.

She palmed him the keys and settled into her passenger seat. She turned on the new alternative music playlist on Spotify.

"New songs today?" Weston asked as he took his usual place in the driver's seat of her car.

"Every week." She pulled up the lyrics and started reciting. Her guilty-pleasure show was "Don't Forget the Lyrics!" She hoped to find her way onto it once she got to L.A.

He let her focus as he pulled the car out of her long driveway, lined with trees, and toward Max's apartment for a Fourth of July party.

San Diego was a military town, home to multiple bases across different branches. As such, the 4th of July was a big deal, no matter where you went in the city. Initially, Amelia assumed she and Madisson would hang out at the Yacht Club with her parents, as they had for the last three years, sneaking vodka into their Cokes and watching the fireworks from the dock, arms slung around each other, blissfully singing along to the radio.

While Amelia had enjoyed their tradition, the way Madisson spoke about the apartment complex party — older guys, excessive alcohol, and beach vibes — swayed Amelia. It was exactly what she had been manifesting for her summer. She invited Weston along, still dancing on the line of together-or-not with him.

When the next song ended, she stole a glance at him. He was focused on the road, slowing as he approached a tight corner. There was a safety in being with Weston that she both appreciated and resented. She liked being cared for, but also wished for more: stolen kisses, darkened hours, exhilaration.

Amelia had grown accustomed to Weston being the driver. She had driven them a handful of times at the beginning of the relationship, and he had sat white-knuckled and pale. Letting him drive was better than his irritated and dramatic response to her driving. There were perks to being chauffeured. Amelia flipped down the visor and pulled out a small compact of glitter from the center console. She dipped her red nail into the silver sparkles and applied them to the crease of her eyelids.

"You look good," Weston said without taking his eyes off the road. Amelia knew she did, but it still felt nice to have his validation. He wasn't one to pay a compliment unless he meant it. She wore a red-and-white striped top with a corset back. It was paired with a navy blue maxi skirt, featuring a high slit that ran up her waxed leg. Accessorizing the outfit, she added dangling star earrings and wedges. Her dirty-blonde hair was pulled into space buns.

For his part, Weston wore a button-down shirt. The left half was blue with white stars, and the right half had red and white horizontal stripes. Throughout their relationship, every dance, every pep rally, every spirit day, one look would confirm that they were together. Amelia may have been the one to reach out to Weston about dressing up for the Fourth of July party, but he enjoyed it as well.

As the beach was the most popular spot to be on a holiday, parking was scarce. Weston found a space a considerable distance from the apartment. Amelia stepped out of the car and put her fingers up as a visor, blocking the direct sunlight. The day was already warm, and she was looking forward to a cold drink.

They talked as they strolled, swapping plans for the week. Amelia had her usual share of workouts, voice lessons, and hopefully, more time with Madisson. Weston had plans to get high and see an animated movie with his friends.

Amelia let her hand brush against his. Their knuckles touched, but he either didn't notice or didn't care. She hated trying to read him, so she crossed her arms as if touching him was never her intent.

"Do you think Max will already be drunk?" Weston asked. Maybe he didn't even notice her casual attempt at holding hands. She shifted her focus to his question, rather than overanalyzing his noncommittal movements. "What time is it?"

"It's-" he started.

"Doesn't matter, yes, he's drunk," she cut off.

Weston laughed, and she smiled at the sound as they stepped into the street to avoid a crowd huddled on the sidewalk. For a split second, she considered pushing the group into the bush, but thought better of it. She was trying to work on her temper. The last time she lost control was during her play finale when her opposing lead forgot his lines. She broke character, eyes narrowed at him. He struggled to find his line, and she repeated his lines to him through clenched teeth.

"That won't work in the real world, Amelia," her stage director warned after the show.

"What the fuck was I supposed to do?" Her voice echoed through the empty theater.

"Help him. Prompt him. Be a partner. Acting is not for the selfish."

"Acting is not for the weak," Amelia snarled. "It's a cruel world. Only the best will make it."

Horror crossed the older woman's face. She said nothing else after that, and Amelia sank into bed that night with an unease she couldn't place.

Amelia and Weston stepped into the courtyard of the apartment complex. Folding white tables were set up for beer pong. An ice chest overflowing with cheap beer sat near a column, and a grill with a propane tank was off to the side. Guests Amelia didn't recognize clustered in groups. She checked her Cartier watch. She was twenty minutes late, but apparently, others would be even later.

As her eyes swept the yard, she noticed Art, standing a full head above everyone else. He carried an armful of beers and set them on the plastic table. He wore a blue striped shirt and black cargo shorts—possibly the most festive he could come up with for the holiday.

She couldn't tear her eyes away. The color of his shirt accentuated his eyes. Bending over the table, he arranged the cups into perfect lines with his firm hands. She had never seen someone so focused on something that would be wrecked within minutes.

He looked up from his cups as she and Weston approached. "You have a car?"

"I do, yeah," Amelia said.

"We gotta go get hot dogs," Art said, straightening up.

"You don't already have hot dogs?" Weston's eyes scanned the setup.

Amelia could have sworn annoyance flashed on Art's face as he gave Weston a fake smile. "No, I don't."

Amelia knew a thing or two about fake smiles.

"I'll get the hot dogs. Can you see if Madisson needs help?" Amelia asked Weston. "I'm sure she's already here." Then added with an empty laugh, "Hell, I'm not sure the last time she even left."

By "help Madisson," Weston would go smoke again with Max, which was fine with her. If there were other guys at the party and Weston wasn't even trying to hold her hand, it would be better if he were high and out of the way.

"She went out to get donuts yesterday," Art offered.

Amelia furrowed her brows. Leaving for a glazed twist hardly counted as actually leaving.

Weston fished her keys out of his pocket and gave them to Amelia. She turned back toward the car, Art pivoting in step with her.

"You're coming with me?" she asked, looking up at him, dark hair falling against his shirt.

"I am." He didn't offer an explanation.

She hmm'd as they started walking. The day was perfect for a holiday, and the sun warmed her exposed skin through the slit in her skirt and along the lines of her corset back. She hoped she wouldn't be murdered by the pizza enthusiast on such a beautiful day. Her mind drifted to Lauren. She was sure her mom would disapprove of her letting a stranger into her car, but there was something about his confidence that drew her in.

He'd been with Max for a few days now. How long would it take living with someone to know if they were psychotic or sane?

"This place is packed," Art observed as they navigated around a tight crowd.

"Oh yes, holidays are one of a kind here." She realized that she had no idea where he was from.

Amelia pushed the key fob twice to unlock the car.

He whistled as her blinkers flashed. "This is yours?"

"Graduation present," Amelia said offhandedly.

He gazed at the white BMW. "Man, all I got was $50 from my grandma." He sauntered in front of her, opening the driver's side door.

"Why, thank you." Her eyes slid up to him as he closed her door. He let himself in on the passenger side. As Amelia pushed the button to start the car, the emo alternative music blasted out of the speakers.

"I'm so sorry." Amelia laughed in embarrassment, reaching over to the speaker knob to turn it down. Before she could move it, Art threw his hand over hers on the volume knob, grinning wickedly as he sang the lyrics.

"You know Pierce the Veil?" Amelia asked, astonished. Most people she knew hated her taste in alternative music.

"Yep, saw them a couple of years ago at a dive bar in L.A."

"What were you, ten?" she teased.

"Fifteen!" He placed his hand over his heart, feigning appalled.

She laughed and turned the volume down when his rendition came to a close.

"So, what's your story?" She flipped on her blinker and turned left at the traffic signal.

"Just moved out here. I grew up a couple of hours to the east. I really wanted to be at the beach."

"Max said he found you on social media," Amelia ventured.

Art laughed. "Yeah, yeah, that's true."

"How do I know you're not a killer?" she said, toeing the line between playful and concerned.

"You don't." He gave a wolf's grin.

Art leaned back, stretching one arm across the seat. "Listen, I grew up with a 10 PM curfew in some bum fucked town. I'm sure you are more dangerous than I am."

She laughed. "I'm killing time between now and when I start at UCLA in the fall."

"No shit," he said, turning toward her. "You're going to Los Angeles?"

"Mhhm. Most of my family has gone there. I was accepted into their School of Theater, Film, and Television," Amelia boasted.

"Damn, L.A. is my plan one day."

"What do you want to do there?"

"Drums, drums, drums."

"Like Travis Barker."

"Like Tommy Lee."

"I'd rather be Kourtney than Pamela."

"Fine, I'll be Travis so you can be Kourtney."

"Thanks." The banter was so easy. She had chalked herself up to being someone difficult to get to know, but maybe it was Weston who made her feel that way.

She navigated the parking lot, swerving around a truck with a few 20-somethings in the back of the bed, sporting China-made USA sunglasses, and pulling drinks from a cooler. She ended up scoring a parking spot near the back of the lot. As expected, it was packed with last-minute shoppers. When she turned the ignition off, Art was already half out of the car. With that saunter, he was over at her side and opened her door again.

"You don't need to do that," she said.

"I was raised to be a gentleman."

It was different from what she was used to. She tried to think back about how Weston had behaved at the start. She couldn't recall if he used to open doors for her, but she didn't think so.

They walked across the black pavement and through the automatic doors into the bright and bustling grocery store. Past the chill of the produce section, they approached the loaves of bread. Art's hand found Amelia's, and he laced their fingers together. It was the most natural thing in the world. Her fingers squeezed between his large ones, making her heart skip a beat.

"Oh yeah?" she asked, looking down. He seemed to do whatever he wanted.

He sang a line about her being able to leave whenever she wanted, then looked expectantly.

"Blink-182." It was an easy one.

This was the summer of adventure after all, and she wasn't ready to leave.

He guided her to the meager selection and picked up a pack of buns with his free hand.

"Why is it always that the hot dogs come in packs of ten, but then buns are in packs of eight?" he asked.

"That is not something I have an insider scoop on," she replied, moving out of the way as a pack of men in red and white striped bandanas barreled down the aisle toward the beer coolers.

"Guess you don't get a bun." He pulled her closer to him protectively and away from the madness. Pressed against his body, she laughed through her nerves and tried to focus on the conversation.

"Me? Why do I have to give up my bun?"

"Fine, fine, I'll get two packs of buns."

"That's wasteful."

"Well, what do you want to do, Princess?'

"Oh, and now I'm a princess?"

"Two packs of both!" He grabbed the buns and led her to the hot dog selection, where he also picked up two packs.

They made their way to the self-checkout aisle, and Art took it upon himself to play cashier and scan the items. There was a flicker of a pause as he didn't reach for his wallet. She slid her phone out of her skirt pocket and tapped it against the screen, paying for the groceries with her parents' American Express card. After he bagged the dogs and buns, they headed back to the car, picking up the conversation.

"What's your favorite hot dog topping?" he asked.

"Ketchup. Is there another answer?"

"Chili cheese. Definitely."

She let out a laugh. "You're disgusting."

When they reached the car this time, she let him open her door.

"Let's take the freeway back, " he suggested.

She obliged, knowing that it would take an extra five minutes. As she approached the on-ramp, he had already connected the Bluetooth to his phone and started playing a band she was unfamiliar with but liked. It was softer, sweeter.

"Who is this?" she asked.

"A Day to Remember," he explained. "I saw them too." He tapped his fingers against his jeans.

"You have pretty good rhythm."

He gave a wicked smile she couldn't understand. "Yeah. I do."

She pushed the gas pedal.

70.

80.

90 MPH.

Art didn't seem concerned as Weston would have. With a tinge of delight, they belted the chorus at the top of their lungs. The adrenaline rush was surreal. Their exit disappeared into the rearview mirror as she intentionally missed it to finish the song. Amelia stole a glance at Art, and he stared back at her, eyes dancing.

Ultimately, she pulled off at a random exit after another duet together.

They had to park too far away again, but Amelia didn't mind the walk back this time.

Art grabbed her as they neared the courtyard entrance. Time stopped as he leaned toward her, and her heart thumped as she tilted her head. He brought his hand to her cheek, and his soft lips met hers. They didn't make out, tongues staying in their respective mouths, but as he kissed her, she longed for more.

When he pulled away, Amelia couldn't help but search those turquoise blue eyes again. He was essentially a *stranger*. What was she doing? And why did she like it so much?

"Ready to party?" he asked.

"Always." The words came out in a faux confidence.

CHAPTER SIX

Top 40 radio played as they reentered the festivities. The courtyard that had been nearly empty when she arrived with Weston was now packed. A group of about twenty people crowded the white folding tables. The onlookers were interested in either the beer pong game or Madisson in her Fourth of July bikini top and white micro shorts. Amelia wasn't sure if Madisson registered the group of girls to the side in low whispers, or if she just didn't care.

Madisson spotted her. "Amelia, this is my third game! I can't keep going!"

Amelia raised her eyebrows. "Stop winning, love."

"You want a drink?" Art asked Amelia, cutting through the noise.

"Yes. What do you have?"

"Who the fuck knows. How do you feel about surprises?"

"You can surprise me." She might as well go all in today. Her life would return to its regular, monotonous cadence tomorrow.

"That's the spirit!" Art squeezed her shoulder, sending a tingle of delight through her.

He walked over to a shirtless neighbor stationed at the grille.

The neighbor wore a backward baseball cap and was holding a spatula. Art dropped off the bag of dogs and buns on the grille ledge, and the neighbor smacked the kitchen utensil against Art's butt. Lifting his eyebrows suggestively, Art laughed. Weston would have *never* let another man swat his butt. He would have been downright offended by the playful gesture. There was a freedom in the exchange. Art was unrestrained by the social norms she had spent her life boxed into.

Weston strutted out of the apartment, brushing past Art. She was relieved that Weston hadn't seen her kissing him. Even though they weren't together, they sometimes were.

Weston strolled over to her. "You want to play a round?" He nodded toward the dueling beer pong table, which had grown an audience. His Ray-Bans covered his freckled face, and, she could assume, his bloodshot eyes.

Amelia slid over to Madisson. "Weston and I have next."

"Thank fucking god."

The table next to Madisson lost first, so Amelia took up her position a few feet to the left of Madisson and Max. Weston was pouring the beer into the collection of red cups when Art came out with her drink.

"What is it?" she asked.

"A punch?" he asked, his left eyebrow raising in skepticism.

"OH! I made a festive punch!" Madisson chimed in.

"What makes it festive?"

"It's red, white, and blue."

Amelia peered into her cup. "It's just blue."

"Ugh. I can fix it. Here, take my spot." Madisson put her hands on Art's hips and pushed him into the vacancy she was leaving. Max nodded at his roommate and new partner.

Setting her punch on the side of the table, Amelia hoped it wouldn't be knocked over. She much preferred a strange punch to cheap beer.

Two shirtless, buff guys with tribal tattoos were on the other side of the long table, starting the game with a dramatized bend in their knees.

"One, two, three, shoot," they said in unison.

They flicked their wrists, and ping pong balls bounced toward the cups. They each made a cup. To some, it was a backyard game. To these guys, it might as well have been a tryout for the NBA. Amelia and Weston traded off turns with their opponents, who clapped for themselves and chest-bumped after they both made the same cup. The most excitement she got out of Weston was a nod of approval when she made a shot.

Amelia's eyes slid to her right as Art made a cup with a light flick of his wrist. He gave her a wink, and her cheeks flushed.

She and Weston had made three cups out of twelve by the time Madisson returned with a Tupperware of strawberries and a canister of whipped cream.

"PAUSE!" Madisson shouted at the table.

The tribal tattoo guys turned into statues.

Madisson plucked a juicy strawberry out and plopped it into Amelia's cup.

A mischievous look crossed her face. "Better open."

Amelia obliged as Madisson sprayed the whipped cream into her mouth. Amelia struggled to swallow, laughing as it overflowed. As she wiped off the extra, she felt eyes on her. While she enjoyed performing, she preferred to be ready for it. Madisson was much more comfortable in spontaneous situations.

"RESUME!" Madisson clapped, dispersing the attention on Amelia.

Madisson stepped up next to Art.

"I made you a cup," he said, extending the ping pong ball.

"Well, aren't you the sweetest?" Madisson asked rhetorically, excusing him from the game as she accepted the ball.

Amelia lost track of where Art went as her game continued. Admittedly, she wasn't good. Weston made some of the shots, but they lost with six cups to drink as the tribal guys pounded their chests, openly threatening whoever challenged them next.

"I'm going to go smoke," Weston announced, downing his loser's cup.

"I'll stay and make sure Madisson doesn't win anymore," Amelia said.

Pleasantly buzzed, she leaned against a pillar, soaking in the summer sun. Madisson and Max started another round as winners, and a breeze brushed her skin.

A shadow came over her, and she deduced it was Art, based on his sheer lanky height.

"You want to have an adventure?" he asked.

"You ask me to go on a lot of adventures for someone who literally just met me."

They have already held hands and kissed. What more could be in store for a second day of knowing someone?

"When I see a good adventure person, I know." His eyes washed over her, and her chest tightened.

She didn't know what kind of adventure he saw in her. Her life was curated with acceptable activities and good enough grades.

"What's in the backpack?" She lifted her chin in its direction.

The frayed black backpack he was wearing had a few band patches on it–Glass Animals, All Time Low, and Taking Back Sunday. His hands gripped the straps, keeping them close.

"Adventure, yes or no?" he pressed.

She glanced back at Madisson.

"Madisson, you're done after this!" she hollered, making her decision. She hadn't been killed by him yet, and the alcohol boosted her confidence.

Madisson gave a thumbs up, then pivoted back to the game.

"I've got her," Max assured.

Amelia didn't believe he had anyone but himself, if that. But, as long as Madisson quit after this round, she would be alright.

"Yes," she told Art and followed him out of the courtyard.

"You don't like Max," he observed.

"I don't know you," she replied in a non-answer.

"You keep saying that. But you're going to know me, Amelia, and you're going to love me."

"You're pretty sure about it."

He shrugged and then nodded.

Amelia let Art lead her down the block. She assumed they were going to the beach, where everyone else was on the holiday. After another block, they spilled into the main road, a sea of red, white, and blue. It was loud, chaotic, and alive. With a tug, Art pulled her into an alley.

He surveyed the area. It was quieter in the strip behind the chain drugstore. He knelt and unzipped the backpack. The bottom was discolored from use. Amelia had traded backpacks for oversized purses in the seventh grade—a new one for each new semester. Art's backpack had to have been worn extensively for years.

He scanned the alley once more before he deemed the area clear, pulling out an assortment of firework packages and laying several on the pavement before him. He picked one out, then tossed the others back in the pack.

"I don't know where you're from exactly, *to the East*, but those aren't legal here."

"Why do you think we're in the alley?" His blue eyes sparkled, and she said nothing else.

Down a few paces, he set the first firework on the ground. Pulling a white lighter from his back pocket, he sparked the flame against the long firework string. As it sizzled, he bolted, grabbing the backpack and Amelia's arm. He yanked them out of the alleyway and against the back of the building. Her heart raced as his chest pressed against hers.

The next flame reached the firework, exploding with a boom and a flurry of white and yellow before dissipating into smoke.

Amelia's eyes widened. "I officially think you're insane."

"I think you're gorgeous."

He kissed her, and she sank into him. Draping her arms around his neck, they kept kissing until her mind spun. The dizziness was more than the assortment of drinks and the sparkle of the fireworks.

He pulled back. "Your turn." He tilted his head toward the backpack of fireworks.

"I don't think so."

"Look, I'll pick a good one for you." He had moved away before she could refuse again and scoured through the backpack.

"This is a Roman Candle." He extended his lighter along with the firework. "Flick, light, then fucking run."

In resignation, she swiped the lighter from his hand, determined not to let him know it was her first time lighting one. Someone else had always lit up for her.

She tugged the edge of her skirt up and squatted. Rubbing her thumb against the gears of the lighter and murmuring a plea, she was grateful when it sparked. The flame danced toward the string, and once it caught, she dashed toward him.

He caught her by the waist and pulled her back to the alley's edge. His fingers tingled against the strip of bare skin her corset revealed. The blue sparks cackled along the pavement, darting in unruly directions.

As it fizzled out, Art turned, placing his hands on the side of her face. He kissed her, stealing the oxygen from her lungs.

"We've been here too long." He pulled away with a devious tint in his eyes. "Let's check out another alley."

Ten fireworks, three alleys, and countless kisses later, they were back at the party.

A pair of girls had taken up Madisson's spot at the table. Amelia scanned the yard for her and instead found Weston. She had forgotten about him, but one look told her that the feeling was not mutual. His eyes darted between her and Art, his lips pushed together.

The unusual jealousy from Weston, tangled with the fireworks between her and Art, propelled Amelia to cloud nine. A perfect feeling that would sour if she stayed there any longer.

CHAPTER SEVEN

Madisson wasn't hard to track down. With a laugh Amelia would recognize anywhere, she found her in the apartment kitchen. She was downing a water bottle, hair frizzing out of the pigtails. Amelia wet her hands in the kitchen sink and patted down Madisson's hair. She rubbed a thumb under her eye to remove the rogue eyeliner.

"There." She admired her quick fix. "How's Weston been?"

She needed to know what she was dealing with. She had made Weston jealous before, but never in a substantial way. He knew she wouldn't have hooked up with the football player at the graduation party. But disappearing with a stranger for who knows how long. Weston could have feelings.

"I don't know," Madisson said, looking around. "I don't think I've seen him?"

"He's out by the beer pong table but looks pissed."

"Where'd you go?"

"Art.... had fireworks?" Amelia leaned against the kitchen counter, resting her elbows behind her.

"Oh my god, that's so fun." Madisson pulled out another water bottle from the fridge. "You'll thank me later."

Amelia drank half of it in one movement, then turned her attention to the living room. Most people were dressed up, and almost everyone had a drink in hand. A circle of people was off to the side of the living room, passing around a bong. Amelia was sure that one guy was asleep as they passed it over his head, unfazed. Every seat on the couch was taken, with giggling girls on laps and dudes lying across the floor.

A few minutes later, Weston found them.

"Let's go," he said, shoving his hands in his jeans. His hair was plastered with sweat from the summer heat.

"I'm not ready to go." Amelia evaluated her nails.

"You haven't even seen the fireworks," Madisson pleaded.

Amelia gave her a grateful look.

"Fine," Weston said with an edge that communicated it was not fine. "We'll stay for the fireworks, then we're going."

After a flash of annoyance at his deciding for them when they would go, she reasoned that they came together. She wouldn't make him find another ride home, especially not with the holiday madness.

For the duration of the party, Weston was there. She could feel him, whether he was next to her or keeping tabs on her from across the room. For a single girl, she had the feeling she was in trouble. Art must have picked up on the energy as he kept his distance the rest of the night. She was dreading having to explain to him why the guy she wasn't dating was weirdly territorial.

When the sun tucked behind the horizon, the night shifted. Scratchy blankets were pulled from the various units in the complex and dragged across the grass. The beer pong champions, with their tribal tattoos, hauled a couch out from their unit —a decision they would regret in the morning when sprinklers soaked the furniture.

"It's time!" Max yelled from atop the folding table, hands up in offering to the sky. He kicked cups from the earlier games of beer pong onto the grass.

"Babe, can you come down?" Madisson asked, her eyes darted from the ground to where he wobbled.

He listened, but as he stepped to get off, his foot slipped on the spilled beer that coated the table.

Madisson raced over to him. He lay, looking up, laughing manically.

"Let's get you inside," Madisson said. She pressed a light kiss to his forehead.

Max pushed himself to his feet, and Art appeared from the shadows. He offered his shoulder as a crutch to help Max get back on his feet.

"I'm going to see the fireworks!" Max insisted, trying to dodge their aid.

The universe did Madisson a solid. A blue explosion boomed overhead.

Madisson sighed in relief as Art hobbled Max over to a plastic chair. Madisson relocated a second chair beside him. They sat together and watched the illuminated sky. Madisson's hand slipped into Max's.

Amelia chewed on the inside of her cheek. She may never understand Madisson's attraction to Max, but Madisson loved him.

Weston moved next to Amelia and reached his arm around her. At his touch, she shrugged him off. It felt wrong; he never loved her in the way Madisson loved Max. She didn't want his feeble attempt at affection tonight. Especially not when she had just been kissing someone else.

"What?" he asked, a smile not reaching his eyes.

"I don't want to right now."

He nodded but said nothing, letting his arms hang limp by his side. It reminded Amelia of when he didn't reach for her hand earlier in the day. A parallel that he would never draw. Likely had no idea of the could-have-been moment from earlier. He had never been observant, certainly not of her.

While fireworks had always enchanted Amelia, the day's activity had caught up with her. She didn't feel as drunk as much as she was depleted from the sun and her adventure with Art. Her shoulders slumped, and during a pause in the fireworks, she turned to Weston.

"Let's go home," she said.

She waved to Madisson. Max was passed out in the chair beside her, head back and mouth open. Madisson gave an apologetic wave back. Art was talking to a couple of other guys near the bear pong table, and she threw him a smile. He wiggled his fingers and raised an eyebrow. The guy beside him nudged his waist, breaking his eye contact.

Amelia and Weston snaked through the crowds, stepping over littered beer cans and red cups strewn around the courtyard. Even after they'd made their way down the block and away from the party, music reverberated in her ears.

"You're good to drive?" Amelia asked.

"Yeah. I mostly smoked."

Once in the passenger seat, Amelia closed her eyes. She must have dozed off, waking as the car slowed to a stop in front of her house.

"You want me to come in?" Weston offered as he stepped out.

"No, I got it. Thanks, though."

They evaluated each other in her driveway, their over-the-top outfits resembling costumes in the late night.

"Goodnight then," Weston said.

"Goodnight," she replied.

He shoved his hands in his pockets and walked toward his house, shoulders hunched forward. It was the right decision.

Amelia made her way through the back gate to her flat. As

soon as she turned on her bedroom light, her parents' light then flicked off. A gentle reminder that someone was always making sure she got home safe. At one point, she had found it overbearing, but tonight, it was comforting. She wondered who would care when she got home, once she was in college —hopefully someone.

CHAPTER EIGHT

A few days later, Amelia slid across the table from Weston at Lilian's Cafe. They could go to only a handful of restaurants without leaving town, and Lilian's was her favorite. She had thought she would be ten minutes late and didn't bother to update Weston. The clock on the wall ticked closer to twenty minutes past the hour, but she didn't care.

Weston's eyes were fixed on the menu, even though he got the same thing every time they came.

"Couldn't bother to shower?" he asked without lifting his eyes.

Amelia's neck prickled with sweat, and the strip of bra underneath her boobs was damp. Her morning pilates had kicked her ass. She swore Lauren took sick pleasure in Amelia trembling through the plank position. Lauren had corrected her three times through it, even though she held straighter than anyone else in class.

"Did you want me to be even later?" she asked.

He didn't give her the satisfaction of a response.

Sitting on one of the green couches, with an elegant chandelier overhead and the sun shining through the arched windows, Amelia felt at home. She ordered an iced vanilla latte with oat milk and the avocado herb sandwich.

"Tell me all about your plans," she prompted Weston after their regular waitress, a southern woman in her thirties, had left for the following table.

Weston sighed and tapped his fingers on the table, trying to decide whether or not she was worthy of a response after she'd made him wait for her.

He must have decided she was.

"I was thinking about joining the chess club. Robotics looks cool, too." His brown eyes lit up as he spoke, his blond hair barely past his eyes.

Amelia had no doubt he would find his niche when he went away. A flutter of sadness filled her stomach. Whatever their friendship was would change when he left. Maybe even disappear. He was good-looking and the most intelligent person she had ever known. He'd find another girl. Her stomach knotted, knowing that she would be replaced.

Amelia took another bite of her breakfast as she tried to think of something else. She did the math on the commute from where she would be at UCLA to San Diego State University to visit Madisson. Two hours max, the way she drove.

Weston ate his chicken wrap and dabbed his lips with a napkin after a bite.

Amelia stirred her latte. When would she ever go to Cambridge?

"Penny for your thoughts?" Weston asked, noticing he'd lost her attention.

"Do you think we will still be friends after you leave?"

"Of course." His brows furrowed.

They hadn't discussed when he reached for her on the Fourth of July. He probably forgot about it. She definitely hadn't told him she'd been talking to Art since the party. Who even knew what it was and what wasn't worth saying? What was worth keeping to herself?

"I'll email you once a week," Weston added, interrupting her thoughts.

He was forever the planner, always wanting his life in a neat, organized box. Which is why Amelia had been sure they were destined to be together. But at some point, he decided she no longer fit into his plans.

Now that she had a taste of what life could be unplanned, with spontaneous fireworks and alley kisses, maybe it was for the best. Perhaps she wasn't a planner like she tried to be with him.

Weston signaled for the server and handed her his parents' card. He had lost her attention again.

———

AMELIA PUSHED inside Art and Max's apartment after her vocal lesson on Thursday, which was far more convenient than the last couple of times she drove to their town from her house up in the hills. For all theater students, it wasn't solely the acting that mattered. You had to be a triple threat–acting, dancing, and singing. Acting was what she loved and what she excelled at. She got by on the dancing because she stayed in shape and had decent rhythm. As for her singing, her parents had paid for vocal lessons for the past four years to make it bearable.

"I'm glad you came," Art said. "Do you want anything to drink?"

"Water with lemon would be great."

They had been texting, and the banter came across as natural through messages as it had in person. A nervousness grew when Art invited her over while Madisson was in

Monterey visiting her cousin. But Madisson promised that Art had seemed friendly so far, and reminded Amelia that she would have Max as a buffer. Amelia bit her tongue. Max was not someone she would count on for anything unless she wanted a poorly drawn tattoo.

Max stood at the kitchen counter with the neighbor who she recognized as the grill master on the Fourth of July.

"Tony," he introduced himself.

"Amelia. Nice to meet you."

She eased down on the couch and twisted her body over the back to watch Art. She wasn't optimistic they had lemon in the house, but, sure enough, he pulled one out of the fridge and grabbed the nearby cutting board. He rolled the lemon with his palm on the board for a moment before reaching for the steak knife to slice into the fruit. He filled a plastic cup of water from the Brita and dropped the slice in.

"You can't bitch about me calling you princess now." He sauntered to her and handed her the cup.

"Fair enough." She sipped the lemon water. "How's your afternoon been?"

"Good, ran some errands."

He sank beside her on the couch and wrapped an arm around her. She had a feeling she wouldn't need to decipher his intentions. He would do what he wanted.

Amelia leaned against him, and he grazed his fingers along her arm, raising goosebumps.

"You're out of your goddam mind," Max said from behind them.

Art and Amelia turned their heads toward him.

"Fuck off. A yeti is far more likely to be real than a Loch Ness monster," Tony responded.

"Yeah, right."

"No, seriously, you can't even see what's deep in the ocean.

People make shit up. A yeti, when people reported they have seen it, they would have to be at a close enough distance."

Max hmped, almost in agreement.

"I'm with Max," Art cut in. "The Loch Ness monster is far more likely."

"You know what, I am right." Max crossed his arms.

"Hey, listen, just because-" Tony started defending.

Amelia nudged Art as the argument restarted, giving a sly smile. He was comfortable making waves.

Ten minutes later, once it was decided that the more believable monster was a yeti, for sure this time, Max made his way into the kitchen. The cabinet doors opened and slammed shut.

He called over his shoulder to Art, "Are we out of liquor again?"

"Guess so." Art turned his head toward Max.

"Alright, Tony, let's take a walk," Max decided.

Tony grunted in response as they headed out.

The door clicked shut behind them, and Amelia mused, "How long do you think they'll be?"

Art grinned as he shifted to be horizontally behind her on the couch. He rested his chin on her shoulder and dragged his fingers along Amelia's stomach underneath her blouse. A sitcom rerun played on the TV as he tested the boundaries. With each movement, her heart raced in anticipation.

Until today, they had kept everything very PG. Well, except for the way his tongue found its way into her mouth as he pressed her against the alley's brick walls. Technically, that was PG, but maybe PG-13.

Against her body's desire, she silently shook her head as his fingers reached the hem of her bra. Weston had been her only experience. As much as she enjoyed being with Art on the Fourth of July and today, she wasn't there yet.

His hand lowered, circling her stomach, his breath against

her ear. She was glad he didn't take her 'no' as meaning she needed to stop altogether. He pulled her closer against him, her ass against the fly of his jeans. As he put his lips against her neck, footsteps approached. Amelia sprang up as Max and Tony flung the door open. The handle thudded against the wall, nicking the paint.

"Ooops," Max chuckled.

Amelia smoothed down her hair as the guys passed her toward the kitchen.

Amelia turned to Art. "Do you want to show me your room?"

While she didn't want to go any further, she wouldn't mind continuing what they were doing in private.

His eyes glanced at his bedroom door.

"Too forward?" she asked, eyes scrunched in surprise, thinking about where his hands had been.

"No, it's not that. Well, come on." He pushed off the couch and extended his hand. Her fingers clasped his, and he led the way to his room.

Inside, Amelia understood his hesitation. There wasn't a bed. There were a few boxes of clothes and a sunset colored drum set, but no bed.

"So the drums are more important than the bed?"

"I mean, I have an air mattress that I get out, but yeah, basically." He combed his fingers through his wavy hair and gave a slanted smile.

Amelia moved to the small stool behind the drums. She spied the sticks between the drums and slid them out. She rubbed her lips together and knocked the sticks around offbeat, eliciting a laugh from Art.

"I'll show you." He gestured for her to stand up.

He snuck around her, sat on the stool, and pulled her onto his lap. With his arms stretched around her, he took the drumsticks and started a ruckus of bangs, chimes, and booms. What began as a joke turned serious as he found a rhythm.

Amelia tapped her fingers against her jeans to match the pattern. She knew it from somewhere.

"*Summer Skin*? Death Cab for Cutie."

"Oh, Amelia, who knew I would find my favorite person when I moved here?"

He stopped playing and wrapped his arms around her. He interlaced his fingers together, holding her against him.

"Do you have a band?" She leaned against his chest.

"Ah, yes. Honey Cat." His breath against her ear sent shivers down her spine.

"Honey Cat? Why?"

"Who remembers? But it sticks with you, right?" He gave a ba-dum-tss with his drumsticks.

She rolled her eyes before kissing his cheek and sliding off his lap.

"Does your band ever play?"

"We're working on getting bookings now. The rest of the guys live in San Diego, which is why I moved out here. Plus, best of all, now I've met you."

"What good fortune you have." She glanced at her watch. It was past eleven.

"I should go." The guilt of her mom waiting up for her seeped in. Lauren was up at 5 AM to start her day and was an advocate of beauty sleep. Even leaving now, Amelia was chipping into Lauren's sleep schedule.

"Wait, let me give you something." He scrambled to his feet and rummaged through one of the clothing boxes. He lifted out a rubber bracelet and handed it to her.

She rubbed her thumb across a logo of a cat licking honey off its hands. "Clever."

"Now you have to come to our first show. You're an official fan."

She liked the sound of that.

He led her out of the apartment and to her car. After two years, Weston and Amelia had slipped into saying their good-byes in their bedrooms.

Instead of getting in, Amelia arched her back against the car. The salty air blew past, and she didn't know if it was from the wind or the proximity to him that raised the goosebumps on her skin. He put his thumb underneath her chin and lifted it.

"I'd like to take you out on a date sometime," he said before kissing her—another perfect, soft kiss.

"I can let you do that." She meant for the words to come out playful, but they were earnest. A date was exactly what she wanted.

He gave her another kiss and opened the door for her. Once she was inside, he outlined a heart on the evening frost on her window. She melted at the gesture.

CHAPTER NINE

When Art wanted something, he made it happen. Whereas Weston would take forever to plan a date, they hardly did more than sit on the couch and watch a movie, or attend the quarterly, obligatory social function, Art planned their date for the following day.

Her morning consisted of a quick coffee with her mom, who relayed that Georgina was visiting a new country (Portugal), then she busted her ass at a boot-camp fitness class. After she got home, sweaty and accomplished, she indulged in a complete girl shower with both a hair and face mask.

In the late afternoon, Amelia barged through the apartment door to find Max on the couch, eyes glazed. His t-shirt had a ketchup stain, and a new tattoo of a PB&J was on his forearm. The bar when Madisson was gone was painfully low.

He didn't seem to notice Amelia's critique of him as he smiled at her, his tongue sliding against his lip ring.

"Ohhhh, Art. Amelia's here," he teased.

Art bounded out of his bedroom and whistled before slinging an arm around her shoulder. For his part, Art was more dressed up than she had seen. However, he wore the same black

Converse. Likely, it was the only pair of shoes he owned. A travesty. She made a mental note to pick him up a more versatile pair the next time she went shopping.

"Ready?" Art asked.

"Always."

They walked out of the apartment, leaving Max to do, well, whatever Max did.

The greatest thing about Art living in a beach town was that there was no shortage of activities.

He pulled her in, his breath tickling her earlobe. "Fucking or friends?" Art started a round of a people-watching game.

His eyes shifted toward a man and a woman outside the 7/11. The woman's arms were crossed, and the man kept fidgeting with his Padres baseball cap.

"For sure fucking. You're not that invested in an argument if you're not getting laid," she reasoned.

"I like the way you think." He kissed the top of her head.

Halfway down to the beach, they stopped at Pizzeria Luigi's. She wasn't surprised by the restaurant choice for their first date. After all, they had only met because he was a pizza enthusiast.

There were a few other customers at the fast-casual shop lined up in front of the display case. She scanned the options, deciding on the Leonardo with pesto sauce instead of marinara. Art chose two slices with bacon and extra ranch on the side.

While Amelia tapped her parents' card, Art picked up two cups for the fountain soda. He pushed the Coke button into his cup.

"Diet, please!" Amelia called to him as she signed Lauren's name on the receipt.

Approaching the table, she caught the glimmer of a flask as Art returned it to his pocket.

His eyes stayed on her with a coy smile as she unwrapped the red straw and punctured the lid.

At the first sip, her eyes widened, confirming what she suspected: he had put alcohol in their drinks.

"You should probably ask people before you do that." Amelia took another sip.

"You don't seem to mind." He leaned back in his chair.

She didn't. She had been craving a summer adventure, not realizing a person could be the adventure.

"Some people may accuse you of being an alcoholic." Amelia sucked the makeshift cocktail through the straw, liking the way the whiskey burned. Madisson, the environmentalist, would have disapproved.

"Some may say I'm always prepared for a good time. Always down, never scared."

She hummed. "There has to be a time when you're scared." She swirled her straw against the chunks of ice.

Balancing on the back two legs of his chair, he folded his arms across his chest. "Fuck no to needles. There has to be a line somewhere, right?"

"Yeah, there should be a line somewhere," she laughed.

"So, where does your experience land?"

"This." She gestured to the cups between them.

"Just drinking?"

"I've smoked pot, but I don't like it," she admitted to him. It was the first time she vocalized the opinion.

"So where's your line?"

Amelia took a bite of her pizza, buying her time to think.

"I guess I wouldn't want to snort anything," she shuddered.

"No cocaine?"

"Nothing up my nose."

"Hmm. Cocaine's an upper. You seem like the type that would like that."

"Please don't give me any cocaine today."

He laughed. "Damn. Left it at home. You'd try hallucinogens?"

"I think so."

"Well, we won't do anything without you agreeing to it."

She put a hand over her mouth and laughed until tears fell. Art glanced around at other customers of the pizza shop who were taking notice of her outburst.

"What's so funny?" His voice dropped, and he leaned closer.

"Oh, I don't know. How, you basically had to tell me that you're not going to force me into anything."

He laughed toward the ceiling, wiping tears from the corner of his eyes.

"No, no. Scout's honor, I'll only do what you're comfortable with." He held up his three middle fingers with his thumb over his pinky nail.

After a few more belly laughs, Amelia regained her composure. She never laughed this hard with anyone aside from Madisson. Her eyes flicked up to him again. Things were so easy.

"Let's get out of here." He shoveled in the last bite of his second slice.

She had eaten half of hers and threw the rest away. Over the years, she had habitually failed to finish a full meal. While her school plays never commented about her weight, she had booked a few commercials, and Lauren made clear what their expectations were. She told Amelia not to give anyone the slightest reason not to hire her. The line between motherly concern and vanity had always been hard to distinguish.

As they reached the boardwalk, Art heeled off his shoes and extended his hand for Amelia's.

They resumed their game.

"Those two." Art pointed to an older woman and a teenage girl, both wearing matching sun hats.

"Russian spies, scheming to take over the world," Amelia answered.

She pointed to a group of guys with rolled-up jeans, gingerly side-stepping clumps of seaweed.

"Poodle trainers. Just won a local competition," Art decided.

She snorted as he gestured to a solo surfer dashing to the waves.

"Trying to find the Loch Ness monster," she teased.

He flashed her a toothy smile.

When the people to watch dwindled, they ventured to an abandoned lifeguard tower, shielding themselves from the boardwalk view. On the perch, their legs dangled. Art edged closer, and her heart fluttered. She reminded herself that she barely knew him, but it felt like a lie.

With her head on his shoulder, they relaxed in comfortable silence, admiring the pink and orange hues of the sunset over the crashing waves.

"There's nothing like a sunset over the ocean. My mom would love this." His words were hardly above a whisper.

"What's your family like?"

His shoulders slumped beneath her.

"My dad left when I was ten. My mom," he wavered. "Well, she did what she could. My brother, Asher, is a few years older than me. Then I have a sister, Aurora."

"Really had a thing for the 'A' names in your family."

"Got room for one more." He wiggled his eyebrows. "You want to be Amelia Anderson?"

A blush crept up her cheeks, and she worked to suppress her smile. "Not today." Then she asked, "Are you close to your siblings?"

"No."

The one-word response didn't deter her. She was also

someone who would keep things surface-level unless pushed. It was good to show people you cared more.

"Why not?" she asked.

His chest fell with a heavy sigh. "Asher was my hero. Then he got mixed up with bad people. He's in jail."

The surfers, no bigger than buoys from their view, bobbed in the sea. Another wave crashed against the shoreline. She wasn't sure what to say. She hadn't been close to people whose lives were so complicated.

"Aurora's pregnant," he said over the waves. "Four or five months."

"And then there's you."

"What do you mean?"

She shifted against the wooden panels beneath her. "Just that they have these circumstances that have mapped out how their lives are going to be. Then there's you- free."

"You think I'm free?" He pulled back in surprise.

"You moved out here all by yourself. You let the band be your only compass. You're not bound by anything." She had UCLA and concrete dreams, for better or for worse.

"Free." He locked eyes with her. "I'm going to write a song about you, Amelia. The girl who showed me I was free. The only chains I have are self-imposed."

She laughed. "Wow, you took that a step further than I did."

He chucked. "I do that." Then added, "What about you?"

"I have an older sister, Georgina. She's currently in Italy."

"Are you close?"

"No." Her lips twitched at the realization that she repeated his answer.

"What about your parents?"

"Lauren and James Cox." She let out a sigh before launching into their resumes. "James is head of accounting in one of those skyrise towers downtown. Lauren teaches pilates in addition to being the yacht club treasurer, flower club member, on the board of the theater company, and I'm sure a bunch of other commitments that she would be offended that I forgot."

"I'm sure they're happy they get to brag about you going to UCLA."

"Honestly, I think they only agreed with my dreams to be a UCLA trained actress, so I'd keep focus on my appearance long enough to get my MRS degree."

"What's that?"

An embarrassed laugh escaped her lips. "MRS, as in Mrs. degree. Basically, go to college to find a husband."

"But that's not why you're going?"

"No. This is my dream. But whatever their reason, does it matter?"

"It matters to me."

His fixed gaze, sincere in its expression, made her heart tremble. It was more vulnerable than she was used to showing. She reached for her drink, but the cup was empty.

"Oh no, guess we will have to drink it straight," he said in mock sadness as he pulled out the flask from his jacket pocket.

Amelia shook her head. "Yeah, I don't think so."

"Then what would you like to do?" He took a swig.

"I think you need to find me another chaser."

"Oh yeah?"

"That's what a gentleman would do."

He took in that information with a bob of his head. "Fair enough, let's go, Princess."

She smirked. She liked that he let her have her way. He didn't argue or try to change her mind.

Art led the way back through the town. They ended up foregoing the chaser and went back to his apartment. Not wanting to push her limit before driving home.

"Do you have time for a movie before you go?" Art asked, reaching for the remote.

She glanced at her watch. "Maybe we could watch part of it and finish it later?"

"Are you making up excuses to see me again?"

"Do I need an excuse?"

"No." Their eyes held, and the electricity between them heightened. When she couldn't take the intensity, she broke contact, pointing to a top ten suggestion on the streaming service. "I've been wanting to see that."

He licked his lips. "Anything else you want?"

Shoving down all the things she could think of that would be far too much, too soon, she replied, "Maybe some water?"

"You got it." He flicked on the film and retreated to the kitchen.

Amelia's phone buzzed, and Weston flashed across the screen. She silenced it and stole a glance over her shoulder at Art. Now was not the time.

Art returned with two cups of ice water with lemon and placed them on the table. As he settled in beside her, she reached under the table for the Christmas crocheted coasters Madisson had made for Max and slipped them under the cups.

She leaned back, resting her head against his chest.

After half an hour, when the on-screen love interests shared their highly anticipated first kiss, her phone alarm sounded, and she groaned.

"Just another reason to see you again," Art reminded her.

He walked her to her car, where they exchanged breathless kisses before he closed her in with another heart drawn on her window.

On the drive home, Amelia played a Spotify playlist Art had created for her: Twin Flames.

CHAPTER TEN

A few days later, Art took Amelia to a dispensary, convinced that the only reason she didn't enjoy weed was that she hadn't *properly* experienced it. She wasn't sure what that meant. She reiterated that she had smoked pot before, but he insisted that she had done it wrong.

In front of the green building, a prominent white warning sign was hung:

21+

No Entry for Minors

The sign reinforced that she and Art, both eighteen, shouldn't have been there. Her chest tightened, but Art forcefully pushed open the door. She quickened her step behind, trusting that he had a plan.

Inside, she choked at the scent. She hated the smell of marijuana in the apartment, but the way it filled the building was overwhelming. Swallowing a cough, she scanned the store. She expected it to be dark and dingy, but it felt sterile with its bright white overhead lighting and glass display cases. R&B music floated throughout.

A middle-aged woman with grey streaked hair stood by the bongs. Or, rather, 'water pipes' was the technical term. An older man with a beer belly was at the checkout counter. A couple of girls, who must have been barely 21, or maybe even younger, like her and Art, giggled while taking selfies in front of an influencer-style green backdrop. She squinted. It wasn't the typical grass background. It was shaped like pot leaves.

Her shoulders eased. Everyone looked so regular. As the beer-belly man exited, a woman in cat-eye glasses walked in and moved to the line for online orders. It was as simple as picking up an everything bagel and butter from her favorite cafe.

Art beelined to the ATM. He explained before they arrived that although weed was legal in California, credit cards were subject to federal law, so the pot shops remained cash-based. The line between legal and illegal, depending on the state and age, was hard to keep up with. Was this right or wrong?

She meandered over to the wall displaying pipes and bubblers in various sizes, shapes, and colors. A handwritten note card accompanied most. She crouched to an opal pipe made of thick glass with fuzzy purple clouds inside. The note-card read:

Tako Glass
$325

Standing back, she folded her arms in examination. While she wouldn't purchase it, she respected an artist with a niche.

Art approached a pretty woman at the checkout counter. Amelia would have bet that the clerk would be an older man with dreadlocks and a tie-dye shirt. The *budtender*, as Art referred to the cashier, wore a thin smile and neutral eyeliner.

Amelia busied herself inspecting a pumpkin-shaped bong as Art pulled out his fake ID and cash. The woman paused, and Amelia's eyes flicked toward them. She swallowed, her chest tightening at the budtender's delay.

"Bummer, you just missed your birthday," the woman finally said, handing the ID back to him and packing up his items in a brown bag. "You get a 25% discount that day."

He laughed and ran a hand through his wavy hair. "Oh man, thanks for the heads up."

Art took his change and shoved the bag in his backpack. It was not what Amelia had expected at all.

Outside on the sidewalk, Amelia's curiosity rose. "Do you get the same thing every time?"

She tucked a piece of loose hair behind her ear.

Art chuckled. "I don't remember what the hell I get from one week to the next." He tightened his grip on the backpack straps. "I tend to go for an Indica-dominated hybrid."

At her puzzled face, he explained, "Indica is a body high. It makes you feel more stoned. Sativa is the other option. It's more in your mind." He tapped the side of his head. "You feel more high than stoned."

Up until now, the terms stoned and high were interchangeable.

Art was still talking, and she strained to absorb the information.

"I enjoy the Sativa-dominant hybrid. But I also want the highest amount of TCH. Not only for the high, but it guarantees that there's not a bunch of other shit in it like pesticides."

"There are pesticides?" Her face twisted in disgust.

"It's a plant," he reminded her.

They turned into a nearby park and took a seat at a picnic table at the far end, tucked between two large oak trees. It was early afternoon, and they were alone.

Art pulled out a tube with a joint inside- a message in a bottle and handed it to her.

She read the disclaimer, "Sativa hybrid. Julius Caesar Triple Burger. Full flower joint."

"It's just marketing." Art whipped out a lighter from his pocket.

He scanned the vacant park, then he ignited the flame, holding it below the edge of the joint. He rotated it in a circle like he was roasting a s'more. As if this was normal, to be out in the middle of summer at a park where children could have been playing and lighting something on fire. Pot was legal in California as long as you were over twenty-one, but she wasn't sure if smoking in public places was also legal.

She wrung her hands together as Art burnt off the last of the paper and reached the weed. He inhaled, passed it to her, then exhaled a moment later.

Amelia inhaled quickly to get it over with, then tried to hand it back to him.

"Princess," he drawled, a smile playing on his lips. "You really haven't smoked before."

"I've done this." Maybe she didn't have the same experience he did, but she did have some.

Art reeled in his enjoyment at her expense. He leaned toward her. His eyes had softened. "Can I give you some advice?"

She met his eyes, knowing he intended to help her.

"Inhale and pause," he instructed. The words 'I know' were on the tip of her tongue, but he cut her off with a raised finger. "Let the smoke sit in your mouth for a minute."

She put the joint to her lips again, inhaling and counting to five. When she opened her mouth, her eyes locked on Art, and the smoke billowed out. A wide smile spread across his face, as if he could tell that his advice worked.

A triumphant smile spread across her face. She handed the joint back, feeling giddy, and the smoke curled into the cloudless blue sky.

They passed it back and forth a few times. Her entire body, from her toes to her fingertips, relaxed. They fell into a comfortable silence, yet she felt his presence more than before. He was right. She hadn't smoked before.

He stood up and extended his hand. "Let's adventure."

She took his hand and smacked her lips together, tasting a fire pit.

She pulled out her phone. Madisson should be home by the time they arrived. But instead of messaging her, she fixated on her thumbs. *Texting was a pretty cool thing she could do. Twenty years ago, people didn't know how to text.*

At least, she didn't think they did.

How long had texting been around? Were pagers considered the first form of texting? What did a pager look like?

Her phone vibrated, but she hadn't been able to text Madisson yet, lost in her thoughts.

WESTON

Where have you been?

Amelia shoved her phone in her jean jacket, which felt like a tent on her. She couldn't think of Weston. She was trying to make sense of the world.

Walking along, she rolled her shoulders.

How often did she go through life without feeling as intensely as she did now? Without noticing how tall the pencil-shaped palm trees were or how wet the puddles looked, mirroring the sky blue above them. What a shame not to notice everything.

They were almost back at the apartment, one block further

to go. Her eyes were dry. While she always made fun of lazy stoner eyes, hers felt too big for her head.

Maybe it wasn't great to feel everything after all. She hated that her eyes were bulging out of her head.

How could anyone love her with her giant bug eyes?

Through the apartment window, Madisson was waiting for them, perched on her knees on the couch. As soon as they made eye contact, she shoved herself off and bounded toward them. She flung the door open, letting it slam into the wall.

"You're back!" Madisson wrapped her arms around Amelia, but Amelia's arms were anchored by her side. She gave a slight nod as Madisson released her.

She couldn't remember how she would have greeted Madisson if she weren't high.

Wait, no, she was stoned.

She tried to remember how Art had distinguished the two.

She crossed to the couch and sank. Instrumental music wafted through the apartment. It must have been something Max put on. Amelia hummed along as she sat on the couch.

She took vocal lessons. Did that improve her humming?

Art slid next to her, his arm draped around her, but it felt unnatural. She dropped further into the couch, the weight of his arm on her shoulders like cinder blocks.

Amelia looked back at Madisson. *Had she even said anything to her?*

"Hi," Amelia squeaked out.

Madisson cocked her head, then her eyes landed on Art. "Oh my god, you got her high." Madisson's hands flew over her mouth in delight.

Art's lips were closed as he nodded up and down, then moved his head back and forth. He rolled his head in a circular motion.

Hunger tugged at the bottom of her stomach. Her chest felt heavy.

Was the weed pulling down her lungs? Was her chest attached to bricks plummeting to the bottom of the Pacific? Nowhere to go but down. Down, down, down, down. That was a Blink-182 song. She wanted to tell Art, but couldn't find the words.

Giving up, she sighed and rested her cheek against his chest as he turned on a show. She couldn't process the graphics. Her thoughts kept pulling her back to the ocean.

When enough time had passed that hunger no longer dominated her belly, and her arms swung freely, she asked Art, "Walk me to my car?"

"Of course."

Crickets chirped along the way to the car, the moon lighting their path.

"So what did you think?" Art asked as they approached the BMW.

The day had been a complete waste. Spending so much time thinking about irrelevant things. What did it matter when texting was invented?

"I don't think I like weed," she said.

"Cool. Are you glad you tried it?"

She grazed her teeth against her bottom lip. "I'm glad I tried it, and I can confidently say that I never want to do it again."

He leaned in and kissed her once.

"I think there's a drug for everyone, maybe you're a hallucinogenic girl."

She laughed and rolled her eyes. "Fuck no to needles is the line."

"Oh fuck no!" Art's laugh reverberated through the evening air.

She pressed a parting kiss to his lips and slid into her car. He drew a heart on her window, then blew a kiss to her and sauntered away.

Amelia turned up the radio and discarded all the thoughts the weed had conjured in her mind. None of it mattered, anyway. Stoned, high, she didn't care–she'd never smoke it again.

CHAPTER ELEVEN

It had been a couple of days since her dispensary experience, and the ease of it was still the strangest part. Lying on her bed in her silk pajamas, she pulled her phone from the charger on the nightstand and checked the time. Still early enough to reach her sister. She tapped the WhatsApp video. It rang a couple of times.

Georgina answered, "Hey, Sis."

"Hey! How's Italy?" Amelia propped the phone up on her pillow. The day was bright on Georgina's end, and she recognized her historic apartment.

"Oh my gosh. The best! Sorry, I couldn't come home sooner." She paused. "Who am I kidding? I'm not sorry. I want to move here one day!"

Amelia stiffened. Their relationship was a predestined obligation, not a friendship. Still, Georgina could shed light on what she had been wondering.

"You went to Amsterdam, didn't you?" Amelia said tentatively.

"Oh yeah, Amsterdam for spring break, Copenhagen for

Christmas break, Paris with this guy Raphael. Did I tell you about him? He brought me home to meet his parents! They were nice and got a good laugh when I asked if we were having escargot for dinner. Apparently, that's not, like, a dinner staple."

"Wait, you have a boyfriend?"

"Oh hell no, who has time for that? I know, the parents would love nothing more than for me to find a nice foreign businessman. Oh well, guess you're their only hope. Mom told me you're still hanging out with Weston. They would plan that wedding tomorrow."

Amelia's head was spinning. This was not why she called. "Okay, back to Amsterdam, drugs are legal there, right?"

"Oh yeah, I'm not sure which ones, but they do have these 'coffee shops'," Georgina used air quotes, "and everyone's high. Also, you can buy a little box of magic mushrooms. It looks adorable, but how wild is that!"

"And everything is safe and legal?"

"Yeah, whatever they sell is kosher. It was a gorgeous city. Everyone was biking over canals. It was a lot nicer than most of the big cities in America." There was a pause on the line. "Why do you ask?"

Amelia's eyes dropped to her nails, a French tip after the Fourth of July to reset her palette. "Oh, I have a friend who's twenty-one, and he was saying how casual dispensaries are. I just didn't know if drugs got a bad rep. If they are fine in Amsterdam, what's the issue in America?"

"Amelia, what's going on?" Georgina's voice dipped, as if she cared.

"I'm asking a question. Just curious about your travels. Is that okay?"

"Yeah, that's fine," Georgia drawled, unconvinced.

"Okay, well, I gotta go. Have some gelato for me," Amelia

plastered a smile on her face and then hung up. So, hallucinogens were approved somewhere in the world. Good enough for her.

She rolled out of bed and looked out her slider door. The pool water glistened under the sunshine. She sent Art a text.

AMELIA

Beach walk today?

ART

Yeah! Swing by around 3? I have band practice and then I need to run some errands.

A few hours later, she approached the complex. Art had his back to the door, a vape cartridge dangling between his fingers. His eyes scanned the courtyard, then a smile spread across his face.

"Hey, stranger," she said, giving him a curious look.

"Hey, you." He took a hit of his vape and then pocketed it.

"Nicotine is terrible for you."

He slung his arm around her. "I'll work on it." His tone was non-committal.

She let him steer her away.

"Are you fucking kidding me?" Madisson screeched on the other side of the door.

Amelia paused, her eyes on the apartment door.

"Trust me, they'll be okay. They do this," Art reassured.

"They do what?"

"They fight, and then they fuck," he said nonchalantly.

Her cheeks grew red, and she forwent any follow-up questions. She knew it happened, but the thought of having sex with Max, who didn't shower half of the time, was disturbing.

They strolled hand in hand down the main strip of road. It was a relatively quiet evening for a party town in the middle of summer. They passed by bars and restaurants where college students were outside vaping, and couples on patios indulged in extravagant towers of tortilla chips drenched with nacho cheese sauce.

The ocean breeze tickled her arms, and Amelia pulled her pink cardigan closer. She almost regretted her choice of jean shorts, but washing sand out of pants was a nightmare.

"Band practice was sick today. Jake, the singer," he reminded, "brought a bunch of new lyrics and they just go there, you know?"

Her phone buzzed, and Weston's name flashed across the screen. She silenced it and put it back. It buzzed again, and she silenced it a second time without looking.

In Weston's defense, she had been uncharacteristically avoiding him. She hadn't seen him since their breakfast at Lillian's, which had been a week and a half ago. They typically saw each other three to four times a week. She didn't know how to tell him about her date with Art, which was the first time she felt like they were completely broken up. Art tucked a strand of dark hair behind his ear. There would no longer be a grey with Weston, she would tell him. Soon.

Art eyed her as she clicked the silence button on her phone for a third time.

She inclined her head toward a large Jenga game on the patio with a couple of girls wobbling out the pieces, attempting to divert his attention.

"There is no way that girl is going to get that piece out," Amelia said. The girl pushed a piece of wood and wiggled it free, instantly destabilizing the entire tower. Wood pieces crashed to the ground and scattered across the patio.

Her friend laughed. "So close!"

"I have to ask about him," Art said, forcing a lighthearted smile.

So he had seen who was calling.

Amelia concentrated on the sidewalk ahead of them. A trash can overflowed on the edge of the pavement, and a squirrel whizzed up to scavenge through it. She had been thinking about how to tell Weston about Art. She hadn't yet considered how to tell Art about Weston. Clearly, he knew something based on them coming and leaving together on the Fourth of July and Amelia's avoidance of Art toward the end of the night when Weston was around.

"What do I need to know?" he pressed.

He stopped walking and waited for her to meet his eyes.

She rolled her shoulders back. How much did she owe Art after a couple of weeks? There didn't feel like a right answer when two weeks felt like two months, so she opted for the whole truth. If Art was who she thought he was, if this was going to go where she wanted it to, he should know.

With a deep breath, Amelia started. "We've known each other since elementary school, but didn't start dating until our Junior year of high school."

Art's eyes were soft as he waited for her to continue.

"I didn't know how similar we were until we started talking about college. He was as passionate about MIT as I was about acting in L.A."

"So the whole time you planned to be across the country from each other?" he clarified.

She tensed. "Well, yeah. But isn't it good that we didn't want to hold each other back from our dreams?"

"Wouldn't it be better to share your dreams?"

She crossed her arms. "We shared our dreams after college. He would move to L.A. or New York, wherever I got my big break. Then we would spend summers in Italy."

"So what ended it?"

She blinked a few times. "He broke up with me the day after

he was announced Valedictorian. He said it was better to end it then and slowly separate than have an abrupt goodbye in the fall. He reasoned himself out of the relationship, which was awful because he knew I loved him."

Art thought that over. "I expect love to be a lot of things. Reasonable has never been a word that comes to mind."

They reached the edge separating the sidewalk from the sand. She wondered what love meant to him. An unreasonable love sounded dreamy.

He knelt to take off his shoes as she kicked off her wedges and hooked her finger between the straps.

"Have you ever been in love?" she asked.

He chuckled, still taking off his shoes. "I mean, you're my first girlfriend, so no."

She pushed her feet into the chill of the sand, enjoying the tingle as the sand engulfed her toes.

"I'm your girlfriend?" She tilted her head.

He stood up. "Aren't you?" His eyes searched hers.

"You never asked me."

A seagull circled overhead, and salty waves crashed behind them as she waited for his response.

"You're my girlfriend." He leaned down and sealed the label with a kiss.

"Not a question, but I'll take it," she teased, pulling back.

There was a lightness in the air as they crossed the sand together, officially a couple.

"Let's race," Art said, then charged toward the water.

"Not fair!" Amelia called after him, breaking into a sprint.

He made it to the water first, and she chalked it up to his gazelle legs. At the edge of the sand and sea, he kicked water onto her bare legs, leaving a trail of goosebumps.

She narrowed her eyes at him as she burst into the shallow water and sprayed him back. He hopped to the side, out of her reach. Tilting her head up, she laughed. Amelia had spent her whole life in a nice, neat package–UCLA-bound, perfect girlfriend, exemplary daughter in Pilates class. With Art, there was an unharnessed burst of freedom.

"Didn't expect you to be a water girl." His eyes washed over her. She reached up to smooth the frizz in her hair. He put his hand gently around her wrist and brought her hand down. He let go.

"You look good the way you are." His comment was light, but it felt heavy in her chest.

"Let's explore," he said, walking along the receding tide.

Amelia could spend her whole summer here with Art and be happy. In fact, that is what she intended to do.

They walked and laughed, soaking up every minute until the red-orange sun started to set.

"Should we turn around?" Amelia asked.

"Sure." Art grabbed Amelia's hand and twirled her in the afterglow of the sunset.

They made their way horizontally away from the tides, back toward the apartment. The stretch of beach had emptied, and stars blinked in the sky one by one. Art stopped walking when they reached the bottom of the dunes.

"What if we sat here for a bit?"

"I can't think of anything better."

Art shrugged off his faded black zip-up jacket and set it on the sand for her. She plopped down on top of it, then smoothed out the lumps underneath.

Her carefully seated position lasted briefly. Art lowered down, placing each knee on either side of her waist. His mouth covered hers, stealing her breath. He took his time kissing her, pulling back intermittently to take her in. He rolled his thumb over her cheek.

"You're the most beautiful girlfriend a guy could have."

She had never felt more desired. As he continued to push his mouth and body against her, she reclined back on her forearms. He balanced on the sand with one hand as the other moved slowly up her blouse.

"Is this okay?" he whispered.

Her throat constricted in anticipation, and she nodded.

His hand moved behind her back and unhooked her bra. For a guy without relationship experience, the ease of the maneuver gave away that he had other expertise.

He leaned her further back until she lay mainly on the jacket, her blouse partially in the sand. His kisses trailed along her neck as he reached for her shorts. Her body tensed, and his thumb waited, pressed against the button of her shorts.

Amelia squeaked out, "Yes," and he continued.

He helped her slide out of her shorts. His cool fingers in the summer evening raised a trail of goosebumps against her upper thigh, and he pulled off her pink thong.

He unbuttoned his shorts and shimmied them down. When he climbed on top of her, her mind was hazy even though she was stone-cold sober. He fished a condom out of the pocket of the jacket and tore the top off with his teeth.

"Do you want to do this?" His voice was low but clear.

If she said no, they would stop and revert to how things were before. He didn't seem like the type of guy who would be mad, which made her only want him more.

"Yes." Her body grew warm as her desire for him intensified. She could barely speak, could hardly breathe, waiting for him.

When he pushed himself into her, and his lips travelled across her body, she didn't think of the public beach or how late it had become. She didn't think about the sand surrounding them. She could only think of bringing them closer and closer together. A moan escaped from her lips, only to be swept up in the crash of the tide.

She learned from movies that the first time is supposed to be special. She hadn't known if losing her virginity to Weston was special until that moment. Now she knew it wasn't. Sex with Art was the most special thing.

He ran his hands through her hair and gently pulled, exposing her neck. He slid his teeth along the skin, and she reached her perfect nails over his back, dragging them over his shoulder. With each thrust into her, her nails dug deeper. Gripping her hip, he pulled her close, his ragged breath against her ear.

They enjoyed each other as long as they could. Until they were panting and the chill of the night overpowered the heat between them. When they finished, Amelia hurried to reach for her underwear, a bashful reddening on her cheeks.

Art cupped her arm. "Wait."

He dragged a finger from her collarbone, between her exposed breasts, nipples perked in the evening chill.

She swallowed.

He pulled away his finger, but she could still feel the lingering touch as his eyes trailed every curve of her body.

"I want to make sure I remember every part of this night."

Her heartbeat raced. She put her hand to his cheek and drew him in for another kiss.

"I'm going to put on my clothes now," she said, leaning her forehead against his.

"If you must." His eyes darkened in yearning.

She gave a coy smile as she grabbed her shorts and shook off the loose sand. Art dressed next to her. He was reaching for the used condom as Amelia shoved her underwear into her shorts pocket. Going commando was better than chaffing due to sandy panties. She tugged on her shorts, then her shirt and cardigan.

"There's sand everywhere," she whined.

The wet spots from their splash fight on her cardigan were now plastered with sand.

Art raised his hands with a devilish look.

"Don't you dare."

He quickly tousled her hair as she shrieked.

"It's going to take a lot of washing to get that out." He didn't sound the least bit sorry.

She swatted him away, and he kissed her.

With Weston, it wasn't that sex felt awkward after, but it didn't bring them closer. It was something they did–usually before or after a movie. Sometimes during, if Amelia was particularly bored by the film Weston had chosen.

Sex with Art was something Amelia wanted again and again. They had connected on a deeper level. It wasn't solely that they had been naked, but it was the way that Art gazed at her like he was committing her to memory. Like she was someone he wanted to know every inch of, inside and out.

She felt the same. He had opened up to her about his family, and he wasn't afraid to ask about Weston. He liked her as much with messed-up hair as he did when she was done up. He saw every part of her and had no reservations. It was that connection that left her desperate for more.

They made their way blissfully back. Past the bars, the patrons, and the moon up high in the sky.

Art walked Amelia past his apartment and continued to her car. She had no idea what time it was, but it had to be late. Later than she should have been out. They reached the car, and Art lingered, brushing his fingers against hers tentatively.

"Would your parents be cool with you spending the night?"

She suppressed a giggle. "My parents aren't the problem."

He thought. "The air mattress?"

"That would be the problem."

"Well, we will revisit that on another day," he mused. "One

day, I'd love to wake up next to you. Make you bacon and pancakes."

"Men and their bacon," she replied, standing on her toes for a kiss. He obliged.

He opened her car door, bid her goodnight, and drew a heart on her window. She loved the growing collection of his fingerprints. A reminder of him every time she left the house.

CHAPTER TWELVE

A few days later, Amelia finally lured Madisson out of the apartment with a promise of matcha and short-bread cookies. She also returned Weston's call and invited him to join. Having the three of them together meant that Amelia could see Weston, stop his incessant calling, and also have a buffer while she figured out how to tell him about her new boyfriend.

In her granny flat, the three sat in a loose circle with a plate of shortbread cookies between them as Amelia distributed their drinks.

"I learned who my dormmates are," Madisson said, taking the cup of matcha and inhaling. "Ugh, this is divine."

Amelia's school was the last one to start, so her roommates were still a mystery. "What are they like?"

"One's a fashion major from Michigan. The other's a graphic design major from Oregon. We have a group chat going."

Weston scoffed. "My roommate is ranked online in Dungeons and Dragons." He brought the paper cup of black coffee to his pale lips and took a sip.

"You're going to need to find friends outside of him. You can't spend your freshman year in some dark room," Amelia said as she nibbled on the shortbread. If it were paired with a scoop of Italian gelato, she would be in heaven. Georgina hadn't reached back out, and neither had she.

"I mean, Weston likes to game on occasion." Madisson took up her role as Swiss. "Maybe Weston could help *him* make friends, too." Her already big eyes widened further with hope.

Weston gave a nod, but didn't continue hypothesizing. Instead, he turned to Amelia. "So where've you been?"

"I've been with Madisson a lot. Sorry."

Madisson averted her eyes, reaching for another shortbread cookie. "Yep. Hey, should we put on a show?"

Amelia pushed herself up and grabbed the remote off the dresser.

"Too busy with Madisson to even answer a text?" Weston's voice remained neutral, but his eyes showed a flicker of doubt.

This was the moment. She should tell him that she has a boyfriend.

"So, I -"

The slider opened, and Lauren was taken aback.

"Oh, hi!" Her eyes lit up. "Glad to see you both here, I know Amelia's been spending her summer with you, Madisson. It's great for you to come here for a change."

Relief flashed on Weston's face, and he offered Lauren a small smile.

"Happy to be here, Mrs. Cox," Madisson stood for a hug. Amelia was pretty sure Madisson hugged her mom more than she did.

"The pool is warmed if anyone wants to take a dip this afternoon," Lauren suggested.

"Yeah, we'll probably do that," Amelia said.

"Well, okay then. Let me know if you need anything."

"Great to see you, Mrs. Cox," Weston said.

Lauren put her hand on her chest. "You're welcome anytime, Weston."

She closed the door and walked toward the main house. When she was out of sight, Amelia snapped her head toward Weston. "Are you serious?"

"It was great to see her. Your mom's really nice."

Amelia tried not to roll her eyes at Lauren and Weston's mutual obsession. Apparently, Lauren had no trouble over-looking that he had broken her daughter's heart, and Weston conveniently forgot all the times that Lauren made her feel like shit about herself.

—

They spent the rest of the afternoon letting the shows run while they envisioned what their college lives would be like, only two months away. Periodically, they would venture to the pool and dip their feet into the salted water. It was warm as Lauren promised.

When the day turned to dusk, Madisson's phone lit up.

"Hello," Madisson drawled, cradling it between her ear and shoulder.

Amelia strained to listen, hearing a man's slow voice.

Max. She shouldn't have been annoyed. She had a full day with Madisson, which hadn't happened since graduation, but she still wasn't ready to say goodbye.

"I'm with Amelia and Weston."

Pause.

"Yeah, Babe, I'll ask them and get back to you."

She hung up after a few minutes of shameless flirting.

"Do you guys want to hang out at Max's?" she asked.

"That's cool." Weston moved off the chair.

Amelia couldn't hear beyond her own heart pounding in her chest. "No."

"Why not?" Weston turned toward her.

Her mind raced with an excuse to avoid Art and Weston at the same place.

"I have plans with my mom," she lied.

Madisson pulled her shoulders back, seemingly realizing the situation she had put them in. "Oh yeah, didn't you have that play together?" Madisson pushed her lips together.

"*Fiddler on the Roof* finished last night," Weston studied her.

Now was not the time for their parents to be on the season pass holders to the same theater.

"There's more than one theater in the world," Amelia said.

"But that's the theater you always go to," Weston pressed. "You hate the community theater." He tilted his head, his face puzzled.

Amelia had been boisterous about her feelings toward the local community theater. She referred to it as lowbrow and commented she'd rather walk on hot coals than go back after a painful rendition of *Hairspray*.

"You're right. I think we already missed the play. Let's go," Amelia conceded.

Weston's eyes searched hers, and then she let her gaze drop. She reached for her keys on the nightstand.

She led them out of her flat and into the backyard, where Lauren was approaching.

"Oh, are you leaving?" She paused by the rose bushes lining the house.

"Yes, mom."

"Great to see you, Mrs. Cox." Weston grinned.

"Of course, I meant what I said about you being welcomed any time."

The group was almost at the ivy-adorned side gate when Lauren called, "Amelia, a minute, please."

Amelia's chest rose, and she turned back. Madisson slipped

past Amelia, and when Weston walked by, he held his palm open. She passed him the keys in a huff.

Lauren's eyes met Amelia's. The woman was unblinking as she waited for Weston and Madisson to be out of sight. The Cox family did not make a scene in front of their guests.

"What can I help you with?" Amelia asked, mouth straight.

"I want you to come to the main house for lunch. You hardly seem to be around this summer."

"I'm here every morning and every night."

"Fine, come for coffee, and we'll talk about your plans for when you go abroad. Georgina said you talked a lot about Amsterdam during your last call, and I'm not sure that's the best place for you." Fucking Georgina.

"Sounds great, Mom. Thanks again for letting us know the pool was warm." Amelia said with her best attempt at sincerity. Right now, all she wanted was to be at the apartment to control the situation between Weston and Art. While Art knew about Weston, she didn't want to blindside Weston about Art.

She flashed a practiced smile. "I'll be home by eleven."

Lauren nodded, seemingly satisfied.

Shuffling down the path around the house, Amelia tried to devise a plan.

She still didn't have one when she reached the car.

"What was that about?" Weston asked.

"She wants me to have coffee with her tomorrow."

She remained quiet the rest of the drive, running dozens of scenarios in her mind: reintroduce Weston to Art, her boyfriend, as soon as they arrived. Text Art and tell him she needs more time to tell Weston they're dating. Encourage Weston to get so high that he would forget that he and Amelia were ever involved.

By the time Weston pulled up to the apartment complex, she

still didn't have any idea how to introduce her ex-boyfriend to her new one.

CHAPTER THIRTEEN

Art was on the phone, a few feet from the apartment door, when Weston, Madisson, and Amelia approached. She gave him a casual wave, and he nodded back at her before dropping his head and speaking into the phone.

It was Amelia's good fortune that the reintroduction was postponed

Not even two steps into the apartment, Max picked Madisson up in a hug. She wrapped her legs around his small waist. There was a new tattoo of a fork and spoon holding hands on his forearm. It was no wonder Madisson never left him alone for long.

She moved to the couch, blocking out the sound of sloppy kissing behind her. Weston took up the space on the far end of the couch from Amelia.

Out of the living room window, a guy she didn't recognize approached Art. They locked hands and then pulled each other into a dude hug.

Madisson plopped herself on the couch between Amelia and Weston. She stretched out her legs and her arms, letting out a squeak, exhausted from a day of alternating bingeing TV and basking in the sun rays by the pool.

The apartment door opened, and laughter from the new dude and Art exploded.

"This is Bryan, my friend from home," Art introduced, clapping Bryan's shoulder with another laugh.

Bryan held a case of beer in each hand. He was a few inches shorter than Art, which was typical for most people. He had a strong jaw, a well-kept mustache, and a buzz cut. He wore a black tank top, showing off his large muscles. Amelia catalogued him, definitely military.

"Are we having a party?" Amelia asked.

"Art and I like to see who can finish more beers in a case first," Bryan replied, pulling up one of the Coors cases.

"This one is a housewarming present," Bryan said, lifting the second one toward Max.

"Thanks, man." Max grinned and took the case, setting it on the table behind him.

"The two of you split a case?" Amelia clarified as Max handed her a can and then reached one out to Weston.

"It's more about the race to finish than the split," Art said with a devious tint in his eyes.

It was the same look he had given her on the beach. A small smile crossed her lips as she recalled their last night together, the tiny sand particles and cold breeze in sensitive places. Art's eyes hung on her, as if he could read her mind.

"Ready?" Max asked from behind the couch, breaking their unspoken conversation.

"Yes," Madisson said.

Amelia started ceremoniously, raising her beer as she recited her portion of the chant. "Here's to you, and here's to me."

"Best of friends may we ever be." Madisson raised hers to touch Amelia's.

"But if we should disagree." Weston raised his to touch both of theirs.

"Then to hell with you, and here's to me!" Max concluded with a Joker's smile as he tapped the beers, and they all drank.

Art and Bryan exchanged a look, then tapped their cans and chugged.

When Max inclined his head toward his room, Weston pressed himself off the couch and followed Max, likely to pack the bong. Worry creased Madisson's face. When Max mixed substances, he could get destructive, like on the Fourth of July. There was also Madisson's eighteenth birthday party, when he punched a classmate who put his hand on her thigh.

"It's been hell being back home," Bryan said.

"Where are you from?" Amelia asked.

"Out in Anza," Bryan said. "There's not much to do. But you can make your own fun."

She had grown up in San Diego, but when Art said he lived to the 'East', he wasn't being unreasonably vague. The furthest east she had ever been was to Julian, and that was because Lauren insisted on getting one of the famous apple pies every Thanksgiving to bring to whatever committee she was serving on. Anza was an hour further with nothing around it.

"Like fireworks for fun," Amelia offered.

"Oh yeah, Art has a real fetish for fireworks," Bryan replied with raised eyebrows and a chuckle.

Bryan extended his hand for Art's empty beer can and then headed for the kitchen trash. She turned her attention to Madisson, who had a distant look in her eyes. Patting Madisson's thigh a couple of times, Amelia mouthed, "You okay?"

Madisson's lips curled, and her eyes flicked to the closed bedroom door, and back again, then she shrugged.

Amelia's mouth curled, and she kept her hand on Madisson's thigh.

Bryan returned with new cans of beer for him and Art. He unclipped his carabiner key ring and flipped a house key out like a switchblade. Stabbing the beer can, he dragged the key in a circle to make a coin-sized hole. Art took the key and followed suit.

"Count us in, Princess?" Art asked her.

Her stomach flipped at the nickname, glad Weston was in the other room.

"Three... two.... one!"

Bryan and Art tilted their heads back, mouths pressed against the holes, and popped the tabs. Within seconds, Bryan finished, a fist raised in triumph. Art followed behind him, brushing away beer from his lip.

Max's room opened, a subtle swirl of smoke releasing.

"Art, you guys want in?" Max's voice was gagged as he raised the bong's stem in offering.

Art crushed his can and shot it into the kitchen trash like a basketball. "Nah, man, counterproductive."

Amelia was grateful for the answer, happy she wouldn't have to worry about him the same way Madisson worried about Max.

As Art retrieved a third beer for him and Bryan, Weston took a seat on the couch next to Madisson, and Max dropped onto the recliner.

Madisson glared at him.

"What?" Max asked with a guilty smile.

Madisson didn't answer. She looked away from him and toward Amelia. "Please tell me something?" she asked.

Distract. Deflect. Avoid. Compromise. They were Madisson's go-to strategies.

"Did you hear Reyna hooked up with Brandon?" Amelia asked. She had caught that gossip at the graduation party.

"But he's dating Genieve!" Madisson's hands flew over her mouth.

"Guess not anymore," Amelia said, pleased with the shock value of her information.

"Damn, Reyna always gets what she wants," Madisson said, impressed.

As they were only a month out of high school, Amelia expected the drama to continue until at least the first semester of everyone's college choices. Only a handful of their graduating class weren't attending a four-year university. Some were going abroad, and one was going to rehab. Reyna was in their direct outer circle. While Amelia and Madisson were in front and behind the scenes of the plays, Reyna was a dancer. The troupe would occasionally intersect with the drama and stage students when the script called for it.

"We should see if Reyna wants to hang out," Madisson suggested.

Amelia smiled tightly. Madisson's natural reaction to help those she deemed in need (case in point: Max) was both Amelia's favorite and least favorite thing about her. Amelia believed in natural selection.

"Yeah, probably." She didn't care one way or the other.

After half the beers in the case were gone, and Weston and Max had smoked another round of weed, Art said, "We're going to go to the beach." He put his arm around Bryan with a sway.

Amelia glanced at her watch. Shit. She had decided when she turned eighteen that she didn't have a curfew, and her parents didn't fight her on it. But she had explicitly told Lauren she would be home by eleven. A cold war would be arriving from her mom if she kept this up.

"We'll probably head out," Amelia sighed and stood. Weston rose behind her, eyes glazed.

Madisson gave them each a hug.

"You're going to stay?" Amelia kept her voice low.

"Yeah, we'll just go to sleep. It'll be fine in the morning," Madisson said.

"Call me if you need anything." Amelia knew she wouldn't, but Madisson needed to know she always had another option.

Art held the door open. Bryan walked through first, then Weston. When Amelia moved by, he grabbed her by the waist and gently pushed her against the wall. He hovered in front of her, chin down. He was so damn tall. The air had evaporated from her lungs as he pressed her harder. He bit his lip, enjoying her squirm in anticipation.

After entirely too long, he kissed her. Slow and deliberate.

"Goodnight, Princess," he purred, brushing back a lock of her hair with his thumb.

"Goodnight," she responded weakly.

He turned and half-jogged a few steps to catch up with Bryan. Not even three feet away, he looked over his shoulder and winked at her. A smile rose on her face.

Until she heard Weston. "What the fuck was that?"

CHAPTER FOURTEEN

A foot from the apartment door, Weston's stoned eyes burned into her.

"What the actual fuck was that, Amelia?" he repeated as if it were a plot twist in what used to be their love story.

She took a deep breath, stilling her rising anxiety. It was no longer about her and Weston.

"Art and I are dating." Amelia forced the words out simply. Direct was always best with Weston. He could never pick up on context clues or subtleties.

"That guy?" He nodded to where Art had been. "That's the guy you want to be with?"

She knew what Weston saw–the long hair, clothes that didn't quite fit right, a pair of tattered shoes.

But she also knew what Weston didn't see. Art would open doors for her, draw hearts on her window, and make a playlist before they even had a date. She had known that Weston wasn't an affectionate person and had grown accustomed to that. But it was nice to have romance.

"You don't know him," she stated, strutting past Weston

toward the car. The sun was long gone, and a gust of wind rubbed against her.

Weston laughed behind her. The sound was sharp and out of character, stopping her in the middle of the complex. She spun around.

"What is your problem?" She spat the words out with arms pulled across her chest to protect her from both the cold and whatever verbal attack Weston was preparing for.

"I have no problem. If that's my competition, okay." There was a smile on his face that she wanted to slap off.

"Your competition?" she asked.

"You've been trying to make me jealous since we broke up. Congratulations, you did it." He walked to the middle of the complex courtyard where she had stopped.

"I'm not trying to make you jealous."

"Didn't you want to get back together?"

Silence stretched across the night. "I did."

"Okay, then we can figure it out." He walked past her to the car. It was settled for him.

"You didn't want to do long distance." She dropped her arms to her side and turned to walk in step with him.

"It's not great, but it'll be fine." For him, the conversation had concluded.

"It'll be fine?" she clarified, eyebrows knitting together.

"Sure, we'll see how it goes."

"You want to get back together, right now?"

The conversation spun in a way that Amelia could have never predicted, no matter how many imaginary conversations ran through her mind on the car ride over.

"That's what you want." He put his hand on the driver's side door.

"You think that my kissing another guy means I want to get back together?"

Weston removed his hand and stared at her. "If you weren't kissing him to make me jealous... then what were you doing?"

"We're together. We're dating. I just told you we were dating."

His mouth parted, and his eyes narrowed. "You're not serious."

She was serious, but something in his tone also made her feel crazy. "I'm serious, Weston."

He thought. "Do you want me to say I made a mistake breaking up with you?" He opened the car door. "Fine. It was probably a mistake."

"I don't want you to say that you 'probably' made a mistake." She pressed her fingertips to her forehead.

"Okay, I made a mistake. Definitely. Can we go now? It's almost midnight." There was an unfamiliar plea in his voice, a softness in his eyes that she hadn't seen since the breakup. He granted her the emotion she had fought tooth and nail for, but it was too late. Why couldn't he have recognized what he had when he had it? Why did one kiss with someone else tilt his whole vision of her?

She inhaled and tried to talk to him.

"I can't be with you. I'm with Art."

"What do you even know about this guy?"

"You've never even regretted the breakup until today. That killed me!"

"No one knows you better than me."

They talked at each other without conversing, as they had throughout their relationship. After a few minutes of trading sentences, she shook her head and gave up talking altogether. She glanced down at the curb against the wheel of her car, feeling helpless.

He whispered, "I love you."

Her eyes snapped to him, and her whole body turned to ice. "What did you say?"

He reached for her hands, and she didn't pull away.

"I love you," he repeated tentatively, earnestly.

Tears rolled down her cheeks against her will. It was what she had spent two years waiting for. And now? The first chance she had to move on?

"It's too late." The words were choked, barely above a whisper.

He let go of her hands and tilted his head toward the darkened sky.

All she had wanted was for him to love her, and he would never say it. He threw out the phrase as a life raft–only when he needed to use it. He couldn't love her.

"Can I have my keys?" She opened her palm.

"I can drive," he said gruffly.

"You're high, and you've been drinking. I had half a beer two hours ago. I'm driving my own damn car."

He hesitated, then took them out of his pocket.

Sliding into the driver's seat, she placed her hands on the steering wheel, thankful for the center console as a forced barrier between them.

After he buckled into the passenger seat, she pushed on the gas. His eyes darted between her and the road ahead of them. She had never seen him destabilized.

Speeding down the freeway, her thoughts spun incessantly.

Why does it take one man to make another realize what he has? Why can't good things happen without something bad to even it out?

Off the exit, she followed the winding road, its scattered lighting rising into the hills. By the time she parked in the driveway, Weston was clenching his teeth.

"Just let me stay with you," Weston said with desperation.

His fingers reached out and touched her knuckles on the steering wheel. The feeling sent her hands recoiling. Despite what he proclaimed about always knowing her best, he didn't. He couldn't read her at all.

"No."

"I promise nothing will happen." His eyes fell to the floor. "Let me stay with you one last night."

"You broke up with me." She pushed her door open, exited, then slammed it shut. Not caring if she woke up the whole damn neighborhood.

Weston flinched at the sound. When he got out of the car, he dragged himself over to her. He wrapped his arms around her, her body stiffening under his touch.

If he noticed her tense, he didn't let it deter him. He pressed his forehead against her hair and inhaled.

"Amelia." His voice cracked at her name.

Anger bubbled up in her. She still couldn't shake off her thoughts from earlier - why now? His emotions were not about *her*; they were about *him*. He was losing something. He wasn't getting what he wanted. The situation broke him. It wasn't about her.

She shook her head and shrugged him off.

He looked at her, as if finally experiencing the heartbreak he had inflicted upon her months ago. He didn't know back then what this pain was. But the hurt was etched on his face now, and she wanted nothing more than for him to choke on the love he supposedly felt. She stomped toward her house and didn't turn around.

She navigated through the ivy gate, past the S-shaped pool shimmering in the moonlight, and to her flat. She stepped inside, greeted by a message from Netflix: Are you still watching?

The message was haunting. How had she, Weston, and Madisson been watching a show together that same day? It felt like an eternity ago.

Amelia clicked it off and sat on her bed. She had had one of the happiest days when Art made her his official girlfriend. Now, she wanted to bury herself under her comforter until the fall. She stood up and paced, trying to make sense of the unruly feelings.

Her eyes landed on the line of photos on her dresser. Family photos from tropical vacations, the opening night of her performance as the lead in *Legally Blonde*, and a collage of her and Madisson that Madisson had gifted her for her birthday.

Then there was the photo of her and Weston at Spring Fling, a month before the breakup. She looked great. Admittedly, they both did. His hair was freshly cut, and he wore a cream suit and a forest green bow tie that matched her backless dress.

They had slow danced to Taylor Swift's "Lover" as she mouthed the words to him. He gave her a dopey smile and held her close. She hadn't interpreted his lack of reciprocation in the words as a warning sign at that point. He merely needed more time. She'd been told growing up that she was a handful. She was sure that Weston would get there.

Amelia walked over to the silver frame and picked it up gingerly. Running her thumb along their foolishly happy faces, her resentment about his declaration of love intensified. Amelia hurled the frame against the wall. The glass shattered on impact.

CHAPTER FIFTEEN

"We need booze," Max said to Art and Amelia, who were cozied up on the couch. She was partially on his lap, a finger twirling his moose brown hair.

It had been a few days since she had talked to Weston, although he had reached out. She left his messages on read, wanting him to know that, yes, she had received his messages, but no, she didn't care.

"We'll go." Amelia decided for them, letting her hand fall. They'd been rotting on the couch for too long anyway.

"If you insist." He smiled. Was there anything he wouldn't agree to?

"Do you want me to join?" Madisson called from the kitchen.

Amelia peered over her shoulder as Madisson snapped a fistful of noodles in half and dropped them into the pot of boiling water.

A few sprays of water jumped, and Madisson shot back. "Fuck!"

"Nah, I appreciate you making food." Amelia had never

learned to cook, not even noodles. She'd much rather get out of the house and enjoy the sunlight.

Amelia and Art untangled and waved a quick goodbye.

When they were situated in the car, she reached into the backseat and pulled out a navy blue gift bag, handing it to him while trying to suppress her smile.

"You got me something?" His chin tilted to her.

A coy smile crossed her face as he ripped out the tissue paper, and she pulled out of the parking spot. He grabbed the shoe box and flipped it open.

"Holy shit," he murmured, removing a black skater shoe decorated with skulls and with black laces. "These are insane!"

She pulled onto the main road, glowing at his reaction. "You're welcome." Then asked, "Where are we going?"

He swapped his old shoes for the new ones. "What are the choices?"

She took his request literally, naming stores as she cruised by.

"Burger King?" she joked.

"You think Burger King has hard liquor?"

"Community church?" She smiled sweetly.

"Oh yeah, they have tons of liquor." He said deadpanned. Her smile grew at their new game.

"Walgreens, Corner Liquor Store, Albertsons, Ralphs," she rattled off as they approached a shopping center.

"Ralphs!"

She was surprised he didn't choose Corner Liquor Store, but the thought was fleeting. She darted into the next lane, cutting off a blue truck in the process. They honked, and she waved her manicured hand in apology.

"Pull up right here," Art instructed as they turned into the parking lot.

She stopped a little before the store entrance at the walkway.

"I won't be long." He hopped out of the car, and she scrolled her phone, searching for an album to play for him.

Less than five minutes later, he was in the rearview mirror. His hair blowing as he sprinted toward her, his fingers in the air, gesturing for her to drive away.

She reached over and popped the door open for him. Sliding into the seat, he slammed the door closed, and she pressed her foot on the gas.

"The alarm went off!" His blue eyes bulged.

"What?" Her eyes flicked to him, then back to the road ahead of them. There was a bump as her car zoomed over the curb, and she merged back onto the main street. Full trees lining the center divider blurred by.

"It's okay, I got it." He pulled out the top of the bottle of Plymouth Gin from his oversized jacket and raised his eyebrows at her. A vindictive smile widened.

"You might want to get on the freeway," he recommended.

"You can't be serious!" She yelled between laughs. "Buckle your seatbelt."

"You're an accomplice, a felon, and you're bitching about my seatbelt?" An amused smile on his face.

"Yes."

He buckled, then turned in his seat, peering over his shoulder. Deeming the coast clear, his shoulders relaxed, and he kicked up his new shoes on the dashboard. "These babies passed their first test!"

It was nice to be out of the apartment and on an adventure together, even if it was ripping off a grocery store. She shrugged off her conscience as she stole another glance at him. He caught her eye, and his smile didn't falter. Adventure in a bottle, and he was hers. They were each others.

She did as he instructed and merged onto the freeway as a precaution.

For all his drama—running and signaling to her, nothing actually happened. There were no flashing lights, no security guard panting after him. She checked the rearview twice on the freeway to be sure. Nothing happened at all.

Amelia pressed her tongue behind her teeth. "This wasn't your first time."

"It was my first time with you, Princess."

When he smiled, she melted.

"Here, I think you'll like this." She turned up an MGK song.

He took it in and found the rhythm tapping against his knee. He squinted as he beat. "Yeah, this is good. You have quite the ear, Amelia."

They cruised the rest of the way back in contentment.

When they returned, Art bounded for the kitchen. Madisson had vacated the area, sitting on the couch with Max. Four bowls of spaghetti were set on the kitchen table, a mismatched fork and a paper napkin next to each.

Amelia plopped on the arm of the couch nearest Madisson and watched Art as he made four gin and tonics, garnished with a lime, then distributed them.

"We are celebrating today." Art raised his glass.

"Because the cashiers at Ralph's don't think you're worth the chase?" Amelia teased.

"Well, yes. But no. I got a job as a dishwasher."

They clinked their glasses together and took a sip.

"You waited all day to tell me?" Amelia asked in disbelief as she found a seat at the table.

"I wanted it to be a moment!" Art gestured grandly.

Madisson clapped. "Oh, that's amazing!"

"Nice, Bro," Max added.

Madisson took another sip of her drink as she pulled out her chair, letting it scrape against the linoleum floor. "Well, I think that's great."

"It's temporary, of course. Until I find something better." Art took the seat next to Amelia.

She put her palm against his cheek. "I'm proud of you."

His eyes left hers as a blush crept up his cheeks.

"Dig in!" Madisson raised her fork.

It felt more like a family dinner than Amelia had had in months.

CHAPTER SIXTEEN

During Amelia's Tuesday morning vocal lesson, she practiced the Alexander Technique, focusing on balance and posture. Coach Patricia circled her like a shark. The woman had curly red hair and a freckled, pudgy face with deep creases. Amelia had always been curious about how old she was. Coach Patricia highlighted her career on Broadway, notably a two-year stint in "Annie," but Amelia knew better than to ask how long ago that was.

"Again." Patricia snapped.

She took a deep breath and sang "Matchmaker" from Fiddler on the Roof. Straightening her back, her voice filled the room. Coach Patricia was the only person in Amelia's life to whom she never spoke back. While Amelia had never been physically harmed in her life, if she had to guess one person who would slap her without thinking twice, it would be Coach.

The woman eyed her carefully.

Amelia belted the lyrics, expanding her entire chest. When her rendition came to a close, Coach Patricia stopped in front of her.

With a straight face, she remarked, "That was good."

Amelia's eyes grew wide. "Acceptable" was the highest compliment she had earned in the four years she had been at the studio.

"You mean it?" Amelia's eyes widened.

Patricia gave a nod so slight that Amelia wasn't convinced she saw it.

"See you next week," Coach Patricia said, dismissing her.

Amelia practically skipped to her car. She had always taken being fit seriously, knowing it would improve other areas of her life. Her singing progress correlated with the time she spent in her mom's pilates class, strengthening her core.

Riding the high from Coach's compliment, she wanted to stay feeling great the way she knew how—more endorphins.

At the apartment door, with a bag slung over her shoulder, she rapped three times.

Max opened the door, with messy hair and droopy eyes. "Amelia?"

She stepped inside. "As I live and breathe," she sang.

He rubbed an eye as she slipped past him and eased open the door to Art's bedroom. He lay stomach-down on the air mattress in a pair of blue checkered boxers. Closing the door behind her, she couldn't help comparing her relationship with Art to the one with Weston. She wouldn't have dared to go to his house uninvited.

Taking a deep breath in the darkness, she tempered her excitement to match the quiet. She set down her bag by the door.

"Art?" she said, rubbing his shoulder.

He rolled over and did a double-take in surprise.

"Amelia," he murmured, a smile playing on his lips.

"I had an idea for the morning," she said.

He reached out for her hand. "Tell me more."

She smiled back, feeling confident in her decision to come.

He accepted her as she was. "I want you to come to my gym with me."

He chuckled. "Sure thing, Princess." He yanked her hand, and she fell onto the mattress with a light thud. She giggled, their faces inches apart.

As he put his hand on her cheek, her body tingled. Kissing her, he pushed himself up and had a hand on either side of her.

"Wait." She giggled. "Class is in forty-five minutes."

"We will do this after." The authority in his voice made her almost second-guess her plans for the day. She nodded; he would sense the hesitation if she spoke.

"Okay, let's do it." He kissed her again, removing himself from the bed. She swung her legs off the bed, picked up her bag, and took it into the shared bathroom, where she changed into her workout clothes.

Forty minutes later, they arrived at the gym.

"I'm not sure you're ready for this," Amelia teased as she evaluated him. He wore loose gym shorts, an A Day to Remember band tee, and his new shoes.

"Oh, you think you'll do better than me?" he asked, resting a hand on his heart in mock offense.

"Yes." Her dirty blonde hair was pulled back into a high ponytail, a few strands left out intentionally to frame her face. Her Nike shoes were pure white. She had a new pair waiting on her bed from Lauren every six months. After all, a good pair of shoes was ready to be retired after 400 miles.

"I'm sure I can handle your pretty little gym," he said.

Amelia reveled in the knowledge that he had no idea what he was getting into with her nationally recognized gym. This franchise location was run by the same owners as the Pilates studio where Lauren coached.

She turned off the car as Art pulled a baggie out of his shorts with blue pills. "Want one?"

Amelia furrowed her brows. "Excedrin?"

"No, Adderall. It'll make you feel like Superman."

Her nose crinkled. "Isn't this for kids with ADD?"

Art smiled. "I was a kid with ADHD. Now I'm a guy with Adderall."

She held out her hand for the pill and then washed it down with her water, curious about the effects. Aside from pain medication, used exclusively as prescribed, she had never ventured into recreational pills. She stuck her tongue out to show him it was gone. He took one himself, stuck his tongue out back at her, then put the baggie into her center console.

"Let's go, Princess. You're going to tear it up."

"I always tear it up." With or without Adderall, she thrived in the gym.

Amelia checked them in with the college-aged receptionist and used her guest pass on Art. Under the dim lights, they headed to the treadmills. Techno music reverberated off the floor beneath them.

"This is the strangest gym." Art nodded in approval, eyes scanning the space. Rows of weights were next to the wall of mirrors. Mats and adjustable benches were lined in front of the treadmills.

"Best boot camp in the country," Amelia quipped.

It was packed for a midday class. The clientele consisted of late-night bartenders, foodie bloggers, and influencers without a niche—the sort of people who walked around with giant headphones and turned their noses up at AirPods. Most were dressed like Amelia with workout sets and luxury shoes. Amelia's eyes drifted to Art, who stood out. His being there, out of his comfort zone, meant a lot to her.

Amelia stepped up onto a treadmill next to Carlos, a peppy regular, who had already started a jog to ease into class. He craned his neck around her as Art took the treadmill on her other side.

"Bravo," he said to Amelia after a heavy scan of Art.

She rested her hand against her chest and mouthed "Thank you."

She had seen the guys Carlos had brought to the gym before. If there was anyone whose taste she trusted, it was his.

The instructor, a freckled brunette with no stomach fat and a round butt, called out the workout. "Incline 5, speed 3!"

Art's expression was more panicked than when he had stolen the liquor. She reached over to his treadmill screen and toggled his incline and speed, then adjusted her own.

She hadn't known what she expected the Adderall to feel like, but as her feet slammed against the black belt, her performance felt different. Heightened. Her heart raced, urging her to push harder. With another tap on the machine, she increased her speed beyond the instruction, feeling unstoppable.

"Bring it back down to a jog!" the instructor hollered after ten minutes.

Carlos eased his pace back down. On her other side, Art had halted his machine altogether. He gripped the treadmill's railing, his head hung low as he panted.

Amelia slowed, her legs trembling, but kept the jog pace. Despite the slight shake, she wanted to hop off the treadmill and run a mile around the block to prove she could. The sound of her shoes pounding and techno thumping was exhilarating.

Art restarted the treadmill, but kept the speed at a walking pace. He wasn't on her same level. It was as if the Adderall channeled what they were already capable of. It couldn't suddenly make him in great shape. His brown hair was plastered to the side of his face, and sweat dampened the back of his shirt. She pulled the extra hair tie off her wrist and handed it to him.

"You're impressive." Art said after a deep breath. He tied back his brown waves into a bun.

"Guess I have you beat." She felt triumphant.

"Yeah, yeah, so you can run. Let's see how you do with the weights," Art challenged.

In the second half of class, they moved from the treadmills down to the benches set up in rows. Instead of her usual 15-lb weights, she grabbed the 18-lb ones. Art pulled a pair of the 20-lb weights to his bench.

Amelia laid out a sweat towel on her bench and then reclined. After the next set of instructions was announced over the music, the coach snaked between the students, adjusting their form as needed. While Art could lift more than she could, her form was better.

"Good job, Amelia." The coach nodded.

She took pleasure in the way Art looked at her as she lifted the weights during a chest press, her arms strong and chest prominent.

When the music softened and the lights brightened, signaling the end of class, Amelia and Art wiped their sweat with towels and waved goodbye to a few more familiar faces that she recognized.

"Bring him again!" Carlos shouted with an animated wave.

Art flashed a smile as Amelia slipped her hand into his and led them out.

"Thanks again," Amelia said as she passed the receptionist. The girl glanced up, then snapped her head back down.

The sun was bright, and the afternoon was just beginning. Amelia tugged Art into a smoothie shop a few doors down. A little treat for a job well done.

His eyes swept the menu, then he leaned forward on his heels. "Peanut butter and chocolate smoothie."

"What are you, five?" she teased.

"And for you, miss?" the woman across the counter asked.

"Green superfood fusion, please."

"What are you, forty-five?" Art asked, mimicking her tone.

"Shut up," she knocked playfully against him.

She tapped her credit card against the card reader. They collected their smoothies, then returned to her car.

They held hands as she drove him home. When she pulled up to the curb, Art got out. "I remembered I have some errands to run, and then I have work. Rain check on the rendezvous?"

"Do people say rendezvous?"

"Rain check on fuck-"

She reached over and jerked his door closed, her cheeks reddening.

Pulling out to the road, her smoothie remained three-quarters full. The Adderall must have killed her appetite.

CHAPTER SEVENTEEN

melia had returned from Art's apartment and walked along the edge of the S-shaped pool in her backyard. She contemplated whether to sunbathe or research UCLA's welcome week schedule. On one hand, soaking up the sun after a gym session and dipping in the pool was the perfect way to spend the afternoon. On the other hand, she hadn't reviewed anything UCLA-related in two weeks and should probably have a better idea of her transition plan. Both of her ideas were shoved aside as she noticed the slider to her room was open.

She strutted into the flat and found Lauren on her oversized plush bed. She dressed in her standard outfit: black Athleta workout leggings and a solid-colored tank top that crossed in the back. Her hair was pulled back into a high ponytail with a sweatband on top. The resemblance between Amelia and her mom was uncanny.

In her hands, Lauren held the broken photo from Spring Fling that Amelia had forgotten on the floor.

"What's up?" Amelia asked. Her eyes lingered on the photo

before returning to Lauren. She hated it when her parents let themselves into her room.

"Who'd you bring to the gym today?" Lauren's eyes lifted to meet Amelia's.

Amelia's chest deflated. It had only been an hour since they had been at the gym. She assumed the word would eventually get around. Amelia had never brought anyone to the gym aside from Madisson once. But Amelia thought she would have time to come up with a story first.

Amelia went with the facts and nothing more. "His name is Art."

"Is Art a boyfriend?"

"Mom, I've had boyfriends before." Amelia slumped.

Lauren tapped rapidly on the man in the framed photo. "You've had Weston."

"What's your point?"

Her mom licked her lips. "Weston wasn't a normal boyfriend."

"And why was that?" She was genuinely curious what made Weston so special to her mom.

"Weston's the kind of guy you marry. Some boyfriends aren't great, and then there's the guy you marry."

"Well, clearly Weston didn't want to marry me."

Lauren hmphed. "Maybe you should see if he wanted to try again?"

"No, mom!" She grabbed the photo from Lauren's hand and slammed it face down onto the dresser. "I'm dating Art. You can't make judgments about someone you've never met."

"Never met?" Lauren scoffed. "I didn't even know he existed until Raquel told me you brought some *guy* into the gym today."

The way Lauren referred to Art, Amelia knew that the description that fucking-front-desk-Raquel had given did not do him any favors. Clearly, Raquel hadn't noticed how sexy he looked with his hair pulled back. She smirked at the thought.

"Is something funny?" Lauren asked, rising from the bed.

"Look, I have a boyfriend. If you have any other questions, ask. Otherwise, I need to get ready," Amelia said, flipping her hand open in dismissal.

She didn't know what she was getting ready for, but she would find something. Staying home for any reason was no longer an option. She didn't want to be around whatever lingering coldness Lauren was sure to exhibit the rest of the day.

Lauren shook her head in disappointment as she left, sliding the door closed behind her.

Amelia collapsed on her bed. Maybe she had been a bitch to Weston, giving him the silent treatment after he said he loved her. Maybe she was a bitch to her mom, too. At what point were you not a bitch to people as an adjective but as a noun?

A heavy breath escaped through her lips, and she picked up her cell phone, clicking on the photo of Weston.

He answered on the first ring.

"You want to get frozen yogurt?" Amelia asked before she could change her mind. She had to get out of the house, and she and Weston had been friends even after the breakup.

"Be there in five," he answered.

Amelia made a mental list of all the reasons she called him as she walked out to her driveway, in case anyone ever asked. Weston lived closest. Art was at work. Madisson was with Max.

The truth was, she needed to get out of the house or risk appearing to her mom like a liar, who was already upset with her. Weston was a safe space, even if their last conversation had been uglier than the breakup.

As he approached, she got into her car, and he followed suit. She was met with a whirlwind of emotions. Guilt for not telling him about Art before they went to his apartment. Sadness that she knew she hurt him and hadn't cared. Empathy that his heart had been broken, as he had slashed apart hers.

Despite Weston's admission, Amelia didn't believe he loved her. Certainly not enough, maybe not at all. This was Weston's first experience with jealousy. Amelia had never done anything to make him feel truly jealous before. It was a gnarly feeling, but it was not synonymous with love. Jealousy happened when there was a lack of control, and Weston had never been in a situation where he wasn't in control. No wonder he spiraled, spouting off anything to get her back to him. He wasn't in love; he was a control freak.

In the passenger seat, he was put together as usual. At one time, she had loved that about him - how organized he was - believing that if someone like that saw something in her, she could be like that too. Put together. Ready for a promising future.

Now, the pretty package of a life he offered her was a cage compared to the freedom she had with Art.

They pulled up to the frozen yogurt shop, and Amelia opened her own door to get out. Weston was oblivious to the small gesture she had grown used to by someone else.

They walked inside and toward the flavor options, passing a group of laughing teenagers at a nearby table. Pulling a bowl from the dispenser, they evaluated the choices. Weston liked to get the same thing—vanilla yogurt with strawberries and granola. Amelia had a habit of mixing whatever nutty flavor she could find with seeds. Today's flavor of interest was pistachio. With full bowls, they took a seat at a table in the corner. The silver metal chairs indented Amelia's thighs.

"Do you want to talk about why you're upset?" Weston ventured, his eyes fixed on his next bite.

"Pissed off my mom again." Amelia stirred the seeds into the creamy yogurt.

"I thought you were going to have coffee with her the other morning?"

Shit. She had forgotten all about that.

"Chalk that up to another reason I won't be winning daughter of the year."

Weston ate a bite, then sat back in the chair. "Do you want to talk about the other night?"

"Nope," she replied with a pop. She wasn't trying to be unkind, but there wasn't a different ending to be had here, no matter how much conversing they did. She cared about him. That wouldn't stop that overnight. But Art had opened her up. The perfectly curated shackles she hadn't known she had been wearing all her life had been unlocked, and Art was the key.

Weston took another bite, then shoved the bowl aside. "We have to talk about this."

"You don't love me." She stabbed her spoon into the yogurt.

"I do."

"You don't suddenly wake up and love someone."

He dragged his fingers through his hair, his voice desperate. "I did. I just didn't realize it until I saw you with him."

"So, what, these feelings were dormant until some sort of twisted jealousy activated them?"

"Yeah, there's probably a science behind it." He nodded as if she was getting it.

Her eyes met Weston's. He was MIT-bound, respectful, and got along with her parents. She understood what her mom meant by 'husband material.' He was great on paper, but in real life, "You're not it for me." Her words were soft. It wasn't his fault that he didn't love her then or that she didn't love him now.

"How do you know?" He leaned closer, his face pained.

"I can't explain it, but I know." It was the exhilaration she felt around Art. The comfort in someone knowing you, without needing to teach them who you are. It was the lightning strike on the lone tree that set the world ablaze.

"Answer me this: you said you loved me only a few months ago." He studied her face. "What changed?"

She gazed out the window of the coffee shop. A small child in pigtails was pulling on her mom's leg, her lip quivering. She looked back at Weston. "I changed."

He scoffed. "People don't change that fast."

She bit her lip. Their conversations were never resolved, and she didn't want to spin in circles tonight. "Can you take me home?"

His eyes dipped to her nearly full bowl of yogurt, but he didn't address it.

"Okay, Amelia." His tone was hollow as he collected both their bowls, dropped them into the silver trash can by the door, and led her outside.

"Promise me something?" He paused as they reached the car.

"Sure."

"Can we keep being friends?" His eyes were clouded.

She'd enjoyed his company throughout the years, and she didn't want to give it up either. "Yeah, I'd like that."

He gave a weak smile.

She was sure he'd find someone new, too, and then he would understand what she meant. Everything would work out for both of them.

CHAPTER EIGHTEEN

True to her word, Madisson had reached out to Reyna. As they hypothesized, sleeping with her friend's boyfriend exiled Reyna from her normal group of friends. And, shocker, Brandon and Genieve stayed together. Which is how Amelia found her own group expanding, with Max, Art, Madisson, and now Reyna, all sitting in a loose circle in the apartment.

Reyna looked comfortable in the group, the type of girl who fit in anywhere. She had a dancer's build with toned limbs, a small chest, and a compact frame. Her hair was so dark it had a blue tint in the right light.

"This is the craziest shit," Max said in warning, but a grin formed from ear to ear.

"Where do you get it?" Amelia turned over the clear package in her hands as she had for the marijuana. The drugs, neatly packaged, offered the illusion that they were safe.

"The smoke shop down the street," he responded.

She and Art passed the shop regularly on their way to the beach. A blush crept up her cheeks as she recalled their last visit. She still found sand particles in her sheets, brushing up against her legs in the dark of the night.

"It's the craziest shit, and yet they sell it legally?" Her face twisted. The rules on drugs varied. Meth, heroin, and cocaine were bad. Pot was acceptable. Shrooms were natural, so that was fine. Acid was chemically made, so it was bad? Salvia slipped into its own dimension. Maybe it was acceptable since it also comes from a plant? She turned the box over again as she considered.

"Hey, I don't make the rules." Max interrupted her thoughts.

"I'll go first," Art offered, hand outstretched to her. She palmed the box of salvia over to him.

"You've done this before?" An uncertainty was building in her chest.

He squeezed her knee reassuringly. "I've done it, and it's over like that." He snapped his fingers.

He pulled out a spoon-shaped pipe and packed it with the moss colored plant. With a flick of the lighter, the bowl glowed. He inhaled deeply. A few hits reduced the contents to ash.

Everyone waited.

Then it hit him.

Art balanced on his fists and knees like a gorilla. He bounded across the apartment, knocking his shoulder into the side of the couch.

"Ohmygod." Reyna giggled. Her almond-shaped eyes focused on him.

Art picked up the Xbox controller and tilted his head sideways at it, as if he had forgotten what it was.

He pointed insistently to various inanimate objects: the ashtray Madisson made, the television remote, Amelia's shoe. The rest of the group eyed each other with giggles, and Art's face pulled back in frustration.

He never spoke a word.

Art was right. It didn't last long. Like a roller coaster, he was up, twisted, and the world turned strange. Then, he returned to Earth as if nothing had happened.

"You ready, Princess?" Art asked with far more amusement than she had.

"You looked crazy," she said.

She wasn't sure she wanted to do it. She certainly didn't want to be bounding around the apartment ape-like. Fear flickered in her chest.

"It was crazy. Then it was over. And I'm alright now, aren't I?"

She glanced at Madisson, who had done this with Max before. Madisson reached a hand out to her.

"We're right here," Madisson ran a thumb over Amelia's fingers.

"Right here," Reyna echoed with a nod.

Amelia looked sideways. She certainly didn't need comfort from Reyna. She shifted her attention to Art, who was already repacking the pipe with another dose of salvia. He extended the pipe out for her turn. She sighed, extinguishing the fear inside her. She would do this, and it would be fine.

With her lips to the pipe, she inhaled deeply. She held it in her chest and counted to three, as Art had taught her about the weed.

When she exhaled, she entered another dimension.

Even after watching the strangeness of Art's trip, Amelia didn't expect it to hit her as it did. She had been staring at Madisson when it took over. Hard.

The room shifted, and things were no longer as they had been. A cold darkness enveloped the room. A red light pulsed from the television, stretching out of the screen and toward her. A red so deep it had to be the flames from every bad, ugly thing in the world blasting toward her.

She gripped Art's hand for protection. The light vanished,

panic taking over. Sweat prickled at the base of her neck. Her mind dizzied trying to keep focus, like a child on a spinny disc at a park.

Please. Someone. Help me.

Instead of help, she was met with a melting gaze from the group, pushing her through the floor and into the ugly red flames.

She shouted for help, then pulled back at the noise.

It wasn't her voice. The words were foreign. Not English, Spanish, or Italian. Not a language she had ever heard.

She was in a foreign drama, another country's telenovela of sorts. No one blinked. Were they filming her? Watching her unravel?

Amelia wanted to run, but her legs were anchored to the carpet that threatened to swallow her.

Max reached over and gently patted her leg.

Panic scurried up her body like a baby mouse. Its claws scratched against her as it raced up her jeans and then into her chest.

Amelia pressed a hand against her heart, her breath ragged, eyes wide, and then the world adjusted back. The red flames had gone. Her body loosened, and her hand fell. She repositioned, extending her legs out in front of her. Her fingers snapped to the back of her neck, still moistened from sweat.

"You're okay," Art said faintly.

Her chest rose and fell.

"You're okay." Art's voice was stronger this time.

He put his palms on her cheeks and turned her head to meet his eyes.

"You're okay." His tone was firm.

Her eyes fluttered closed. When she opened them again, he was still looking at her.

"I was on drugs." She sought validation. She needed to know

that she was not in a telenovela. No red flames were coming for her. The world was not opening up into another dimension. None of it was real.

"Yes." Art said.

"But I didn't remember I was on drugs. It felt real," she insisted.

"Ah, that is the hype of salvia." He let his hands fall from her, satisfied that she had returned from her trip.

"How long was it?" she asked.

Reyna checked her phone. "Ten minutes."

Fuck. She would have believed Reyna if she had said hours.

Art handed the pipe and salvia to Max, who packed the bowl for Madisson.

Amelia was still, as everyone else took their turns tripping on the drug, but she couldn't focus.

She didn't laugh with the others, and she didn't try to ground anyone. She was locked in her mind, trying and failing to make sense of her own experience.

Her fingers twitched against her chest, as if the mouse would reveal itself and she would learn that the drugs were real, and the reality with her friends in front of her was the false world.

Everyone else moved on after their turns, as if what had happened wasn't terrifying. Maybe it was fun for them. Maybe it wasn't meant to mean anything. But to her, it did. The world could be terrifying, and dancing in delusion could have consequences. Warning bells sounded, and she promised herself that she would never smoke salvia again.

Amelia didn't linger at the apartment. After everyone took their turns, she let Art walk her to her car before the sun had even set. He drew a heart on her car, but the parting kiss felt hollow as her mind lingered on the salvia experience.

On the windy drive home, she wondered what Weston would think of her now. She had changed, she had warned him.

He was better off without her. He had a path ahead of him, as she once had. Now she was walking in the dirt, trudging her own path.

This was what she had wanted - an adventure. Then she would get right back on the straight and narrow for UCLA.

Amelia parked and walked into her back house. Not a minute later, the light from her parents' bedroom turned off.

Going through all the motions of what she should do: putting on her nightgown, washing her face, drinking a glass of water, the feeling still lingered that she was in the wrong reality.

When she folded herself into her sheets that night, she dreamt of a better time. She and Art, running on the beach, toes squishing into the sinking sand. They laughed, hair blowing.

She pushed out any other dream sequences involving a blond boy with disappointed eyes that tried to make their way in.

CHAPTER NINETEEN

A few days later, Amelia pulled up to the front of the fast-casual Mexican restaurant. Balancing on the toes of his skater shoes, Art waited on the curb with his dark hair blowing in the beach breeze. He leaned in and kissed her before sliding into the seat, resting a takeout container on his lap.

"Hope I didn't make you wait too long." The dashboard clock indicated that she did.

"Gave me more time to perfect your nachos." His smile was easy, unbothered. "I sweet-talked the cook into giving me extra jalapeños."

She smiled and tapped her freshly manicured nails, pink with gold flecks, against the steering wheel.

"Buckle up," she reminded him as she drove toward the apartment.

Amelia had shoved the salvia trip to the fringes of her mind and was content to forget it ever happened. Her UCLA welcome week activities were finalized, including a tour of the theater and a university housing move-in. She'd spent an hour by the pool, listening to the finches rustling the trees, and letting the sun bronze her skin. She was back to normal and at peace in reality.

Art led them inside, and Amelia did a double-take at Madisson and Reyna at the living room table playing cards.

"Hey?" She quirked an eyebrow as she sat on the couch, placing her nachos down.

"Hey!" Madisson responded.

"Good to see you, Reyna." Amelia gave a tight smile.

"Did you know Renya's going to SDSU too?" Madisson asked, her doe eyes shining.

Reyna reached for her hand. "I'm so excited. We found out we've been assigned the same building! How lucky is that?"

Amelia looked between them. "Super lucky." She scraped a tortilla chip against a blob of cheese and crunched into it.

"SDSU is hosting a live art show next week. You totally have to come with me." Reyna looked at Madisson.

"That sounds like fun. Have you ever been?" Madisson asked Reyna, reaching over for a chip.

A smug smile slid across Reyna's face. "I modeled in one a few months back." She settled back on her forearms.

Madisson's hands covered her mouth, then fell. "Dude! That's incredible."

"Didn't all the dancers do that?" Amelia asked.

Reyna side-eyed her. "Yeah, but not all the dancers were invited to do it a second time."

Amelia didn't say anything else. She fingered a jalapeno from the bunch and popped it in her mouth. Madisson caught her eye and raised an eyebrow. Amelia pretended not to notice.

Tapping her fingers against the table, Madisson suggested, "How about we play a game of King's Cup?"

"Sure," Amelia said.

"I haven't played that in forever!" Reyna added.

Probably because she had no friends left.

Madisson called over her shoulder. "Hey, Babe, can you get beers?"

"Sure, Babe." Max opened the fridge.

Madisson's inviting Reyna over twice in one week was overly generous. Reyna slept with her best friend's boyfriend. Who's to say she wouldn't sleep with one of *their* boyfriends?

The guys in the kitchen worked in tandem, pulling beers from the fridge and stacking them.

On second thought, she couldn't picture anyone aside from Madisson sleeping with Max, and Art only had eyes for her. Maybe they were safe, but still. She turned her attention back to the girls. Madisson doubled over in laughter at something Reyna said, and Reyna's head tipped back as she swiped the tears rolling from her eyes.

Maybe she wouldn't be a boyfriend stealer. Maybe she would be a best friend stealer.

Max approached with an armful of Natty Ice beers and distributed them among the group. When he settled on the floor, Madisson crawled into his lap. Reyna sat in front of the short end of the table.

One by one, they pulled playing cards from the ring around the middle and acted according to the number or face card they drew. They poured some of their beers into the middle whenever one of them pulled a King card.

Madisson pulled a seven.

Amelia moved her hand to Art's thigh, her fingers walking underneath the gap between his shorts and his skin.

With her free hand, Amelia pointed to Heaven, echoing Madisson's movement and the directive of the card.

Art, preoccupied with Amelia, missed the instruction. "You tricked me!"

"I helped you." An innocence in her tone.

"How so?" He leaned closer, and she felt warm and reckless.

She kissed him. "I knew you wanted to drink." Then she pulled away and hunched forward for a card.

He hmphed and peeked at her card. "Six. Chicks." He nodded at her to drink.

"Six. Dicks," she challenged.

The group looked around at each other. No one was confident in the correct rule.

"Everyone drink!" Max decided.

Amelia rolled her eyes and lifted her beer to her lips. She set it back down as Reyna pulled an eight.

Reyna pointed at Madisson. "You'll be my mate!"

Madisson giggled and raised her beer in solidarity as the pair sipped. Amelia shifted on the couch. Art tilted his head at her discomfort, but she offered a closed smile, and he let it go.

The drinking game carried on for a dozen more card pulls. Amelia had hoped she'd loosen up with the alcohol, forget about Madisson and Reyna's newfound closeness. But the alcohol exacerbated her insecurities. She paid more attention to them than to the game.

Twenty minutes later, Max drew the final King. He chugged the center beer, then let out a proud belch, marking the end of the game.

Amelia leaned toward Art and lowered her voice. "Can we get out of here?"

He gave a nod, then stood, reaching his hand out to help her up.

"We're going for a walk," Art announced to the group.

He grabbed their jackets and slung his arm around Amelia's shoulder. She leaned against his chest and breathed him in.

Max, Madisson, and Reyna offered a chorus of goodbyes and headed into the kitchen, presumably for their next drink.

Outside, Amelia shivered in the sudden temperature drop from the cozy apartment. He stepped behind her, rubbing the pink fabric against her biceps. His head bowed, his cheek against hers.

"Let's warm you up," he murmured, sweetness in the words.

She tilted her chin up. The stars shimmered above, and a crescent moon shone brightly in the sky. A promising new act of the night.

They walked, hand in hand. No predetermined destination. Not a care in the world. As long as she was with him, they would have a good time.

"Tell me what's going on," Art encouraged, slowing his saunter to match her pace.

The streetlights hummed on with a tinged, yellow glow. She exhaled and met his turquoise eyes. He always looked at her earnestly; she never had to fight for his devotion. He handed it over as easily as he breathed.

"I feel like I'm losing Madisson to Reyna," she admitted. Then, caveated, "I know it's silly. It's only been a few days, but they're both going to SDSU in the fall. They're making all these plans, and I'm going to be gone. Madisson will move on without me. And I don't know a single person in L.A."

As she spoke, she realized the truth was buried beneath the Reyna excuse. It wasn't about being replaced. It was about being left behind. It brought her back to when Georgina left for college. Then to her parents, who acted like their job of raising kids was done. It was about Weston, who broke up with her casually.

Dabbing the corner of her eye, she was careful not to smudge her eyeliner.

He halted. "Hey, Princess, it's okay. Madisson talks about you all the time. Also, you'll make so many friends in L.A. I'm the one who should be worried." He gestured to himself.

"You're worried?" Amelia gazed up at him, her spirits down.

"Of course I am! My hot girlfriend is moving to L.A. and will have all these actor wannabees all over her. I want you all for myself." He cupped both sides of her face and kissed her deeply, possessively. Butterflies released in her chest.

When she pulled away, her hazel eyes searched his ocean blue ones. "You know no one could ever compare to you."

A dopey smile formed on his face, and they strolled with a weightlessness between them.

"Tell me about your day," she prompted. She wanted to know every piece of his life that she wasn't there for.

"Well, the dishwashing job is... It's gross. It smells terrible!" He covered his nose to prove the point. "I spend as much time scraping food into the trash as I do washing dishes. It's such a waste." He emphasized the last word in disgust, then continued. "It's fine, it's a job, right?"

"It's a job." She shrugged in agreement.

"Honey Cat was supposed to practice this week, but Evan-"

"The guitarist?" she clarified.

"Bassist. Super smart. Like, he reads Moby Dick or some shit. Anyway, he woke up late, missed the bus, and his brother was supposed to give him a ride, but then he had work. We didn't get to practice today, but we'll make it happen on Thursday, and it's going to be insane. I've been working on new beats, and they're so good."

She loved the way he rambled when he got excited. "That'll be good. The band is solid?" Her Honey Cat bracelet dangling on her wrist served as a reminder of her status as a day-one fan.

"Yeah, I would've moved out here regardless, but there's a lot of talent. It's something special."

"I'm sure it is." Her worries about the future softened in the glow of his positivity.

They wandered, zigzagging through the streets, until they stumbled upon a hopscotch grid and a plastic bucket of chalk. Art bent down and grabbed a handful of pastels.

"What are you doing?" Amelia asked.

He flashed a mischievous grin, then grabbed her hand and led her into an alley. Art crouched down and chalked a cat licking honey off its paws.

He wasn't too bad an artist—another talent of his.

As he stood, he admired his work. Then he led her down half a block, stopping in the next alley. "Your turn."

"I'm not an artist. That's Madisson's gift." Madisson did woodworking behind the scenes at the school plays, built bridges, and painted backdrops. It's why Amelia had trouble supporting her relationship with Max. Madisson could do better than a guy without a job or an education, relying on his parents. She was gifted.

Art handed her a purple stick of chalk. "Do something simple. We're having fun."

She tapped her lip, then crouched. Tracing a purple heart with an arrow through it, she scrawled "A + A" inside.

"Like we're wounded warriors," Art mused. He folded his arms together and nodded in approval.

"Like we are meant to heal each other."

"Such a romantic."

He lifted a flask from his jacket pocket, took a swig, then offered it to her.

"How do I never notice when you have this?" she asked.

"Like fucking Mary Poppins," he agreed. "Does Miss I-need-a-chaser want some?" A smile teased on his lips.

She narrowed her eyes and swiped the steel container from his hands. She took a gulp, too fast, and her hand rose to her chest as she choked on the burn.

"What is this?" She coughed.

"Fireball."

"What's that?" Her words were barely out before she coughed again.

"Cinnamon whiskey."

"Fucking whiskey," she muttered. The spicy taste of cinnamon coated her tongue.

Despite the cough, they passed the flask back and forth, stopping for their "Art work" as Amelia coined it.

He answered that with a mocking "har har" laugh and another swig.

With each sip, the liquor went down smoother. They were lost and carefree when a flash of metal caught her eye.

"Art?" Her eyes fell to a pair of Razor scooters lying on an unkept lawn.

"Oh fuck yeah." He picked one with blue handlebars up off the grass.

"Is this wrong?" Amelia asked.

Art moved swiftly. "Here we'll trade." He set the chalk in its place as an offering.

She eyed the second scooter and the chalk, still unsure.

"Don't hesitate." Art warned, "The second you hesitate, you've lost."

Amelia grabbed the second one and started sliding down the sidewalk, wanting to be out of sight before a front door crashed open and she needed to explain to a pair of elementary school children what she had done.

Art followed her, then sped past her, leading the way down the middle of the vacant street. One foot on the metal platform and the other pushing off the sidewalk, she picked up speed, gliding into the ocean breeze. Her lungs expanded with freedom, and the liquor warmed her chest. She couldn't remember the last time she was on a scooter. She and Georgina had them as kids, but how long had it been since she was a kid?

A few blocks down, a three-story building sat among the houses. The windows were boarded, and the stucco was streaked grey. Art stopped ahead of it and shoved his scooter into a thorn bush that perimetered the area. Amelia stalled behind him, scooter in her hand, as he surveyed the structure.

"Aha! Amelia!" he called over his shoulder.

Where he saw adventure, she saw concern. A ladder hung from the second floor, not quite reaching the ground.

He bit his lip, stepped back a couple of feet, then sprinted and jumped to reach it. With his height and subsequently long arms, she was sure this wasn't his first time breaking in somewhere.

His hand gripped the ladder as he lifted himself a rung. His shirt rose, revealing a strip of exposed stomach that clenched with every pull closer to the top.

"Where are you going?" Amelia whisper-shouted.

"I have no fucking idea, but you're coming with me."

The nearby houses were dark, leaving no witnesses for their breaking and entering. He swung his body with enough momentum to pull himself up to the platform of the second story.

"Fuck it," she said with a whiskey-fueled confidence.

She let go of her scooter and narrowed her eyes in determination.

"You're going to run and grab onto this bottom one," Art instructed, pointing to the ladder.

"You're overestimating my upper body strength."

"I'm not. I saw you at the bootcamp class."

She took a few steps back and then ran. Jumping forward, it was just out of her grasp. She stumbled before regaining her balance.

Art howled and doubled over in laughter on the perch. "I get it now," he teased, "I was overestimating your coordination."

Amelia glared at him as the moon glowed behind him. His dark hair and dark jacket formed no more than a captivating silhouette in the night.

She stepped back a foot, prepping for another attempt, when a flash of red and blue lights penetrated through the other side of the building.

"Oh shit," Art muttered. He jumped off, landing with a hand on the ground.

"Follow me." He took off, his long legs extending with every step. Amelia barely had time to react before he raced past her.

She sprinted to catch up. The police lights rounded the corner, silent and alarming.

Her heart raced faster than her legs. After the weed and the thieving and the salvia, their good luck had to be running thin.

"Down!" Art hissed, then dropped to his stomach on the street, hidden behind a dark green sedan, or maybe it was grey. She had trouble distinguishing colors in the black of night. She crept down beside him, then lay flat against the ground. The loose gravel scratched against the side of her hair, smelling of dirt.

The police car slowed as it passed, but didn't stop. She inhaled sharply.

They waited.

She released her breath. In the dead of the night, her pulsing heartbeat felt too loud.

She counted to ten. Then fifty. She moved her hand and pushed herself up half an inch when Art grabbed her wrist.

He shook his head, eyes firm, and she released back down.

The police car circled the block another time.

Fuck, how did he know? Anxiety built, and a tense silence stretched between them. It was the stillest she had ever seen him.

She counted to a hundred.

A hundred and fifty.

At two hundred, Art spoke, "We're clear." A vindicated smile slid across his face.

She slapped her palm against his arm playfully. "You did not enjoy that!"

He reached over and ran his thumb across her cheek, then leaned in and kissed her.

"I wouldn't have enjoyed it if we got caught," he responded. "Now let's go."

He rose and extended his hand to hers. She took it, then dusted off her jacket.

"That was insane." Amelia crossed her arms.

"That was exhilarating." He kissed her. "That was intoxicating." He kissed her again. "That was-"

"Asinine." Amelia finished.

"Great way to keep up the alliteration. You could be a songwriter."

"You've hidden from the cops before."

"A few times."

"Have you ever gotten caught?"

Her question hung in the air as they walked.

After an infinite stretch of time, he answered, "I was there when Asher got arrested."

"Oh shit, what happened?" She reached for his hand.

He interlaced their fingers. "He was selling drugs."

"Did you know?"

"I knew." He squeezed her hand. "I told him not to. That's why our dad left. He got caught up with bad people. He thought he was putting us at risk, and it was better to leave. I didn't know what Asher was doing at first, but when I figured it out, I told him to stop. Told him it wasn't worth it. But apparently, he disagreed. He was selling to a friend of mine behind my back, and that's when he got busted."

"I'm so sorry."

He offered the flask to her.

She took it and raised it. "Here's to staying far away from

drug dealers and police cars." After a generous gulp, she handed it back.

"Here's to never getting caught!" He took a swig.

It took them half an hour to find the apartment. They stumbled together, making up stories about the sleeping homeowners. The small house with a white picket fence contained backyard Labrador breeders. The home with a Tesla out front was full of assassins.

When they finally made it back, the apartment lights were off. Art let them in, and Amelia pulled out her phone and texted Lauren, cringing at the time—2 AM.

AMELIA

Be home in the morning

She turned off her phone, too embarrassed to want to be alerted to her mom's surely disappointed response.

"Can I stay with you?" Amelia whispered to Art.

His smile took over his entire face as he led her into his room, then moved the drum set against the wall. He was wrestling the air mattress from the closet when Amelia said, "I'm going to get us some water," and slipped out.

She opened the fridge with a soft creak, its light illuminating the space. She grabbed two water bottles and returned to Art's room. After she drank half of hers, she set them both down, proud of her foresight to combat tomorrow's hangover.

Art bent over the bed, fully inflated, and fastened the sheets to the mattress as it lifted. As he focused on keeping the edges in place, she began to undress. When he finished and turned around, she was down to her matching pink lace bra and thong. She offered him what she hoped was a sultry smile as she flipped off the light.

He moved quickly, stripping off his shirt and stepping out of his jeans, leaving them piled on the ground. Grabbing her by her arms, he turned her around. He guided her backward, step by step, onto the bed, towering above her. She stifled a laugh as he removed one hand to step out of his Captain America boxers.

His intensity filled the room, evaporating any humor.

His mouth crashed into hers, and she reached her fingers through his hair.

Sex on the beach had been magical, but the experience without the sand and open air was even better. There was a demand in his body, but as he brushed back her hair, he gave just as much sweetness. A dichotomy of beauty.

When they were finished, they stayed entwined. She drifted to sleep, lulled by his arms into a contented haze and the light sound of snoring.

CHAPTER TWENTY

Amelia squinted at the morning light. The mattress pulled underneath her weight as she turned. It had lost some of its air in the night. Art's arm was slung across his face, forehead pressed into the crook of his elbow.

She took him in. The light highlighted a few stray freckles. His chest rose and fell, a peace she didn't often see from him. She reached for her phone and braced herself as she turned it on. A photo of her and Madisson on her parents' pontoon illuminated the background, and she swiped away to the home-screen. Her stomach dropped.

She expected a text from Lauren and had already prepared a series of excuses and apologies. It was even worse. *Nothing.* Lauren hadn't responded at all. Amelia was used to pushing boundaries, but not going home and not letting her mom know was barreling right through them.

The mattress shifted again as Art turned over. She set her phone down and rolled to him. As she brushed her fingers along his cheek, he opened a blue eye halfway.

"I have to go." Her voice was soft and regretful.

He opened both eyes, then blinked a couple of times. "I could make you breakfast?"

"No, I should go." She smiled faintly. "More bacon for you."

One day, they would have a full sleepover, complete with bacon, morning sex, and a walk on the beach at the crack of dawn. But today, she had to get home and make things right. While she and Lauren weren't close, she was better off keeping the peace with her parents.

He nodded, and his eyes fell closed. "Next time," he murmured.

She leaned in and kissed his forehead, then slipped out of bed and gathered her phone, purse, and keys.

In the living room, Max's door was closed. She could only assume Madisson stayed the night. Amelia passed by the couch, a petite leg dangling from beneath a blue blanket. She hadn't noticed Reyna last night when they came in. Amelia chewed on her cheek and snuck out the front door.

In her car, Amelia pulled down the visor mirror to assess the damage. She had missed her whole night's skin routine again, and her makeup was smeared. Yesterday's blouse was crinkled after being strewn on Art's floor.

Despite her appearance, the clock on the dashboard indicated she could still make Lauren's mid-morning Pilates class. A workout and a quick apology, two birds with one stone.

Large windows, framed in navy blue, showcased the Pilates studio. Amelia inhaled through her nose and exhaled through her mouth—the perfect Pilates student.

She had stayed the night with her boyfriend, but she was safe. She had done nothing wrong. Except for not telling her mom that she wasn't coming home, the excessive drinking, and the hiding from cops after stealing scooters and public intoxication. But, still. She was a typical teenager. She was sure this was what other students were doing when she was busy, focused on

Weston and UCLA. She was just catching up with her peers. After all, come September, she wouldn't be coming home at all.

Absolving herself of any guilt, she reached for the door handle, then hesitated. She popped open her center console. Fishing out the Ziploc filled with blue pills, she reasoned that if there was a day for a little extra help, it was today. She threw back the Adderall and washed it down with water.

The receptionist was reading a smutty book as Amelia walked past into the studio and into the locker room. She changed, thankful for the growing collection of clothes in her car, and then joined an Aztec-tall woman in the fitness room. After choosing a reformer at the back, she stretched, loosening up. While she usually claimed the center spot, where Lauren could point her out as an example, today, she didn't have it in her. The rest of the students trickled in over the next few minutes.

Lauren entered with her head high, ponytail swinging. She smiled as she passed people with a "great to see you!" and an "I'm so glad you came!" When she arrived at the front and surveyed the class, she spotted Amelia. An involuntary scowl crossed her face, then was replaced by a large smile.

"Thank you all for being here today!" she said. "And most importantly, thank yourself. You are doing something great for your body, and you should be proud of yourself."

Throughout the class, Amelia kept her head down and followed the cues, sliding her left leg out and pulling it back in. Her movements were slow and deliberate. She clasped her hands behind her back to steady her core, isolating the burn in her thighs.

She didn't know if it was the whiskey hangover peeking through or if Lauren was going hard, but she could feel the sweat from her underboob. The variety of exercises continued, and the Adderall helped her concentrate. She stiffened as

Lauren pressed a hand to the small of her back to adjust her stance.

She narrowed in on the self-inflicted punishment at hand. She was unstoppable as she moved the booty bands above her knees and started donkey kicks. Butts like hers and Laurens weren't hereditary; they were made.

Lauren wiped the sweat from her brow. "Whew, last one!" She removed her bands and grinned at the class. "Great job, ladies! I'd better see you again soon!"

A few women chuckled and promised she would. They left in clusters, chatting about weekend plans and exchanging green juice recipes.

Lauren shmoozed effortlessly. It was a charm that Amelia had tried—and failed—to replicate.

A thick silence spread across the room when everyone else had vacated. Lauren didn't look upset, but she was good at harnessing her emotions. It was another area she advised Amelia to work on.

"Let's go to lunch." Lauren gave her the same practiced smile she had shared with the women in the class

"True Foods?" Amelia offered.

"Sounds lovely. I'll get my things."

As Lauren disappeared to the locker room, Amelia peeled off her sweat-soaked tank top and swapped it for a fresh one from her bag. She walked over to the mirror and adjusted her ponytail. Pivoting, she examined her profile. She looked good, but a voice in her head whispered: *Are you good enough for L.A.?*

———

True Foods was a health-conscious restaurant located around the corner from the Pilates studio, making it an after-workout favorite.

Lauren ordered her usual chicken salad with dressing on the side. Amelia opted for a protein açaí bowl. She was sure she would be throwing up whatever she ate later. Smoother food was better for her to absorb nutrients while she could.

"Why didn't you come home last night?" Lauren asked. Her head tilted down to peer at Amelia over the frame of her black designer sunglasses.

"I drank. Didn't think it was a good idea to drive." She should get points for being responsible.

"So you decided to drink and then couldn't drive home. I waited up for you."

Guess she wouldn't be getting kudos on that decision.

Lauren took a sip of her tea, then set it down. She clasped her hands and leaned in. "I'm worried about you being able to make good decisions in college when you're by yourself."

"I'm practically by myself now." Amelia crossed her arms.

Lauren's voice was low. "By choice. You could have dinner with your dad and me. You didn't join me for coffee. You've been so distant, and I don't know why." The last word came out as a pout.

"You don't know why?" Amelia gave a hollow laugh. "How about because when I'm around you, you're so critical."

"Critical?" Lauren's eyebrows pulled together.

"Yes! You're constantly on me about my appearance and what I'm eating and Pilates and needing to do a skin care routine and whatever else."

Lauren scoffed. "Honey, that's not critical, that's care. What I wouldn't have given to have my mom take me to get my eyebrows done in middle school before a classmate told me they were bushy. I do all of this, pay for all this," she gestured up and down Amelia, "because I care. You have every opportunity in the world to be-"

"Your clone," Amelia cut in.

Lauren leaned back, smug. "You want a life where you can choose to work, not be forced to? Do you want to vacation abroad? You want a boat on the bay?"

Amelia's eyes scanned hers. All of those things were what she wanted, but without being forced into it.

The server placed their meals in front of them and brushed away.

When she was out of earshot, Lauren continued, "You want a life like mine. I wish I could clone my life and give it to you. It all happens when you find a good husband. It's the most important decision you'll make in your life, and it's not going to be with the guy that gets you too drunk to get home." She picked up her fork and took a bite of salad.

Amelia couldn't find a response. To her parents, the most important thing was attracting a husband who would provide for her. She tried to think of a comeback. That she could take care of herself. How Art didn't force her to drink last night.

"Did I tell you I have this new private coaching client?" Lauren asked between bites.

The moment for a response had been swept under the rug. The Cox approach to conflict.

"No?" Amelia pushed her spoon into her açaí bowl.

"She was going to the regular class, but she's four months pregnant. We've been able to make good modifications for her."

Amelia's phone buzzed, and she pulled it out, ignoring her mom's narrowing eyes.

ART

How do you feel about raves?

AMELIA

Those are the places where you dress up and dance?

ART

Among other things.

AMELIA

I'm down.

ART

Cool, it's on Saturday.

She smiled up at Lauren. "Just so you know, I won't be home on Saturday night. You don't need to wait up for me."

She would be doing things her way, not Lauren's.

CHAPTER TWENTY-ONE

A few days later, Amelia lay on the tanning shelf of the pool. The summer rays warmed her skin as the Honey Cat demo played from her phone. Straining to listen, she isolated the drum sound from the other instruments to focus on Art's contribution. She rubbed the Honey Cat logo on her bracelet, smiling at the memory. Her boyfriend, the one-day rock star drummer. She sent him a text.

AMELIA

The demo is so good!!!

ART

Thank you! We're crushing it today. Jake came with these sick vocals.

AMELIA

Another text popped up.

WESTON

Can we hang out today?

Amelia lifted her designer sunglasses. She might as well. There were no other plans for her day, and band practice would take hours.

AMELIA

Sure, come on over.

She pushed up from the shelf and grabbed a towel from the rack nearby. She had rinsed off and put on fresh clothes when Weston was knocking on her slider.

"You don't need to knock all the time." She called from the bathroom, towel-drying her hair.

He slid it open. "How's it going?" He lowered to the lounge chair and crossed a leg over his lap.

"Can't complain." After she twisted her hair up into a bun, she plopped on her pink comforter and asked, "What have you been up to?"

"Gaming. Hung out with the guys from the Honor Society." He shrugged. "What about you?"

"Pissing off my mom."

"Are you serious? I don't know why you're always hard on them."

"I'm not." Her nostrils flared. It was like him to assume she was the problem in their relationship.

"What was it this time?"

"I'm going to a music festival this weekend. Lauren's not happy about it."

"A rave?"

"Tomato tomato."

He brushed his blond hair back. "With Art."

"And Madisson, Reyna, and Max."

He looked around the room, his eyes stopping at the pictures on her dresser. There were a few photos of them together in coordinated outfits that she hadn't taken down.

"You're going to dress up?" His words were laced with accusation.

"Of course I'm dressing up."

He sighed dejectedly. "You're going to dress up with *him*."

"I mean, we haven't discussed it yet."

Weston raised an eyebrow knowingly.

"Yeah, we will probably dress up together." She dropped her eyes and smoothed out the comforter. "I don't know how to do this."

Having a new boyfriend while remaining friends with her ex was impossible. If she could make it work for the rest of the summer, it would resolve itself in the fall.

Weston didn't say anything further. Instead turned on one of his anime shows, not bothering to ask her what she wanted to watch.

First love was a different kind of love. It was innocence and comfort. The thrill of brushing fingers while reaching for popcorn in a theater and the exhilaration of being asked to the Homecoming dance with Hershey kisses.

Amelia unequivocally wanted to be with Art, but that didn't erase the feelings of comfort Weston brought to her. They spent two years together. Dating or not, she valued him in her life. She didn't want to hurt him just because she had moved on first.

There was a knock on the slider door, and Amelia's eyes broke from the TV screen and his silly show.

"Weston! What a pleasure to see you." Lauren glowed.

Weston stood with his shoulders back, the epitome of respect. "You too, Mrs. Cox."

"Are you staying for dinner?" Lauren looked between the two.

It would be an olive branch, and Amelia had nowhere else to be. Lauren had given her the silent treatment for a full twenty-four hours after Amelia announced she wouldn't be home on Saturday because she was attending a music festival.

"You'll learn that I'm right," were the last words her mom spoke to her that day.

Weston looked at Amelia, and she shrugged in indifference.

"Yeah, I'd like that," Weston told Lauren.

An hour later at the dinner table, Amelia's parents asked Weston about MIT. He beamed as he talked about his next chapter. They laughed when he admitted he was more nervous about the cold than the classes. He asked about Lauren's clients, cracked jokes with James about AI, and went back for seconds. Their voices filled the dining room, and Amelia tried to remember the last time she'd made the effort for a family dinner.

Across the table, James leaned toward Weston, chin resting thoughtfully on his knuckles. "So what do you think about the U.S. getting involved in this war?"

"There's a lot that we aren't privy to, but from what I've learned, it could have been avoided," Weston retorted and shoveled another bite of lasagna.

Amelia and James had little in common, but when James spoke with Weston, she had his approval. The two shared similar interests, and Weston was the kind of person they wanted her to marry. They made that perfectly clear.

After an apple turnover dessert, Amelia walked Weston to the edge of the driveway.

He pulled her into a tight hug, and she breathed him in. It wasn't a quick hug. Maybe she should have let go, but she remained in his arms. At the edge of her old life, she let her cheek press against his chest and stayed, enjoying the warmth.

When his arms fell to his side, his eyes fixed on hers, searching.

"You're going to be okay without me," she said, the words for both of them.

"I've only got a few more weeks before I go," he said. He dropped his gaze as he kicked a pebble and then looked back at her. "I want to see you again."

She nodded, and his mouth twisted in the corner, like he wasn't sure he believed her.

In the soft glow of the street lights, he shoved his hands in his pockets and headed for his house. The path they had walked together hundreds of times, he walked alone.

Back in her room, the silence was crushing. She called Art, but he didn't answer. He must have still been at band practice.

She called Madisson, who did answer, but was flirting with Max during the call. Amelia hung up on her.

She settled on turning on an HBO drama for background noise to keep her company. Lying in bed, she imagined various scenarios of bringing Art to her house. They could skinny dip in her pool. They could fuck all day in her California King bed and break to make margaritas and towers of nachos. They would laugh, and at night, he would tell her his plans to take her on a tour of the world with him. A summer trip abroad. Tuscany on a Tuesday. The fantasies played as she drifted to sleep.

CHAPTER TWENTY-TWO

On Saturday, after the group had joked, dressed, and gathered their snacks for the rave, Amelia drove Max, Madisson, Reyna, and Art the three hours to the venue. Art was Amelia's best copilot. He had the map pulled up on the dashboard screen and took music requests from the back seat. At a red light, he passed Amelia a lemon chapstick, which she used, then traded it for an Arizona green tea. He anticipated her needs before she did.

Madisson, Max, and Reyna shared the backseat. They sang off-key to The Chainsmokers, high on anticipation. Art and Max volleyed questions from the girls about what it would be like. This was the first time any of the girls had gone to a rave, but the guys had each been to a few. The group was too young for the bars but too old for the bowling alleys. A festival was the in-between. Amelia was most excited about dressing up—the glitter, the fishnets, the chaos of it all. Madisson had booked the hotel room with Max's credit card so they wouldn't have to worry about getting home.

Art peered over his seat and asked Reyna, "So... what inspired the panda?"

Black glitter ringed her eyes in a smoky mask, and her hair was pulled up into two tight buns. The rest of her outfit consisted mainly of lingerie, with faux-fur accessories.

She tilted her head and smiled. "Oh, because I'm Filipino, I can't be a panda?"

"No!" Art threw up his hands in submission, "You look great. That's not what I meant-"

"Oh, I know, I look great."

Besides the dancer's physique, the playful teasing attracted men to Reyna. Amelia just wished it hadn't been with her boyfriend.

Mr. Brightside came on next, and Art turned wickedly to Amelia. Serenading her to the lyrics, she bit back a laugh, loving the attention in front of everyone.

"Amelia!" Madisson shrieked.

A jeep ahead of her drifted into her lane. Her hands gripped the wheel, steering into the next lane where the neighboring truck lay on its horn. She spun the wheel back and eased behind the jeep, heart pounding.

"Fuck!" Madisson exhaled.

"I dropped my Swedish Fish." Reyna pouted.

"I'm Mr. Brightside!" Art concluded the song.

Max slapped Art's shoulder from behind him and snickered.

"How much longer?" Amelia asked, counting from ten and letting her adrenaline come down a few notches.

"We're getting close," Art said.

Amelia's stomach rumbled, and she took another swig from her tea. Art had warned her that eating would slow down the effects of the drugs. She wanted to do it right and feel its full effects.

"Take this exit," Art directed, pointing ahead of the ramp. She followed the road to the traffic signal.

"There," he said.

The light turned green, and Amelia pulled into the parking lot of a gas station.

"We'll be back," Art told the backseat.

"But I have to pee," Reyna whined.

"Me too!" Madisson seconded, clapping her hands and leaning forward, her zombie face poking between Amelia and Art's seats. She and Max dressed as a zombie bride and groom, and she had spent hours perfecting both of their makeup down to their collarbones. A zombie suited Max.

"Fine, fine. You guys go. Just be back in ten," Art allowed.

Art climbed out of the car, and Amelia trailed behind him to the side of the building.

His dark hair was pulled back into a bun, and his aqua-blue eyes lit up. A prison cap pushed back at his forehead, and he wore a black-and-white jumpsuit.

"First, you look insane," Art drawled, pulling her against him as he leaned against the brick building.

"Thank you," she breathed.

His finger against her skin through the hole of her fishnets sent a jolt up her body. He walked his fingers up, underneath her blue police skirt, right below her butt cheeks. Leaning into him, she pressed him harder against the wall. They kissed deeply in the broad daylight, in the same place that the homeless probably relieved themselves, and yet she hadn't a care in the world. She could never get enough of him.

Too soon, he released his grip on her. He pulled out a baggie from his jumpsuit, filled with green pills stamped with a paw print.

"You're going to tuck these under your tights. No one will notice." His voice was low as he placed the bag in her hands.

Amelia froze, and he folded her fingers around it.

They hadn't talked about this part. She knew they would be taking ecstasy, and had been exhilarated by the way Art spoke about how happy she would feel on it. But, sneaking it in?

His hands stayed over hers, a plea in his gaze.

"A hundred other girls are doing this same thing tonight." His voice was soft. "It's our best option."

She took a deep breath, and he let go of her hands.

"Where did you get these?" she asked.

"Oh, they are totally safe. I tested them."

"You tested them?"

"Sure did, Princess." He rubbed a finger against her cheek. "I would never put you or anyone else in danger."

"Okay." She willed her heart to steady.

Gathering her courage, she separated from him. After she rounded the corner, she walked through the automatic doors into the store. Reyna and Madisson emerged from the bathroom, arms interlocked, barking with laughter.

She tried to smile at them as she walked past, but a bitterness grew in her stomach about Art's unilateral decision-making. She wanted to be carefree like Reyna and Madisson.

Amelia locked herself in the bathroom. It was tight, the wall had brown stains, and a mirror was missing. The right place for this activity.

She pulled out the ziplock bag of pills, then slid down her skirt and fishnets. She placed the bag between her fishnets and underwear. Unless she was getting a strip search, there was no way to tell she was smuggling them in. Like a felon, the thought crossed as a joke, but without Googling the answer, which could incriminate her if things went south, she was almost positive a bag full of illegal substances was a felony. An unshakable weight pressed against her chest.

Once they were back in the car, Art resumed the music. Amelia stayed quiet. One wrong step and her whole future could be in jeopardy. He squeezed her knee, an acknowledgement that he knew what he was asking of her.

Amelia parked at the hotel, within walking distance of the venue. They followed a trail of mermaids, circus animals, and characters from Alice in Wonderland who spilled into the streets. All of life's misfits had a place. Amelia had felt torn between her put-together life and the excitement of who she wanted to be. The rave was where it intersected.

They passed under a twinkling yellow archway that separated reality from imagination.

Fortunately, Art was right, as he usually was about these sorts of things, and security was a breeze. The line moved quickly as the girls filed together. The boys were ushered into a second line. Amelia hadn't brought in a purse to search, so she walked through and then stood with her arms raised like a football post, her phone in her hand. A female security guard patted her down carelessly.

The beat of the music reverberated through the ground beneath Amelia's feet. Art gave her a nod as he waited with the group, and she beelined for the rows of porta-potties.

Costumed attendees filtered in and out. She walked into one, flipping the lock. Pulling down her layers, she removed the bag from its hiding place. With clammy hands, she plucked a green pill and chomped it into pieces. Art had advised it was quicker for the drugs to take effect that way. Her face distorted in disgust at the chalky taste. He had also said that most people preferred to swallow it whole and let it take its time rather than deal with the taste. Amelia was not one of those people.

She exited the porta-potty with the ziplock bag balled up into a fist. Three steps later, Art caught her by the waist and pulled her into him. She slipped the bag back into his prisoner's pocket.

"That's my girl," he murmured into her hair. Goosebumps

rose along her skin, and her guard dropped. It would all be okay, as he had promised.

Within ten minutes, the group smiled guiltily at one another.

The rave was reminiscent of a theme park. The first activity was the giant swings.

Amelia and Art buckled into the blue and red harnesses next to each other, hands gripping the chain links as they were pulled into the air. Higher and higher they went, the ground shrinking beneath them. Everyone below was dressed up and happy.

Art had assured her it would not be like the salvia. He promised her profusely that she would be able to feel it; she would recognize that she was on drugs. He told her she would love it.

He was right about it all.

As the swing reached its peak, so did Amelia. The ecstasy took hold of her while they were high in the grey-blue sky. The air was lighter, the sounds richer, the lights more vibrant. She released her grip and stretched out her arms like a child pretending to be an airplane. Art mimicked her, arms outstretched, laughing as they soared higher. She wasn't sure if it was the whip of the wind or pure bliss from the drug, but tears slid down her cheeks.

After the swings, Art and Max led the group to one of the massive stages, where oversized metal boxes vibrated with the bass of the techno. Max lifted Madisson on his shoulders. In Amelia's chest was an unexpected pang of happiness for Madisson. She was supported, lifted by Max. Reyna trailed behind the double-stacked couple, eyes wide and pupils dilated. In slow motion, she flicked her toes out with each step, twirling, then continuing.

Amelia's gaze wandered, her senses heightened. Two men dressed as ringleaders worked in tandem on the stage, their hands moving swiftly across a massive switchboard. One put his hand on the side of his oversized headphones as he bobbed with the music. The crowd in front of them was ten people deep, sweat dripping, bodies lurching with the beat.

Lights flashed to the side, coming from a man in a massive pink bunny head with a slender body and white-gloved hands. He made eye contact before returning to a pair of tie-dyed ravers sitting in front of him.

Time slowed.

She forgot where she was, who she was, or why she was there.

Art tugged on her hand, snapping her out of her trance. In the real world, staring at another guy might have been concerning for a boyfriend. But here, Art took it as a sign for an adventure.

"Let's go!" Art steered her to the Pink Bunny and his group.

They plopped down beside the couple, whose eyes were stuck on the Pink Bunny's gloves. Amelia shifted, her skirt barely covered her ass from the sticky floor, and her fishnets did nothing to help. The Pink Bunny stood above them and danced his gloved fingers close to her face. He pulled back and traced intricate patterns in the air, weaving through the lights. The tips of his fingers flickered in time with the beats of the music. Blue, green, red. Her heart beat quickened, and yet time stopped. Each movement was a new layer of reality. The universe was unfolding at his fingertips.

The Pink Bunny's hands stopped. He bowed in a sweeping gesture. Without a word, he turned and walked away, disappearing into the crowd. She had a feeling that he had probably forgotten his audience. Yet, for the rest of her life, she would remember the Pink Bunny.

"That was amazing," Amelia whispered.

Art responded with a kiss.

Back on their feet, she scanned for Madisson, Max, and Reyna. They were gone. Underneath her pounding heart, deep sorrow filled her chest.

Art pulled her through the throng of fairies. A ghost in a sheet with only the eyes cut out brushed past her, then stopped and stared her up and down. She was sure he saw through her. She tilted her head at him, then her hand yanked forward as Art dragged her into a dark corner.

The music quickened, and Art's eyes were a deep blue, full of desire. Pulling her against his chest, he snaked an arm around her and rested it on her ass. They kissed as the lights pulsed above them. Mouths open, tongues exploring. He dragged his fingers down her neck as she let out a moan. They could never be close enough.

Amelia turned around. With her skirt lifting against his crotch, she grinded to the rhythm of the music, feeling him pressing against her. After years of dance classes, she enjoyed showing off. She flashed him a devilish grin as she rubbed against him. He brought his teeth to the side of her neck and bit gently. Her heart exploded as the sensation of teeth against flesh rippled throughout her body.

Her friends were both out of sight and out of mind, with his body against hers.

The invincibility from ecstasy was different from what she had with Adderall. Instead of feeling like she could do anything, she felt like nothing bad could ever happen. Nothing in the world could ever be wrong. Everything in her life would be flawless.

She pulled back from Art and smiled ecstatically, understanding the word exactly as it was meant to be. The bass dropped, and like a tidal wave, everyone else dropped with it. She scanned the crowd of happy strangers. But were they strangers at all? Or beautiful people she did not yet know?

Resting her hand on her heart, love and bliss filled her. Nothing could match this. This was special.

A few songs later, Art laced his fingers through hers, to their next adventure. They vacated the DJ room and stepped out into the cool night. The stars and moon peeked through the dark sky. They stopped off in the back of a line for refreshments.

A clown wobbled by on stilts. Batman and Robin made out. When they reached the front, Art asked for a blue Gatorade, and Amelia had to be nudged to stop staring and pay. They were given the drink back without a lid.

"They don't want you chewing on the caps," Art explained, noticing her perplexed face. His answer didn't confuse her any less.

At a lake in the center of the venue, they took a seat. Her fingers glided through the dewy blades of grass. Art leaned in for a kiss, and she was pleasantly surprised when he tongued her another pill. He broke away, and she chomped again.

"You're a beast," he said.

She glowed at his praise. Swallowing the pill fragments, she reached for the Gatorade to neutralize the bitter aftertaste.

Amelia had no control over her eyes. They wandered and lingered in her surroundings. When her eyes tilted downward, she found that she had a death grip on Art's prison cap. She didn't remember taking it, but she understood why she would have. If it were left to him, it would get lost. Amelia had an instinct to protect him and all of his things. She didn't want him to be lost. In such a short time, she had become attached to him. They were in this together.

Art slipped an acid tab on his tongue. "Candy flipping."

Maybe next time, she would try that, too. But not tonight. Tonight was perfect as it was.

"How many pills have you had?" She rubbed her arms, enjoying their softness.

"Five." He smiled.

Five pills of ecstasy. *Damn.* Her mouth vibrated after only two.

Amelia could picture her plump PE teacher telling her health class that every time you take a pill of ecstasy, you're taking an ice cream-sized scoop out of your brain. Just in case, Amelia took a heavy gulp of the Gatorade bottle, convinced the electrolytes could cancel out the ice cream scoop chunks she'd carved out of her brain.

Art put his hand on her cheek. "Release."

She hadn't realized her jaw had been clenched until then. She obeyed with a yawning motion. Her teeth throbbed.

"Keep reminding yourself to relax," Art instructed.

The blue of his eyes started to disappear as his pupils dilated.

She rolled her shoulders back and wiggled her toes. Lifting her hand to his chin, she rubbed her thumb across his cheek. He was naturally beautiful. Tonight, the ecstasy further accentuated it. She'd never known anyone more perfect. Black, soulless eyes and all.

Time slipped by, and Art extended his hand to her. As she stood, he took both her hands in his. They faced each other like a couple standing under a flowered arch, ready to exchange vows.

"Amelia, I love you so much. I know it's too soon to say that. I know it is. But I can't help myself. You're unlike anyone I have ever met. From the first time we were alone, we planned our future–you will always be my Kourtney. I know we're going to be together. You're not judgmental. You don't care that I prefer a drum set over a bed or that I'm washing other people's dishes for a job, or all my family bullshit. You believe in me more than anyone else ever has. I want all of you. God, I love everything about you."

He paused.

When he spoke again, the words were slow, heavy. "I love you."

She didn't consider that she was on drugs when she responded, "I love you, too."

The words encased her heart in pure, elated happiness. Nothing could have been truer.

"Let's adventure." His grin was wide and infectious.

Art snaked through the crowded grounds. At one point, he let go of her hand for a sip of Gatorade, but she never lost sight of him, her love.

They made their way into another stage room. According to the map, there were three stages surrounding the central lake.

They passed go-go dancers in nothing but tutus and matching bras with friendship bracelets around their wrists, necks, and stomachs. Amelia considered it divine intervention when she spotted Madisson. Her petite best friend stood next to three angels, all a different version of blonde. Madisson, with her jet-black hair and zombie bride makeup, was a stark contrast.

"I thought you were gone forever." Madisson's voice was sad, and her eyes wide.

She looked half-crazed, but Amelia was sure she didn't look any more put together after hours of damp air and sweat.

"I'm here," Amelia responded.

The words were a well of depth. She was with Madisson, physically, emotionally, and spiritually. She would always be with Madisson. The girls held each other while the world around them danced and shifted.

Art headed to Max, then to Reyna. She forgot that she had the man with the pills. This would help Madisson feel better.

She grabbed Madisson's hand and led her to Art. "Her turn, please."

He discreetly brushed his hand against Madisson's, then handed her the Gatorade.

"Thank you, thank you so much," Madisson said as if it were the nicest gesture someone could make.

The rave pounded on.

Art checked his phone, then instructed Amelia. "Open."

He placed another pill on her tongue. Three. She needed to know how much was the right amount.

Her hips swung with the music as she chewed. Max was locked in a deep conversation with Ninja Turtles. Madisson and Reyna giggled, trading bracelets with a group of forest animals. Everyone was reminiscent of a drunk girl in the bathroom line—complimentary and overly touchy.

Max grinned as Madisson and Reyna danced together, then Reyna pulled Madisson toward her, pressing a kiss to her lips. In the regular world, the kiss might have raised eyebrows or lasted too long. But here, under the glow of strobe lights and thudding bass, everything was right. Max stepped closer, wrapping his arms around them, and they swayed.

When they parted, Reyna drifted toward a nearby pirate who'd been watching them.

Was this what dancing was like in the olden days? Going from one partner to the next, leaving pieces of yourself with each one?

She didn't feel the same need to drift. Art was all she wanted.

"Come here," Art purred.

He led her into a crowded corner. She expected more kisses, but he took his keys from his pocket and squatted down. He scanned the area twice, then shoveled a salt-like substance from a ziplock bag.

A wave of guilt washed over Amelia. She'd been bothered that she smuggled the ecstasy in, not knowing that Art had other things he was also taking through security. There was more. Always more. Of course, he needed her help.

Amelia glanced at the bag, then met Art's eyes. She hadn't done anything like this before. She'd told him once that she wouldn't ever snort anything. But how long ago was that? And those were ideas from a girl who had no idea what she was talking about. Practically a lifetime ago.

Art brought the key to his nose. He inhaled, head tilting back, then exhaled through his mouth. He scooped out another bump and turned to her, waiting. Up close, the crystallized particles were smaller than a grain of salt.

"Cocaine?" she mouthed.

He shook his head, and relief expanded in her chest. As long as it wasn't cocaine, whatever it was would be fine. She trusted him.

Amelia crouched beside him, tucked out of sight. He held the key up to her nose, and she inhaled. A menthol smell filtered through her nose and clung to the back of her throat. She rolled her head in a slow circle.

When Art and Amelia returned, the group had grown to include an assortment of zoo animals in colorful, oversized, furry boots, who had joined them. Everyone sat in line on the black floor, forming a circle. Each faced the person's back. Their hands were on the next person's shoulders, thumbs massaging into the shoulders. They made room for her and Art, and she placed her hands on his shoulders, thumbs pressing into his blades. He let out a soft moan. She didn't know or care whose shoulders he was massaging. Everyone was together as one.

The tension in her jaw and shoulders dissipated. Whatever he had given her had started to take effect. She was floating. Pulling her hands away from Art's shoulders, she stood. The lights hit a neon orange. Her nails were sharp. Shaking her from side to side, she tried to stabilize.

"Are you okay?" Reyna asked.

Amelia blinked, unsure where she had come from. "Yeah, I'm like really good." Then added, "Are you okay?"

"I don't know." Her head tilted. "Do you hate me?"

She stared at big, panda eyes. "Are you trying to steal Madisson?"

"Am I... What?"

"Madisson is my best friend." Amelia touched Reyna's hand. It was small and soft. "Please don't steal her."

Reyna rubbed the top of Amelia's hand. "I don't want to steal her. It's been a shitty summer, and Madisson's been so nice to me."

Amelia nodded profusely. "Madisson is the nicest."

Renya bounced on her feet, then threw her arms around Amelia. "Thank you for letting us all be friends."

Tears streaked Amelia's face, filled with relief. She wouldn't have to worry about Reyna taking Madisson away. The world was beautiful, so full of love, like her and Art.

Amelia flinched as the music cut, and the floodlights overhead switched on. The abrupt change was unwelcome.

The rest of the group stood, breaking their chain. The new friends were already gone and forgotten. Attendees drifted out from corners of the venue and returned to the archway where it all began. The elaborate costumes of the start were now remnants of smeared glitter, tangled hair, and dulled eyes.

"Where's my hat?" Art asked Amelia, running a hand over his head as they walked.

She was empty-handed. "I don't know," she said softly, disappointed in herself for losing it.

They walked to the hotel in silence, but the music echoed in Amelia's mind the entire walk. The bite of the early morning left a trail of goosebumps along her arms. She rubbed them, but the soft sensation of her skin had vanished. Her lips pulled downward. Art put an arm around her, drawing her close and keeping her warm.

Even twilight, with its moon and clusters of stars, was unable to stop Amelia's downward spiral.

How could the magic be over?

The boys stopped by Amelia's parked car and pulled out the overnight bags. Their room was on the second floor, and each step felt like a small mountain. Amelia was grateful she wasn't carrying anything. Her arms felt made of stone.

Max tapped the lock on Room 21 with the hotel key linked to his phone and pushed the door open. A blast of A/C greeted them.

"Fuck no." Madisson flipped it off as if it were a personal attack.

The room had two queen beds and a couch for Reyna. It was a near-impossible feat for everyone to change out of their costumes and into their sleeping clothes. Reyna was the only one who bothered to wash her face.

Amelia slid into bed beside Art, cocooned between crisp linens. His face was only inches from her. His dark hair had fallen out of its bun and was a mess on the pillow. His eyes were starting to get their blue back.

She whispered in sudden recollection, "What was that powder?"

"Ketamine."

"What the hell is ketamine?"

"Horse tranquilizer."

"You gave me a horse tranquilizer?!"

"You liked a horse tranquilizer?!"

Amelia smiled weakly. They didn't speak again. They didn't even bother to hold each other.

CHAPTER TWENTY-THREE

In the morning, Max checked them out of the hotel, looking worse than usual. Amelia was too tired to critique him, but she was sure she could have come up with something good about his deadbeat attire.

Art tossed their barely used overnight bags into Amelia's trunk as she started the car and blasted the A/C. The car reeked of dried sweat. Aside from snacks the day before, no one had eaten in close to sixteen hours, twenty for Art and Amelia. Her whole body ached, and an emptiness she couldn't name occupied her stomach. It was Art's idea to grab breakfast at a nearby Denny's before they hit the road home.

Half an hour later, they were seated with hot plates spread out before them. The vivid colors of last night had faded. The world morphed to grey, and the infectious energy had been wiped. Madisson's eyeliner was smudged. Amelia's hair, pulled back in a ponytail, was limp. Max kept his sunglasses on, and Reyna couldn't stop her leg from shaking. Even Art, the ball of sunshine, had succumbed to darkness, his voice dipping to a monotone level as he asked for another pot of coffee from an overly chipper waitress.

"I don't know how you slept," Madisson muttered to Amelia when the second pot of coffee had been placed on the table. "I stared at the ceiling for five hours."

Reyna dipped her chin, her own expression equally hollow.

Amelia squinted, unsure. Art caught her attention and sniffed.

Oh. The horse tranquilizer.

That's why she slept, and they hadn't. She shook her head in contemplation. How anyone found the right combination of these drugs was beyond her. She was glad she had Art, who always knew what to do.

Max and Art eyed a stack of fluffy pancakes, but neither reached for it. Instead, Art reached past Amelia and picked up the refilled pot of black coffee. He topped them both off and nudged one toward Amelia. She mixed in a packet of sugar as she reflected on their declaration of love. She tried to smile at the memory. But as quickly as her lips turned upward, they immediately fell back down. The come down from the drugs had taken away her ability to smile, even while she was in love.

Her eyes swept around the diner and its patrons, who had no idea what the group had been through the night before. They could have been arrested. They could have died. The possibilities of the consequences were crushing.

She picked up the coffee mug and took a sip. The warmth, combined with the ketamine, clung to the back of her throat.

Horse tranquilizer. Would she have done it if she had known what it was? She set the mug back down.

She was trapped in her mind and barely heard Madisson's small voice. "Can we go home?"

"You girls get in the car. We'll be out," Max said, lounging back in his chair.

The trio of girls pushed back their seats and rose. Amelia hadn't spoken the entire breakfast. Reyna grabbed a chocolate muffin, which she had only taken one bite out of, and shoved the rest into the front pocket of her SDSU sweatshirt.

Amelia's feet were heavy as they approached the car.

She slid in and started the ignition. No one reached for the music. Her ears still rang.

"Aren't we waiting for the boys?" Reyna asked as she buckled, and Amelia pulled out of the space.

Madisson and Amelia exchanged a look in the rearview. Sweet Reyna. Even without being told, Amelia knew what was happening. The reason Max had excused them first. Her thoughts flickered back to the bottle of gin Art snatched from Ralph's. Stealing when you were underage and couldn't get what you wanted was one thing. They *could* have paid for breakfast. Annoyance washed over her. Art and Max enjoyed the thrill. Their budding friendship didn't bode well for her. Even still, she pulled the car around to the back exit near the restrooms. She left it in drive, her right foot hovering over the pedal. It was her job to be the getaway driver. She'd done it before.

Art sauntered out first, shoulders back, arms swinging lazily at his sides. He slipped into the passenger seat. He didn't look guilty, but the way he forwent his usual kiss with Amelia indicated that there was a layer of nervousness.

"Buckle your seatbelt," she murmured.

As Art's seatbelt clicked, Max burst through the restaurant doors. He reached her car and flung open the back door, then dove across Madisson and Reyna's laps. Madisson yanked the door closed.

Amelia was already zooming away.

Horror covered Reyna's face as she said, "We did not dine and dash."

Max repositioned himself upright, and a wild, proud smile spread across his face. Amelia didn't feel the humor or thrill.

Madisson shifted, her eyes flickering with shame before she

reached into the seatback pocket. She pulled out a Burt's Bees chapstick, coating her raw lips —a distraction. Madisson passed it around the car in silence.

Eventually, someone put on music. Amelia didn't notice who. She stopped caring about the music or what Madisson was thinking. She stopped caring about her own numbness. All of her caring had been exhausted.

Three hours to the apartment dragged. By the time she parked, she still hadn't said a word. There was nothing left to say.

Max, Madisson, and Reyna mumbled a thank you and exited the car. Max pulled out their bags and limped them into the complex.

"Amelia?" Art asked.

"Art."

He swallowed. "I swear it wasn't the ecstasy. I love you so much." His sincerity echoed her feelings. His eyes, back to their ocean blue, met hers, a look of hope and fear in them.

"I love you, too," she murmured.

The words felt new. She had said them to Weston on their sixth-month anniversary, but now they carried a heavier weight, a mutual promise. With Weston, it had seemed like the right time. They had had sex for the second time, which in hindsight was more mechanical than passionate. But then, she imagined that was how it was supposed to be. She lay in his arms, naked under the comforter, and the words tumbled out–I love you.

He said nothing, and his eyes found the ceiling. Her saying it was a new problem for him to solve, to make order out of. She wanted to take the words back at his silence, rewind, and shove them down. Bury them. Forget it ever happened.

"I don't expect you to say it back," she had told him quietly.

It was a lie, of course. Who says "I love you," without believing it was reciprocated? She thought she had loved him.

He made her feel safe. He listened to her complaints about her family. He tutored her to make sure she was accepted into UCLA. They enjoyed each other's company. She loved that he dressed up with her. He came to the opening night of her play with flowers. He accompanied her to whatever function their parents insisted they attend. He was dependable and kind to her. That was the love that her parents shared.

She couldn't fathom how Weston didn't love her. There was no past trauma to untangle- both of their parents were happily married. She and Weston rarely fought and never over anything of substance. They lost their virginity to each other.

It was all important to her. She loved him, and he did not love her. She let the words slip two more times before he broke up with her. Words he never said. Not until he saw her with someone else.

With Art, her perspective had been altered. While she didn't doubt that she had loved Weston as much as she could, there were various types of love. There was a heated passion and effortless understanding with Art. It was an adventure, an experience, a high she'd never felt before. She would meet many more men like Weston, who were great on paper. She would never meet someone like Art again, who was right for her soul.

CHAPTER TWENTY-FOUR

Amelia rolled over, squinting her eyes open. She stretched for her phone on the nightstand and swiped at the screen. *Shit.* She had been asleep for sixteen hours. How was that even possible? There were two missed calls from Weston and a slew of texts.

WESTON

How was the music festival?

Did you get home safe?

If you don't answer, I'm calling Lauren.

Lauren said you're in your room sleeping.

Can I see you today? You know I'm leaving soon.

She shot Weston a text before he summoned another wellness check for her.

AMELIA

Don't text my mom again, weirdo. Can't today, but I'll see you this week.

She slammed her phone down and got out of bed. Her body cramped all over, and it took an embarrassingly long time to reach the en-suite.

Opening her medicine cabinet, she pulled out a variety of pills in different sizes and colors. On the counter, she spilled the Adderall that she had removed from her car, a birth control pill, a multivitamin to help mitigate the damage she was causing in her life, and two Tylenol pills to help with the body soreness.

How many people took this many pills? Without them, who would she be? Someone different? Someone better? Someone worse?

She tossed them down her throat, chasing them with sink water, ending her internal self-analysis. An assessment was better for a day when she didn't feel like death.

Stepping into the shower, she cranked the heat and set the steam. It was the closest she could get to a spa without leaving the house. She fought to remember the last time she had showered. It had been before the rave, which was now, she countered, two days ago. Had it really been two days?

The water beat against the glass door, and she leaned into the calming sound. A break from the perpetual chaos she had been living in. The steam filled the shower, clouding her vision and activating a rose-petal shower bomb. She inhaled, thankful the residual ketamine had finally subsided. She would put herself back together again, one piece at a time. Her fingers raked through her dirty blonde hair, and she massaged a hair mask to the frayed ends.

Scooping out clay for a face mask, she took her time, rubbing it into each area: cheeks, nose, chin, and forehead. Letting the charcoal detoxify her skin, she worked on her body.

With every inch, she recalled the sticky rave floors, dried sweat, and hungry kisses. She rinsed and slid her razor against her legs, section by section. Her routine was slow and methodical, peeling back the layers until she felt new.

While it didn't fix everything, Amelia felt better than she had in days. Almost normal. She didn't know how much she enjoyed being normal until she spent so much time unlike herself.

Dressed in loungewear, she fell onto her plush mattress and called Art.

"What are you doing right now?" She inspected her nails, the next order of business.

"Running errands, then I have work." As an afterthought, he added, "Hey, you want to drop acid tomorrow? I still have some left."

She scoffed. "I don't think dropping acid should be a casual plan you make."

"Okay, I formally invite you to go on a trip of a lifetime tomorrow. No passports required. Bring an open mind and your beautiful face."

The way he teased her made every bad idea sound like a good one. She paused in consideration. Her body still felt like it had been in a head-on car crash from the ecstasy.

"It's not like it's needles. It's a little tab for an epic adventure." His words were gentle.

Art had done both at the rave. Certainly, taking one drug would be fine. Then, she would take a break. She would eat clean, hit the gym, and avoid all brain-altering substances. Be a better daughter, be a better friend to Weston.

"I can be there at ten?" she asked.

"Better make it noon. I have the late shift tonight."

"Cool, will do." Then she asked, "Cherry red or indigo for my next nail color?"

"Cherry red, definitely. They'll still be like that for my show, right?"

The inaugural Honey Cat show was coming up, and she buzzed in anticipation of Art's big performance. "Cherry red for Honey Cat it is."

"Dope. Love you, Princess," he drawled out the term of endearment.

"Love you more."

CHAPTER TWENTY-FIVE

The next afternoon, Art and Amelia met at the picnic table. The same one where they had smoked weed a month ago. A group of surfers walked by, then the park remained eerily empty.

Art took out a purple blotter paper with white psychedelic swirls. He carefully pinched the strip of acid, which resembled a Listerine strip more than it did a drug. Unlike the rest of her experimentation, this was the first one she couldn't see. Her chest pounded, warning her this was not a good idea.

"Tongue out." His words would have been authoritative had he not looked positively giddy about it.

Everything in her body screamed that this was too much, too soon. It had only been days since the ecstasy and ketamine. She swallowed her panic and stuck her tongue out. She would be fine. Everything would be fine.

Her tongue tingled as the acid dissolved.

"What now?" she asked him.

"Another." His teeth showed through his smile.

"I don't know." Her voice was thin, the pounding in her chest impossible to ignore.

His smile vanished. He put his thumb underneath her chin and tilted her head up to meet his eyes. "Listen, Princess, you never have to do anything you don't want to. My recommendation is two for you." He shrugged, casually offering her back control in the situation. "It's always your choice."

"How many are you taking?"

He smirked. "Four."

She bit her lip. She was only doing *half*. Her feelings were an overreaction to the concern of doing multiple drugs so close together.

With her tongue out, she accepted, and his smile erupted, spanning from ear to ear. She would burn the world down to watch him smile. Burn down her own world.

He placed a second strip on her tongue and then took his fourth.

After it dissolved, they both stuck their tongues out at each other. The energy vibrated between them. It wasn't serious. It was one afternoon of fun, and like all drugs, it would be over. The highs never lasted.

Thin clouds stretched above, none dense enough to block the warmth of the sun. A restlessness built in Amelia as she waited for the effects. After the miserable experience of salvia, she was begging for this hallucinogen to be good.

"So, what have I missed?" Art asked as he tapped a rhythm on the picnic table.

"I enrolled in my UCLA classes. I'm stoked about Acting for the Camera and Costume Design, but I don't know why I need a Freshman math class. All I want to do is act. What's the point of the rest?"

"Maybe you'll need to count the minutes between your scenes so you know when to enter and exit on time."

She narrowed her eyes. "You think I'll be standing around counting the minutes?"

"I don't know! I'm trying to help." He reached his hand over to hers on the table.

She sighed. "Anything new in your world?"

"Asher called me."

"From jail?"

Art nodded and rubbed her hand. "He said he might be getting out soon for good behavior."

"How do you feel about that?"

His eyes wandered to the treeline. "I don't know. I mean, it's great to have him back, right?" His eyes returned to Amelia, awaiting her to affirm his feelings.

"I mean, you watched him get arrested for dealing drugs. That's traumatic."

"Yeah." Art's shoulders slumped. "But, also, I think he did it because he had to, you know?"

Amelia scoffed. "Nobody has to deal drugs."

He bobbed his head. "Yeah, you're right." After another pause, he said, "It would be nice to see him again, though."

She offered a reassuring smile. "Of course it would be."

He didn't say anything else, so she shifted the conversation. "I think I'm going to go to L.A. this week to check it out. I don't want my first time exploring to be when I'm trying to move in." Then she added, "I want to find all the best spots to bring you!"

She had already pictured it. He would visit on the weekends. They would sneak into dive bars near the college, watch live music, and spend the night together in her apartment-style dorm.

"That sounds rad. You want company?"

Amelia chewed on the inside of her lip. "I was thinking of inviting Madisson. This was supposed to be our summer together, and we haven't had any one-on-one time."

Art's eyes shone a glacier blue, specks resembling diamonds within them. "That's cool. Bring me back something, alright?"

"Of course! Gift giving is my love language."

She loved that he didn't feel the need to be attached to her.

"Whoa, check out those daffodils!" Art pointed where the concrete slab met the grass.

The plant was a neon yellow and moved up and down, waving to her. She gave a polite wave back, then gazed up at the plum-tinted sky.

"Let's lie down," Art suggested.

He moved onto a patch of lime green grass and patted the spot beside him. She stripped off her UCLA sweatshirt and smoothed it out on the grass before reclining on top of it. The blades were sticky in her fingers. Similar to the effects of marijuana, she felt things more individually, like an isolated muscle at the gym.

A kaleidoscope of flowers sprouted all around her—daisies, roses, violets, and lilacs. The colors and shapes formed again and again. Circling her wrists, flower bracelets wrapped around them like silk. A flower crown landed on top of her head. She was a live-action garden goddess. Careful of the imaginary crown, she rotated to Art, keeping her fingers pressed against the top of her hair.

While she may have been a goddess, his beautifully tanned, smooth skin resembled more a god than she had ever known— the Greek mythology sort. Tall, with a strong jaw, and the perfect wavy hair flowing past his shoulders. Her eyes raked him top to bottom, then stuck to his shoes. The whirls of skulls spun and weaved into hearts, then stars. They left his shoes and floated to the sky. She lay flat on her back, and the sun vibrated, warming her skin.

Time blurred. She had no idea if she had been there for a minute or for an hour. A squirrel scurried down an oak tree and swiveled its head. The fur on its back stood. A nervousness bubbled in Amelia's stomach. *It's just the drugs.* But the critter, whose mouth opened to showcase its sharp teeth, felt real.

Another squirrel zipped down. Then another. Amelia popped back up on her sweatshirt. Angry squirrels were overrunning the park. She pulled her bare arms in a hug, feeling exposed and vulnerable. She wanted to shrink herself, assure the squirrels that she wasn't a threat.

Another came. And another.

Her throat constricted, and her heart beat wildly. If she didn't do something *now,* her heart would fly out of her chest, and she would die. They'd put her in a graveyard where the squirrels would be waiting and seeking revenge on her for being in their park and invading their home. She didn't belong here.

"We need to go," she croaked.

Art took his time, blissfully unaware that a mob of angry squirrels was getting ready to end his girlfriend's life. He squinted at the sun, then stood.

Pivoting toward her, he extended his hand, large and comforting. She squeezed his hand tightly, distracted by his beauty.

Was he a god or a knight?

Was he everything that's ever been good in the world made into one person? Would he protect her from an army of angry squirrels?

She snapped back to the dark world in front of her.

Amelia tugged on her sweatshirt, not slowing to dust the grass off. It was another layer of protection against the rabid critters coming for her.

Hand in hand, they made their way to the sidewalk. Every few feet, another person passed them. It was to be expected on a summer day in a beach town. In fact, it was one of Amelia's favorite things, always an opportunity for her and Art to continue their people-watching game. But today, the people passed by rapidly. She couldn't get a good look at one person before the next one came. It was dizzying. People were small, large, old, and young. They had piercings and slicked-back hair.

Paranoia flooded her chest and tightened her throat.

They were out to get her. The squirrels had sent them.

With her left hand, she flashed the peace sign and hurried. Surely, they knew that she wasn't looking for trouble. She was peaceful.

But there were so many of them.

Panic engulfed her, forcing tears down her cheeks.

She gripped Art's hand tighter with her right hand. He was the only thing that could save her from this disintegrating world with its plum skies and angry squirrels and too many fucking people.

She opened her mouth to tell Art they needed to run, to find a side street. If they could find the alley where they had set off fireworks, or stolen chalk, or kissed against the chain drug store wall. Somewhere that happy memories would surround her.

Despite her mouth agape, Amelia was voiceless.

She couldn't remember how to form words. She snapped her mouth closed, desperate for the trip to end.

When things couldn't get worse, Art's hand slipped away from hers. He brushed his dark locks out of his face, then let his hand fall to his side. Forgetting all about her. The physical separation was equivalent to an emotional separation. Her heart corroded at the rejection.

She tried to understand why they were no longer in sync. The best she could come up with was that she was a train, rushing straight ahead, wanting to be anywhere else. He was a boat. Bobbing along as the current moved him. They were both modes of transportation. Momentum was the shared goal. But they were too different.

He was a boat, and she was a train, after all.

The door to Art's apartment was in front of her. Were they back?

He opened the door, and she barged past him to the bathroom with an urge to splash water on her face. If she could cleanse the whole experience, she could wash away the paranoia, fear, and guilt of being a train.

She jerked the door closed behind her, the slam deafening. Turning on the faucet, she counted to ten, held her breath, then counted down to one.

Water swirled down the drain, each droplet on its own path.

Conceptually, she understood that what she had seen hadn't been real. Numbers, though, those were real. A flicker of amusement pulled at her lips as she recalled Art's earlier comment about how she could apply math to her acting. The absurdity that now, while tripping on acid, she could use something she had deemed to be pointless, made her laugh manically, silently. Air pushed out of her mouth, but still. There was no sound.

Cold water splashed over her face, then she toweled dry.

Her reflection was in the mirror. *Wasn't there a rule not to look in the mirror while you're on hallucinogens?*

She remembered too late.

The mirror latched onto her.

"It's a cruel world. Only the best will make it," Mirror Amelia said.

It was harrowing. The exact words she had been shamed for saying to her stage director, now being hurled at her.

"You could be better," Mirror Amelia said. "You're pretty enough. You're smart enough. You could manipulate people. Distort their emotions like putty." Mirror Amelia smiled like a vixen, her eyes an emerald green.

Her hands flew over her face to protect herself from the mirror bitch, tears blurring her vision. She pretended not to know the girl in the mirror, but what if she was her? What if there was an evil side of her locked away, demanding to escape?

Squeezing her eyes shut, she turned the bathroom knob.

"Accept your destiny! You're too great for that pathetic world!" Mirror Amelia yelled.

One step in front of the other, she inched out of the bathroom and slammed the door closed behind her. Locking Mirror Amelia in.

The door crashed into its frame, but Art didn't flinch from where he sat on the couch. Vacant eyes fixed on the TV. Not the black eyes from ecstasy, but a new sort of emptiness.

Weston's eyes were bloodshot whenever he got high. Her eyes had threatened her in the mirror. Art's eyes were hollow. Had the person who coined the phrase "eyes are windows to the soul" partaken in drugs? Surely, you could determine what drug someone was on by their eyes.

How many drugs had she done?

For the second time in twenty-four hours, she told herself that she needed to slow down. Take a break. Be herself.

Amelia sat beside him as tears rolled in quiet agony, dampening his shirt. His arm limply rested on her shoulder. She wished both trips were over and that they would return to normal. There was an unshakable terror of Mirror Amelia escaping, and Amelia being the one trapped inside the glass.

CHAPTER TWENTY-SIX

A few days later, Madisson's feet were kicked up on the dashboard as she scrolled through the Spotify playlist she had curated for their day. The window was open, sunlight casting a light shadow on them.

Amelia hadn't told her about the acid trip. When Madisson and Max returned to the apartment, she and Art were sober, wrapped in the safety of each other's arms on the couch. She had no interest in bringing herself back down by rehashing the day and wasn't sure how she would describe it anyway. Angry squirrels, colors so vivid they didn't have a name, and her evil alter ego?

No. It was better to pretend it never happened. Art had said that bad trips sometimes happen and held her close, stroking her hair until her tears dried. But the scariest part of the trip was losing him. He wasn't himself, couldn't comfort her until it was over.

As they passed the exit for the Hollywood sign, on cue, Miley Cyrus's Party in the U.S.A. blared from the car speakers.

Amelia laughed at Madisson's perfect timing. "You're cheesy."

A normal day, a one-on-one best friend adventure had been sorely missed.

"Of course, honey." Madisson squealed, her arm hung out the window, and she splayed her fingers, letting the wind blow between them. "We're going to have the best day ever!"

L.A. was vast, and there was no way Amelia could even scratch the surface of what she wanted to do. She narrowed her itinerary down to four spots. Their first was Erewhon, the luxury grocery store Amelia had only seen on Instagram and was dying to check out.

An hour later, Amelia strolled the refrigerated aisle, tips of her fingers trailing the fruit selection.

"I could live here," she gushed.

Madisson was a step behind her, looking at the pyramids of fruits and vegetables. Amelia leaned closer to the peaches, smooth and blemish-free. They resembled kids' play food.

"It looks like a Kardashian's fridge times a billion," Amelia said.

"How do you know what a Kardashian fridge looks like?" Madisson laughed.

"Instagram." While she had long enjoyed Kardashian antics, she had started replaying old episodes more after she and Art decided they would be the next Kourtney and Travis. It was looking into a future version of herself, one she desperately wanted to be: the closet and that rock star wife life.

Madisson grabbed a green apple, rubbed her thumb across the skin, then bit into it. She pulled back, wide eyes with spit glistening on her lip.

"Holy fucking shit," she murmured. "This may seriously be the best."

They spent twenty minutes exploring the store, with Amelia on alert for a chance at a celebrity encounter. Anyone in a hat, she paid special attention to. She scrolled enough gossip websites to know that celebrities honestly believed they wouldn't be recognized with a ball cap on.

After touring each section, ogling the low-ingredient lists and meticulous packaging, the girls meandered to the cafe section. Ultimately, Amelia forwent the legendary Hailey Bieber smoothie. She would want something to bite into at their next stop, and Madisson bought both of them a turkey wrap and a chocolate chip cookie to share.

Madisson connected her phone with the directions to Griffith Park, three miles away. With traffic, it took twenty minutes. They filled the drive by belting along to Madisson's overly popish playlist.

In the parking lot, they rubbed on tanning sunscreen. Amelia looped her hair through a snapback, trying to still look good. She preferred her hair down and out, but didn't want it to get sweaty for the rest of the day.

Madisson had her hair tied back into two long braided ponytails. She was applying sunscreen to the strip of exposed stomach between the sports bra and biker shorts, while Amelia packed their sandwiches into the black backpack.

Madisson eyed it. "Is that Art's?" Her tone had a trace of judgment Amelia couldn't place.

"Yeah, I didn't want to mess up any of my purses on the trail."

Her shoes would already need cleaning when she got home. Locking the car with a beep, she zipped the keys into the backpack, and they fell into step on the dirt trail.

"How long have you been together?"

Amelia talked it out loud: "Let's see. We met on July 1st. We had our first kiss on July 4th. He told me I was his girlfriend on July 11th. So six weeks or so. It's crazy how I dated Weston for so much longer, but it feels right with Art."

Madisson rubbed her lips together.

"How long has it been with Max now?" Amelia asked. Too

long was the answer, but she couldn't remember when they got together. Max had always been around.

"Just over two and a half years." Madisson smiled lightly.

"You think you'll be able to make it work when you're at school?"

"Yeah, I do."

Amelia wished she were more sunny. Nerves about moving away from Art crept in her stomach with each passing day. Things were great, but even if she saw him on the weekends, it would be hard to keep everything the same while moving two hours away.

"I set the expectations that we won't be hanging out all the time as we have been this summer," Madisson continued. "It will be more like when I was in high school—I'll see him some nights and on the weekends. He signed up for a welding class at the community college, which will help keep him busy."

"Wow." Amelia was impressed that Max was doing anything at all.

They fell behind one another when they passed a hiker and a husky dog with a tie-dye handkerchief around its neck. A few clouds hung above them, occasionally covering the sun and providing relief from its glare.

"How was that show with Reyna?" Amelia asked. After the rave, any lingering jealousy of Reyna had faded. She and Madisson would always be best friends, and they would both grow their friendship circles in college, not cutting each other out.

"It was amazing!" Madisson's hands pinched together in the air, trying to hold on to the magic. "I got a new bracelet from the coolest chick. She had her dreads wrapped up and told me that she also does aura paintings and that my color was a bright yellow."

Madisson continued talking, and Amelia smiled. It had been

so long since they had the simplicity of being two girls catching up, not trying new substances together. They reached the Hollywood Sign on the eastern side of Mount Hollywood, as a plump man fell to his knees dramatically and screamed, "I did it. I made it."

Amelia rolled her eyes and surveyed the area. Aside from the Hollywood sign, there wasn't much at the top. The view below was the draw. Amelia leaned over, taking in the enormity of urban Hollywood. Soon she would be a speck in this larger-than-life city, but pursuing her dreams with millions of others was comforting, less lonely.

She unzipped Art's backpack and pulled out her Rumpl blanket, which featured hues of teal, blue, yellow, and orange. She smoothed it out on the dirt, and Madisson plopped down beside her. They took out their wraps and enjoyed a few bites in comfortable silence, the breeze dancing across their skin. A hunger had been gnawing. She'd taken an Adderall pill before she picked up Madisson and skipped breakfast. There were only a few left, and while she was sure Art would get her more, that seemed like crossing the line from summer fun into something serious.

Madisson reclined on her forearms, tanning her midriff while Amelia sat cross-legged.

Amelia leaned over. "What do you think their story is?"

A blond couple with matching navy-blue workout sets stretched nearby.

"I don't know. They're probably dating."

Amelia smiled and raised her eyebrows. "Wouldn't it be funny if they actually came up here to fight a bear?"

Madisson eyed her quizzically and tilted her head. "I guess?"

Amelia pulled out her phone.

AMELIA

> I miss you and I love you so much! I wish you were up here to watch this couple take on a bear.

ART

> Are you sure it's a bear and not a Veloster Raptor?

> Also, glad you texted. I was thinking about how much I miss your–

Amelia slammed her phone down before she finished the message, a blush creeping on her cheeks. While she enjoyed sex with Art, she was not comfortable sexting next to Madisson.

"Ready?" Madisson asked, blissfully unaware, crumpling up the parchment paper.

"Let's do it." Amelia stood.

They tossed their wrappers into the metal bin and set Madisson's phone on the nearby bench. She set the timer and backed up so they were in front of the Hollywood sign. Amelia's arm slung over Madisson's shoulder, and Madisson's arm outstretched diagonally to the sky. The phone shutter clicked.

"For our dorm rooms," Madisson said.

"For our dorms," Amelia promised.

They chugged their water bottles and made the trek down.

CHAPTER TWENTY-SEVEN

At the base of the hike in the parking lot, the girls pulled new clothes from the car, then changed in the restroom at the trailhead. While it wasn't sparkling clean, nothing could be worse than the portapotties at the rave. They tossed their dirty clothes and dusty shoes in the trunk—A problem for later.

Twelve miles and fifty minutes later, they arrived at one of the many UCLA parking lots.

"You might want to consider biking or something when you move up here," Madisson suggested.

Amelia quirked an eyebrow.

"Yeah, probably not. Plan ahead so you can be on time!"

Amelia kept her eyebrow raised.

"Oh well, you'll get to class when you get there, right?"

"That's the one." Amelia pointed a finger. Being on time was never going to be a priority for her.

Last year, Amelia had toured the school with her parents. The tour guide with a crew cut and khakis pointed out the significant buildings, rattled off the extensive histories, and boasted about the published professors. James embarrassingly quizzed him on all the information. Was Royce Hall built in 1929 or 1939? The guide had it right in 1929, but her dad sought an opportunity to show off. Amelia rolled her eyes when James, as expected, told the guide that he had gone to UCLA back in 1990. Then, of course, *his* father had been here in the 60s. The guide responded. "Wow, that's so cool, you could probably give this tour."

Amelia wanted to throw up at the predictability of the response and the entire day. She learned nothing that couldn't have been found in the UCLA brochure.

Today, Amelia was excited to have an experience with the things she cared about. Exploring with Madisson would give her an idea of what school and the people would be like in September.

They headed to one of the university apartments. Amelia wasn't thrilled about sharing a room. As much as her parents tried to secure a single room, they couldn't. In fact, she was initially supposed to share a triple room with bunk beds. The promised double room was at least a step up.

They walked along the concrete stamped path to the side of the Gayley Heights apartment complex. The day had remained beautiful. She was glad the L.A. climate wouldn't be a change for her. The weather mirrored what she was accustomed to in San Diego.

Her mind drifted to Weston and the cold of Boston. Would he adapt or despise it? More preparation would be required for his daily routine there. Screw the umbrella in his car; he would need a whole snow set. She wasn't quite sure exactly what that entailed. Her snow experience was limited to cabins in Lake Tahoe, where the hired help handled shoveling and whatever else needed to be done. A guilt that she still hadn't seen Weston tried to creep in. She pushed him out of her head. She would see him at some point. She was pretty sure about it.

Benches and bistro tables surrounded a bubbling fountain in the apartment courtyard. Tall trees wrapped in fairy lights perimetered the area, their branches extending partially over the tables. A student was hunched over a large textbook at a table. A pair of guys slouched against a wall, passing a joint back and forth. She crinkled her nose at the skunk smell. It was quaint, but quiet. She had expected it to be more lively than this. Summer classes were still in session, and there should have been hustle and bustle.

"Come here." Madisson shout-whispered, waving to her from across the courtyard, her foot propping open the door to the lounge area. A petite girl passed by Amelia, clutching the straps of her backpack.

"Good call." Amelia followed Madisson inside.

The common area had more activity. The conference room was laid out with purple carpeting. A group of nerdy guys reclined in the plush, computer-style chairs. The decor could have been fabulous and funky, but came across as tacky. A pair of yellow couches was pressed together in the center, with a girl on each, both lying horizontally and wearing yoga pants. One was reading a book, while the other was napping with her hands interlaced behind her head.

"This is pretty cool!" Madisson commented.

Amelia wished she shared the same enthusiasm. She wanted to come here to see what her life would be like in a month. She couldn't tell where she belonged at all.

They wandered down a hall, an elevator closing in front of them.

"Hey!" Madisson yelled. A hand intercepted the doors, triggering them to reopen.

They stepped inside, and two guys decked in lacrosse gear moved to the left.

"What number?" asked the taller one with oily skin.

"Five," Amelia lied.

He pressed the number, and the elevator rose.

"If you ladies aren't doing anything later, we're on floor seven." The shorter one with a bowl haircut winked at them.

The girls smiled politely and scurried off at the fifth floor. Art had nothing to worry about, that was for sure.

Madisson led the way, skipping down the hall. "I can't believe you'll be living here! We have to make our plans for me to visit."

Doors were propped open as they passed the rooms. They were identical and cramped. She would hardly be able to bring any of her things. She poked her head into one of the rooms. A girl sat on the couch with a book on her lap.

"Excuse me?" Amelia asked her.

Madisson returned to her side when she noticed Amelia had broken off.

"Yes?" The girl's eyes rose from her book.

"I know this is a super weird question, but I'm moving into this building in a few weeks."

"Oh?"

"Yes, can I see your bathroom? I want to prepare for how much space there is," Amelia hurried. It was necessary information.

"Um, sure." She stood. "I'm Scarlett, by the way." Scarlett extended a hand, and Amelia and Madisson shook it, then introduced themselves before following her a few steps into the bathroom.

"Here are the luxury accommodations," Scarlett joked, gesturing to the small space. It had a shower, a toilet, and two sinks. Organizer containers were on the counter, and an over-the-door rack was filled with perfumes and lotions. Scarlett and her roommates did a good job maximizing the space, but it must have been impossible for multiple girls to get ready at the same time. Amelia interlaced her fingers and tapped her thumbs as she mentally redecorated.

"How do you like the place?" Madisson asked.

"Oh, it's good. I mean, this is the newest undergrad apartment, so everything's nice. The floor itself is pretty quiet, though. Most people who party are in the traditional dorms on campus, but I couldn't imagine sharing a triple."

Amelia nodded with the sentiment.

"Well, thanks for letting us in. We will let you get back to..." Madisson glanced down at the book she was reading by Sarah J. Maas.

A deep blush crept up Scarlett's cheeks. "Oh, you know." She waved her hand.

They thanked Scarlett and returned to the hallway.

Madisson asked, "Did you want to check out the deck on top?"

Amelia was quiet, then sighed. "No, no. I have seen enough."

She had no idea what she was going to do, but living in the apartments was not an option. She wouldn't survive being on top of others without all her things. There was downsizing, then there was living like she was in the military.

"On to the next stop!" Madisson proclaimed and led them back to the elevator.

Once again, they were left waiting on a stranger's mercy to unlock it. Madisson started a game of rock-paper-scissors, winning both rounds, until a plump girl in a UCLA sweatshirt came by to open it. They followed the next stranger into the elevator.

She offered them a small smile. "Going down?"

"Yes, thanks so much," Madisson answered.

They reached the ground floor and followed the resident out of the elevator. When they returned outside, Madisson looped her arm into Amelia's. The last stop was the one Amelia was looking forward to the most, and she had to change her mindset. L.A. was going to be great. She would just need to figure out her living accommodations. She took a deep breath, then had an idea of how to make their last destination the very best.

CHAPTER TWENTY-EIGHT

Crossroads Kitchen, the vegan restaurant owned by Travis Barker, was located a few miles from the campus. But first, Amelia needed an item she couldn't legally purchase there. At a nearby liquor store, Amelia flipped down her visor. She fished lip gloss from her center console and reapplied the pink stain.

"What are we doing here?" Madisson chirped, looking around.

Amelia puckered her lips. "I've been obsessed with their menu- it changes constantly," Amelia explained. "I want the pasta, but what's the point of pasta without wine to go with it?" She smirked.

Madisson shifted. "I guess. But how are you going to get wine?"

"Oh, Art's taught me how to do this. He points out a buff guy in the store, and I ask them to buy it for me."

Truthfully, Art had only told her she could probably pull it off. She hadn't actually attempted it before, but she needed to be confident for this to work. Admitting to Madisson that it was her first time would let the doubt seep in.

"Are you sure?" Madisson's voice was edged with concern.

"Totally. Be back in a sec." Amelia responded before she lost her nerve.

She left Madisson and stepped out of the car. Straightening her back and rolling her shoulders, she channeled Mirror Amelia from the acid trip. If anyone could pull it off, it would be her scary and overly confident alter ego.

A bell dinged overhead as Amelia shoved the liquor store door open, and she scanned her options. An older woman in her mid-forties who was grabbing milk, no. An elderly couple purchasing lotto tickets, definitely not. A man who appeared homeless standing in front of the energy drink cooler, maybe. He'd probably do it, but that was way too weird.

Then she found him. Her target appeared to be in his early thirties, with a thin mustache, and was reaching for a bag of Flaming Hot Cheetos. Not exactly a muscled hero, but he would do.

She adjusted her V-neck. Showtime.

"Excuse me, sir, can you do me a huge favor?" Amelia asked, her voice an octave higher than usual, as she approached him.

He took her in, eyes pausing where she knew they would. Her stomach turned.

"Sir?" he asked with a smirk, enjoying the word too much.

She forced a flirty giggle. "I forgot my ID, and I was hoping you could grab me a bottle of Pinot Grigio."

They referenced the wine on a Bravo show she watched with Lauren. She had no idea what the differences were between wines. She mostly drank beer or mixed drinks, whatever was handed to her at a party. But her first day in L.A. was the occasion for something sophisticated. Adult.

She pulled out a $20 bill and handed it to him.

The man licked his lips, and Amelia smiled through her disgust.

"Sure, sweetheart. I'll see you outside." His voice was slow, and she was itching to put space between them.

"You're such a lifesaver." Amelia turned, feeling his eyes on her ass as she exited the store. Only when she was out of sight did she exhale and let her shoulders drop.

She had done it; Art would be proud.

Madisson caught her eye from the car a few stalls away. She shifted her thumb up and down in question.

Amelia thumbed up and mouthed, "I think."

Madisson nodded, but her body was stiff.

A few minutes later, the man approached with a brown bag. "I hope you don't mind," he said with a slight grin. "I kept your change as a finder's fee."

"Oh yeah, totally," Amelia said, reaching for the bag. He released it, but didn't move away.

"So where are you headed next?" His eyes raked over her again.

"Oh, out with my friend. Great meeting you!" she said, then spun on her feet and beelined for the car.

She had left the engine running for Madisson's music, which made it easy to get into the car and then quickly reverse. From the rearview, he kept his eyes on her. While she accomplished her goal, she also felt slimy. It had worked, but Amelia wasn't disillusioned that it was a good idea.

"I'm definitely going to need to ask Art where he got his fake ID." Amelia forced out a laugh.

Madisson bit her lip. "Are you sure that's a good idea?"

Amelia's face contorted in confusion. "Much better than asking random men to do it."

Madisson averted her eyes and picked a new song on the playlist.

Amelia shrugged off her lack of agreement. Madisson didn't need to worry about it. Max was nearly twenty-one, and all of his friends were older. Amelia didn't have the same advantage.

When they pulled into the Crossroads parking lot, Madisson asked, "Do we need a wine opener?" She pulled the white wine bottle from the brown bag.

"Oh shit," Amelia responded, taking the bottle from her. Relief filled her when she realized it was a screw top. She twisted it, breaking the seal, and returned it to Madisson.

Madisson wiggled her eyebrows devilishly at Amelia and took a sip from the bottle.

"That's my girl!" Amelia proclaimed. Finally, whatever was eating at Madisson had faded. Madisson passed the bottle back to Amelia. She took a swig. It didn't burn in the same way liquor did. "Not actually great," she admitted to Madisson.

Madisson snorted. "Nope!"

After Madisson unscrewed her stainless steel water bottle, she poured the liquid outside the car. Amelia handed the wine bottle back, and Madisson replaced the water with the wine.

"You're basically Jesus now," Amelia remarked.

They burst into a fit of giggles.

Inside, a hostess, who could have also been a model, escorted the girls to their table. There were hundreds of dangling lights, all of different lengths. Little lamps on the table provided a soft glow in the moody ambiance. When the hostess eased away, their server, a man with coiffed hair and a perfect smile, set down two crystal glasses of water on the cream tablecloths.

He handed them menus. "Please let me know if you have any questions."

"So hot," Madisson whispered as he moved to the next table.

"I assume everyone in the restaurant business in L.A. is hot. Most are trying to break into the entertainment industry."

"Oh, I'm definitely visiting you."

"Shall we?" Amelia asked, raising her water glass.

"Yes, ma'am," Madisson said, raising her own.

They quickly drained their cups.

Amelia glanced around, deemed the coast clear, and whispered, "Go."

She poured the wine from her water bottle into the empty glasses. Madisson put her water bottle back in her purse and nudged it under the table.

They smiled and raised their glasses for a second time.

"Here's to you, and here's to me?" Amelia asked with a smile.

"Best of friends we'll always be," Madisson confirmed.

They let the cheer end there. Who needed the boys and their second half anyway? It was more positive without damning the other person to hell.

The girls gossiped while enjoying their pasta and a side of baby zucchini. If their server registered that their water now had a yellow tint, he didn't say.

"Reyna and I are hosting a College Kickoff Party at the apartment," Madisson said.

"Ooo, I'll help decorate." Amelia imagined red and gold streamers and lots of sparkles. She could get her nails done to match.

The server swung back by their table, and Amelia asked to purchase one of the shirts she had seen hanging in the front.

"What if we did a Madisson Mojito?" Amelia suggested after he had left.

"Renya Rum Punch?"

"SDSU whiskey sour?"

"Get the Fuck Out of Town, Tequila Slammer?"

The waiter returned with the medium shirt. "Can I interest you in a cinnamon pecan sponge cake?"

They exchanged a look. Whether it was the wine or his

smile, the girls took his recommendation and inhaled the dessert.

On the ride home, Madisson's L.A. playlist had concluded, and she switched to the radio. Amelia cruised down the freeway, glad to be out of the glacier-speed L.A. traffic.

"Am I taking you to your parents or Max's?" Amelia asked as they passed the sign for the San Diego county line.

"My parents." Her voice was small.

Amelia couldn't remember the last time she had been to Madisson's house. Madisson remained quiet for the rest of the drive, staring out into the dark of evening. The city lights blurred by. A blanket of exhaustion fell over Amelia; with all of their activities, it had felt like ten days in one.

She pulled into Madisson's driveway, ten minutes from her own.

"How often have you been staying here?" Amelia eyed her.

"Not often."

Amelia nodded in sympathy. As much as her parents annoyed her, at least they noticed when she was gone.

Madisson leaned over to hold Amelia's hands. "I need to tell you something." Her voice was barely above a whisper.

Amelia's hands went limp.

"You're scaring me." Amelia tried to laugh, but the sound was hollow.

Madisson glanced away, then back again as if searching for the words.

She swallowed. "Honey, Art is a drug dealer."

Amelia's brows furrowed. "What?" she asked. It was the strangest joke Madisson had ever told. It didn't make any sense, and it wasn't funny.

Madisson hesitated.

Was she serious?

Amelia retracted her hands from Madisson's as if she had been burned.

"What the fuck are you talking about?" Amelia asked, her voice raised.

Madisson folded her hands in her lap. "I wasn't sure how to tell you. If you already knew?" There were deep creases in her forehead.

"It's not true," Amelia defended. With Asher in jail for dealing drugs, Art would never do that.

Madisson shifted and bit the edge of her lip. "It is true. I've seen him."

"You've *seen* him deal drugs?" Amelia asked, incredulous.

Madisson nodded.

"No, you haven't." Amelia shook her head in disbelief. "I don't know what you think you saw, but you didn't see that."

Rage boiled in her chest. Sure, Art made lousy choices, but he wasn't an idiot. He knew the consequences of doing something that dangerous. His brother was the obvious example. No. He wouldn't risk it.

"Are you calling me a liar?" Madisson's tone shifted to offense. But if anyone should be offended, it was Art. And now, by proxy, Amelia.

She held her stare.

Madisson let out a breath and tried again. "There is nobody who loves you more than I do. I'm here, protecting you. How long have you known this dude for?"

"You know exactly how long I've known him. Regardless of the time, I know him. God, he's not even here to defend himself." It was absurd. She knew him. It was Madisson who didn't.

"I didn't think he needed to be here. I wanted to make sure that you knew. I care about *you*."

The car was too small, the day too long. She had been backed into a corner with wild accusations, and she was done.

"Get the fuck out of my car."

Hurt covered Madisson's face in a way Amelia hadn't seen since their fight two years prior. She didn't say anything else. Madisson let herself out as Amelia gritted her teeth.

As the door clicked closed, Amelia slammed her foot on the gas and sped out of Madisson's driveway with a screech. She didn't bother looking back.

Amelia's thoughts tangled as she barreled home. Sure, he did drugs. He got them drugs. But selling? That was different. He had a job at the restaurant, which surely didn't pay much, but he still went to work. That was his job. She knew everything about his life. They saw each other nearly every day and talked in between. If he were dealing drugs, she would have known about it.

She was still fuming when she returned home.

Amelia stormed into her room and paced. She picked up the television remote from her nightstand. Turning it over in her hand, she thought of what Madisson had said. How sure she was. How the entire perfect day they spent was tainted.

How had things gone so wrong? She threw the remote as hard as she could against the wall.

There were several dings in the once-pristine walls. But who cared? Who cared about a wall when your best friend accused your boyfriend of being a drug dealer?

She texted Art.

AMELIA

Just got home, you at work?

He responded with a selfie of himself in the restaurant kitchen.

ART

Here till midnight. Have good dreams princess.
Love you.

AMELIA

Love you more.

Amelia placed her phone with the screen down. Madisson was crazy. Whatever she believed she saw, she was wrong.

Amelia was ready for the day to end. She went to her bathroom, pulled out a bottle of Tylenol PM, and took a dose more than the recommended amount. It didn't take long. As she slipped into her bed, her eyelids grew heavy. She drifted off to sleep, away from the horrible accusations.

CHAPTER TWENTY-NINE

The next day, Amelia stood on the sidewalk outside of Art's apartment complex in nervous anticipation. Art had already confirmed that Madisson was over, and Amelia wasn't ready to face her yet. She needed to hear the truth from Art first. She had been in a gunfight and not just without a knife; she had nothing to use at all. If this were an argument she was to have again, she would be armed with all the facts to counter Art's character assassination.

Her body relaxed at the sight of him. Strolling toward her, his lanky arms swung at ease by his side. He didn't look at all like a drug dealer.

He handed her a thermos filled with vodka, Sprite, and grenadine. She spent her childhood with Georgina drinking Shirley Temples—always with two cherries—at her parents' functions. She unscrewed the top and took a big gulp.

She choked at the cough-syrup taste. "What the fuck?" she asked.

She expected it to taste sweet and nostalgic. Maybe Art had made it wrong, or maybe it was a disgusting drink.

"You need a chaser for your cocktail?" he teased.

"Keep up the sass, and I won't give you your present."

Amelia set the thermos on the sidewalk and reached into her purse for the white shirt. It featured two steak knives crossing each other with a red, green, and yellow color scheme. It read: WORLD PEACE BEGINS IN THE KITCHEN.

"It's from Travis Barker's restaurant," she explained.

"This is so fucking sick!" He picked her up and spun her around. "Thank you so much!"

She laughed at the sky, filled with delight. He set her down, and she already missed where his hands were squeezing against her.

He admired the shirt again. "This really is the coolest. You're the best girlfriend ever."

Reaching back, he pulled off the Deadbeat Nightlife shirt he had been wearing. Her eyes lingered on his flat stomach before he covered up with the Travis Barker shirt. Maybe she'd see him shirtless later. Although there needed to be an alternative to the air mattress.

Down toward the beach, they played their favorite game of people watching. Two middle school boys skateboarded by—headed to ballet class. An elderly couple splitting a plate of nachos—scam artists.

The wannabe Shirley Temple concoction became bearable the more she drank. A lightheadedness and giddiness in her chest.

Stepping off the boardwalk, they headed toward large boulders. Art climbed up on one and outstretched his hand for her to join. She scrambled up with his help, and they sat slightly off kilter. Resting her head on his shoulder, she breathed him in: woodsy body soap and vodka. A salty breeze drifted past them, and the sun's orange glow began its descent behind the ocean.

It wasn't until the sun had dropped entirely and the vodka had emptied that she was ready to talk. She nuzzled against his shoulder, carefully situated. There would be nothing worse than him lying to her face.

"So, Madisson said something strange." Her words wavered. She was no more put together than the ocean.

"Yeah." He stiffened underneath her.

She brought her head up. "You know?"

"I mean, yeah. You didn't want to see her today," Art started. His chest fell, his eyes fixed on the horizon ahead. "I asked her what was up, and she told me."

"Madisson said you were dealing." Amelia forced a laugh.

"Yeah." Even if he hadn't admitted it, she would have known. His face creased, his ocean blue eyes haunted.

She pulled her back. "Yeah?" Her voice cracked.

This was not going how she expected. She had thought they would laugh about it, and he would assure her that Madisson was wrong. They would get drunk, make love, and bury the accusations under the rug.

He gently reached for one of her hands, rubbing his thumb over it. She let him.

"It's just enough to get by. I need new music equipment. I need to pay rent."

"But what about Asher? Why would you do the same thing that got him locked up?" It didn't make any sense.

He ran his free hand through his hair in anguish, and it pained her to see him distraught.

"It's a little on the side. Nothing dangerous like what he was doing. Only people I know. Friends of friends and coworkers, and their friends. It's nothing crazy. I swear to you that I would never do anything that would put myself or anybody else at risk like he did. You know, I want to pay you back for everything. It weighs on me that you always pay. I know you don't mind. But I promise you–one day, I'll make it big. I know you know that too. You believe in me."

His voice was choked, and his eyes shone with tears. He kept talking. She wasn't sure if he was trying to convince her or himself that what he was doing wasn't horrifying and dangerous.

"One day, you'll be with me. You'll be on the side of the stage, living out the Kourtney dream. I can't wait for you to come to my show this week–to see me in action. You're going to be so proud of me, Princess."

He kissed her tentatively. When she didn't pull away, he moved a hand to her cheek. They kissed hard until she couldn't breathe, the kisses drowning her sorrow. She loved him. She would continue to love him more than she could hate him for what he did. She kept kissing until she was crying.

When she broke away, his cheeks were tear-stained as well. She had never seen a grown man cry before. Her dad never did. Weston never did.

"I accused Madisson of lying," Amelia said. Guilt filled her chest. Fuck. Why hadn't she believed Madisson?

"I should have told you. I'm so sorry." Art brought his thumb underneath her eye and wiped her tears away. "I'll stop if you want me to. I'll do anything for you." His words were quieter, pure.

She wiped his tears as well. She'd never doubted he loved her, and even now, his words were heavy with honesty.

Her head dipped, whether in acceptance of his stopping or acknowledgment of the offer, she didn't clarify. She never envisioned she would be in this situation.

Amelia's fingers trembled as she raised the thermos to her lips again, only to remember it was empty.

"We need more." She struggled to breathe with the weight of his confession.

How had she not detected it? It made sense. He always had access to every drug. When he told her he was running errands, she never asked what that meant. It was foolish for her to assume he was getting Top Ramen or buying toilet paper. Then there was the time he told her he tested ecstasy.

She struggled to breathe. He was an anchor, and she let him pull her down to the ocean floor.

"I love you, Amelia. No one has ever believed in me until you."

The Honey Cat bracelet hanging on her wrist confirmed it. She was his day one.

He leaned his forehead against hers. She forgot how broken he was. He kept it together, his pain wrapped tightly in positivity, silver linings, and optimism. It suffocated the messy truth of his past and what he allowed his present to be.

"It's more than love," Art said. "We're twin flames. It will always be us."

"Twin flames," she repeated. The rare type of love that burned and danced.

She settled into his arms as they listened to the crashing waves in front of them, drowning out their sniffling. Crying together, the salt of their eyes and the sea were indistinguishable. It was more intimate, more raw than sex. Amelia had to come up with a plan for them. Whether he knew it or not, he needed her help. She was the one who believed in him, after all.

CHAPTER THIRTY

It was the day of the inaugural Honey Cat show, and Amelia had the same level of excitement for Art that she held for all of her plays. As such, she had the perfect day planned out, concluding with Art's opening night and the two of them celebrating.

In the morning, she went to pilates. She honed in on her butt and thighs, the Adderall pushing her through the pain, and she lapped up the attention as Lauren used her as the example. The rug of unspoken conversations between them grew with each day.

She went to her nail appointment and chose Cherry Red as Art had requested.

"Seriously, check him out. He plays the drums." Amelia slid her phone over, showing a photo of Art at band practice that she had taken the previous week.

Amy, her nail technician, nodded enthusiastically, "Like a rockstar!"

After her appointment, Amelia swung by the mall. She weaved around the crowds and meandered into all of her favorite stores: Dolce & Gabbana, Bottega Veneta, and John

Varvatos. Kourtney Kardashian was her outfit inspiration. Sifting through the racks of clothes, her eyes fell to a black Dolce & Gabbana corset top with a sweetheart neckline. It was perfect. She smiled at the sales associate who rang her up and charged her parents' card without checking the cost.

Amelia shoved the armful of shopping bags into her trunk, moving aside hers and Madisson's dusty hiking clothes, then got in the driver's seat and blasted the Honey Cat demo. She tapped her nails against the steering wheel, eager to hear the songs live.

At home again, she changed into a striped bikini and settled onto the sun shelf of the pool. Tonight would be everything Art had been working toward, and she supported. After this show, he would book more gigs, and then it was only a matter of time before Honey Cat was discovered. Amelia daydreamed under the palm trees, sipping on water with a lemon, until it was time to do her hair and makeup.

——--

At dusk, Amelia slammed her car door shut and walked over to Art, who leaned against the wall smoking his vape.

"I can't believe you're here." Amelia grinned as she approached. The neon lights on the side of the building flickered, a few letters dark. It was iconic.

"Me either. This is insane." His smile was infectious as he pocketed his vape.

He extended a hand out to her and pulled her against him. His kisses tasted of nicotine and whiskey. She wasn't surprised he had already kicked off the party.

"You need to stop smoking."

"After all we've done, smoking remains my biggest issue for you?" An amused smile on his lips.

"You could die!" Her eyes went wide.

"Princess." He flashed a knowing smirk.

He was right, of course. There were plenty of other things that could get him killed, like dealing drugs. Her stomach twisted, and she changed the subject. They hadn't talked about it again. She believed him–it was temporary while he figured out the music. She needed to get him out of San Diego and toward his dreams.

"What if you came to L.A. with me?" She floated the idea to him.

"To your dorm?"

"What if we got our own place?"

"You want to move to L.A. together?" His face remained perplexed, with a half-smile frozen.

"Why do you keep questioning what I am saying?" She laughed nervously. She had thought he would agree immediately. One of their first conversations was about his wanting to be in L.A.

He folded his arms across his chest as he leaned against the wall. He must have concluded that she was, in fact, quite serious.

"I want nothing more than that. I just... financially..." He tucked a lock of brown hair behind his ear and dropped his gaze.

"My question isn't how we can afford it. The question is, will you come?"

This was the only path she could see. If she could get him to L.A., he could work on his music, and best of all, they could be together. While they discussed seeing each other on the weekends, he didn't have a car, and who knew how much free time she would have? It would be best for both of them.

After she visited L.A., she also desperately wanted to avoid an apartment-dorm situation. She didn't want to be stuck in a crowded place without her stuff, assigned to a random roommate.

"I'd follow you to the ends of the earth." He looked back at her.

A smile erupted on her face. Everything would be okay. "Great! Now show me around."

His hand engulfed hers, and he led her toward the back door of the building. Art nodded to a large, bald man with a shirt that read "Security," who opened the door for him without a word.

"You even have security. How impressive," Amelia teased.

"Pretty sure that's more for the venue than for us, but yeah."

The bar counter was located to the left, a stage was situated in the center of the back wall, and tall cocktail tables lined either side. A few patrons leaned against the edge of the bar, talking with the bartender as alternative music played from the speakers. The dive bar was precisely how she'd imagined it from the movies. It was dark and moody, with fairy lights strung overhead. Obscure picture frames decorated the wall.

Amelia immediately liked it, her imagination running wild with all the places Art and his music would take her. He'd play a sold-out show in Italy, and they'd elope in Tuscany on a Tuesday. They would make it back in time for her to walk the carpet with him by her side for her movie premiere. Together, they would be unstoppable.

Art wrapped his arms around her from behind. His sunset colored drum set was in the corner of the stage nearest the bar. A mic stand was front and center.

"Ready to go to the green room?" Art murmured to her neck.

Goosebumps trailed under his warm breath.

"You're so fancy," she said.

He led her down a short hall to a back room with a table and a few worn couches. The rest of the band was already there, and she was the only girl. One day, she was certain, this room would be filled with groupies. She was a day-one fan, the bracelet on her wrist with the Honey Cat logo serving as proof.

Art introduced his bandmates, sitting on the couches beside the table.

Jake, the singer, was a bit older. He had a beard, light brown eyes, and a sleeve of tattoos. They were far more artistic than anything she had seen on Max. He grumbled a hello.

Logan had tousled platinum blond hair. "Thanks for coming!" he chirped.

Evan was pale and freckled. He nodded a hello before his eyes wandered around the room.

After introductions, Art pulled out a baggie from his jeans pocket, and each of the guys threw a twenty-dollar bill on the table.

Amelia's throat caught. While she wasn't surprised by the whiskey, she hadn't anticipated this. Maybe it made sense. A way to celebrate his first show. But she couldn't pretend he didn't deal now. He wasn't just generous with drugs. This was a job for him.

She took a seat on the far end of the couch and willed herself to calm down. She knew he did this.

Art cleared the table and shook a white substance onto it. He pulled out his wallet and slipped out his ID card. With the thin side, he used the ID to chop the clumps of white and smooth them into a horizontal line. Then, he sliced into the powder again, smoothing it more and scraping his ID against it vertically, reforming the line.

After ten lines of cocaine were arranged, he peered at Amelia.

She could do this. She had done the ketamine. She could be part of his group.

He rolled up one of the twenties and then offered it to Jake. Amelia used to think Art was a gentleman when he opened doors for her. The gentleman's act apparently permeated all areas of his life.

Jake pushed himself off the couch and knelt next to the table. He put one end of the dollar to his nose and the other to the chalky substance. He inhaled. He rubbed his nose and passed it to Evan, who inhaled the following line with ease. Evan passed to Logan, who moved slowly. When it was Art's turn, he took his line with an overly dramatic inhale. She usually found his theatrics endearing, but she was too focused on her upcoming turn to feel anything but the rising uncertainty. It was the line she said she would never cross, yet now it was the next step. Not so far from the things she had already done. Once you've snorted something, does it matter what the substance was?

Art finished his line and gave her a curious look. She could say no. He only encouraged her to do drugs because he thought she would enjoy them. Her eyes fell to the powder. She had to make the decision now. It would be fun. Right?

Just once.

She held her hand out for the bill, and a flash of pride crossed Art's face.

The paper scratched against her nose as she inhaled. As with the ketamine, it burned all the way up her nose and then caught in the back of her throat. Unlike Ketamine, her eyes went wide like she had taken a shot of adrenaline.

"Fuck," she couldn't help but say.

The band politely laughed, and Art put his arm around her reassuringly. "It's good shit."

They went around the table again, each inhaling their second line. The guys made conversation about a video game they had played earlier that day.

Amelia's leg jittered. It was like Adderall times ten. She babbled to the group about how *cool* it was to be there. How *impressive*.

She stared at Evan, who was reclining on the couch. "How tall are you?"

"Uh, 5'9." He chuckled and glanced around the group, as if unsure what to make of her interest.

"Same as me." She nodded eagerly and stood, nearly knocking into the table. "Stand up."

"I'm good," Evan chuckled before looking at Art.

That was fine.

Who cared about him? She didn't want to be confined to the room any longer. Energy pulsed against her chest; she was a lion in a cage. She needed out. *Now.*

"I'm going to get a drink," she announced.

Art kissed her on the cheek, then returned to the conversation with the band.

She walked to the door, then, as an afterthought, called over her shoulder, "Break a leg!"

At the bar, Amelia ordered a double gin and tonic. As she had already gotten past the bouncer at the back, the bartender didn't know to ID her. Regardless, Amelia was sure she didn't look eighteen. Her lips were a dark red, she wore her favorite Good American jeans, and her new black corset top pushed her boobs up. In hindsight, the bandmates had gotten a show when she leaned over to snort the cocaine. A smile crossed at the idea of being desired. She was fucking invincible.

Amelia took a spot in the growing crowd next to a tall guy dressed in jeans and a black Guns 'N' Roses shirt. He had cropped blond hair, and the curve of his biceps stretched against his sleeves. They stood off-center from the stage, with a direct view of the drum set. The guy nodded at her, and his steel blue eyes lingered on her chest before he raised a beer to his lips.

"What brings you here?" she chatted.

"My brother's in the band." He smiled at her.

A guy used to attention. While he wasn't quite as tall as Art, he was still over six feet. In another life, perhaps she would have found him attractive. But in this life, cocaine fueled, with her amazing boyfriend going to be playing his first show, her thoughts were leashed to Art.

"Wait, that's cool! My boyfriend is in the band! Who is your brother?" She grabbed his arm, thrilled by the coincidence that they both knew members of Honey Cat.

He glanced at her hand on his bicep, then back up at her. A smirk on his lips. "Evan."

Amelia removed her hand quickly. She hadn't meant to have her gesture misread. "Yes, he plays one of the guitars."

"Bass," he clarified.

"Sure, sure." A guitar was a guitar. "What's your name?"

She hadn't asked, and she needed to know. She wanted to know everything, experience everything. Fucking fly. She was larger than life, surely, too big to be standing on the ground.

"I'm Joe." He extended a hand to her.

"Amelia." She shook it, then turned back to the stage. She lifted her drink, and her tongue circled the straw. She slurped her gin and tonic. She couldn't wait for Art to be on the stage, drumsticks flying.

"Well, I'll see you around, I'm sure." She heard Joe say. She had already forgotten about him.

She gave a bright smile. "See you, Joe, brother of Evan!"

He gave a nod and walked to a cocktail table nearby. A girl was waiting, her eyes darting around nervously. She could probably use a line.

The crowd hollered, and Amelia's attention snapped. On stage, the four musicians of Honey Cat filed out.

She cupped her mouth and whooped along with them. Ready for the best show of her goddam life. She dumped her empty drink into a trash can, then squeezed between the crowd, positioning herself at the front.

"Watch it," a boulder of a man growled as she pressed by him.

Anger budded up at the casual rudeness. She bit back a response, fighting with a guy twice her size before the band started was a bad idea. She closed her fists, and her nails punctured her palms. Releasing her hands, she shook them out. She was here to have fun. Here to support Art. She had to get her temper under control before she lost it.

Amelia glanced around for a distraction. Joe and his girl each took a shot of honey colored liquor. On his tiptoes, she tried to find Max. Art said he had invited him weeks ago. Amelia could only think of one reason Max-without-a-job would miss a night out. While she still owed Madisson an apology, Max could have come alone. It was pretty shitty of him not to be there. She winced. She'd broken a nail with her balled fists again.

Art caught her eye from the drum stool, and relief filled her lungs. He was here. She was here. It was all okay. He blew a kiss to her, and she pretended to catch it, holding it against her chest.

With a strum from Logan and Evans' guitars and a flick from Art on the drum set, Honey Cat began.

The pulsating music took over, Jake's raspy voice, Art's practiced movements, and the guys on the guitar. The songs blended in harmony, one flowing into the next, without distinct beginnings or endings. Watching Art play in his bedroom and listening to the demo incessantly was one thing. Seeing how all the other members came together live was quite another. They had a roaring talent in their own ways.

Holy shit, they *would* make it big. She had thought it, supported it, believed in it conceptually, but in front of her now... This was their first live show, yet it was as if they had done this a million times.

Art built up steam as the set went on. What had started as a gentle flick of his wrists tapping the drumstick to the drum turned into an all-out warfare. He threw himself into the movements, sweat dripping from him. Jake raised the mic and clapped above his head, leading the crowd. Once they caught on to the beat, he brought the mic to his grizzly face and screamed.

Pulling back, the crowd formed a circle. Men ran around the perimeter of it in a frenzy, slamming against each other as they circled. She released her fists. *That* was the place she wanted to be. Rounding the circle, she let herself knock into the men who gently shoved her back, an acceptable place to let out pent-up aggression. The circle was electric, unstoppable. Between the bumping of the music and the pulsing of her heart with cocaine, she radiated with an unparalleled liveliness.

After a few laps, she pulled out of the circle, panting and eyes wide with excitement. On stage, Logan put his foot up on a black box and bowed deeply as his fingers slid across the strings. Evan was at the back, so focused on playing that she only saw his eyes lift once- to the girl seated with his brother, Joe.

Amelia jumped up and down, thankful she didn't have to temper her excitement. Her arm raised, she flicked her fingers with the beat. Her head rolled from side to side. Closing her eyes, she let the music consume her.

A flash blinded her, interrupting the moment. A short girl with a nose ring and a tattoo of a butterfly on her forearm lifted her hand in apology, then took off with her camera.

"Thank you, San Diego," Jake drawled.

The show may have been over, but she wasn't ready to come down.

Her eyes flicked to Art, who gestured for her to go backstage. She pointed to the bar, and he thumbs-upped.

She ordered two Jack and Cokes and tipped the bartender with a fifty as a secret thanks for risking his job by serving an underage girl. The more she got away with illegal things, the more she was inclined to push the envelope. She could understand why Art pushed boundaries. It was the thrill.

The band was in the green room when she returned, white lines on the scratched table. A twenty-dollar bill was currently pressed against Evan's nose. Art and Logan leaned against the black chalkboard wall. She handed Art a drink, and he kissed her on the cheek.

"You can't be serious that you think Ruffles are superior to Lays chips," Art said to Logan.

"Of course they are. They have ridges," Logan responded.

"Do you want another one?" Evan looked to her.

"Yeah, yeah, I do." She was untouchable after the last one.

He lined up two more for her as she sat on the couch beside him and placed her cocktail down.

Amelia tapped her nose. "You have a little something."

"Oh, thanks." Evan wiped the residue off his nostril and rubbed it against his gums.

She would have to ask Art later what benefit that served.

"I met your brother out there," she said.

"Yeah, it's cool he came." Evan handed her the bill.

She leaned forward, inhaled through the rolled money, then tipped her head back.

Her eyes bristled with tears as clumps of cocaine burned through her nose. Swallowing, she choked it down the back of her throat.

"Fuck," she dragged out. It made sense as to why Art worked to smooth out the lines.

After regaining her composure, she asked, "Was that his girlfriend with him?"

As he answered, she took the second line, prepared for the burn this time.

"No, that's his roommate, Izzie. She tries to hate me." He chuckled.

"Why?" Amelia asked, salivating at the chance for gossip.

"She has a misguided idea of who I am." He said with a sniff that inhaled a few more particles from the rim of his nostril. Then he conceded, "I'm also crashing on the couch."

"I mean, Art's on an air mattress, not much better."

Evan's lips parted in a slight smirk. Art may not have shared that tidbit of information with everyone else.

She quickly returned to the prior conversation. "Do you think she's attractive?"

If Joe hadn't claimed her and she was living with both of them, this could cause a brotherly divide.

His eyes met the ceiling in deep contemplation. "Izzie has a myriad of attractive qualities. Her looks are unarguably one of them." He looked toward Amelia. "I'm going to head out."

Amelia took no offense as he left. She'd definitely be asking Art if he knew anything about the brothers and Izzie's situation. His aptitude for learning drama matched hers. He would love this.

She scanned the room for him, an eerie quiet expanding as she realized that everyone was gone. All that remained of Art was an empty whiskey glass.

CHAPTER THIRTY-ONE

With her Birkin slung over her shoulder, Amelia hurried along the carpeted hallway. A folded bill, shining with a residue of white powder, was shoved in her back pocket. Art wasn't at the bar. He wasn't at a table. He wasn't hanging around with fans.

Dashing towards the door she came in, she passed the bald security guard. With all her body weight, she threw herself against the heavy back door and was blasted by the chill of the night. It would have been sobering had she not inhaled two more lines like Pixie Sticks.

"You look like a slut! Why are your pockets longer than your shorts?" She could hear him before she could see him.

Art towered above a strawberry blonde. The girl's eyes darted to Logan, then back to Art. The photographer from the show stepped in between Art and the girl.

"Don't talk to her that way," the photographer said. She was a tiny thing, but if the tattoos and nose ring conveyed anything, she wasn't one to put up with shit.

"What the fuck?" Amelia stomped over to Art, intervening before things got worse.

Art turned to her with a wobble, as if just realizing she was there. "Amelia!" A smile broke, wide and unbothered.

"What. The. Fuck," she repeated.

Confusion crossed his face, and he pointed at the girl. "She looks like a slut. She knows that."

"Don't call her that," Logan said, finding his voice.

Art spun. "Do you like sluts?" There was a challenge in his voice that made Amelia's skin crawl.

Logan stepped closer to the girl, and her gaze dropped to the ground.

"Not another word," Amelia barked at Art. Turning to the girls, her voice dropped. "I'm sorry. We're going."

Grabbing Art's hand, she dragged him into the parking lot.

"Your boyfriend is a dick!" the photographer called after them.

Amelia clenched her teeth. Another day, she might have snapped back in his defense, but she had to get him out of there.

Crossing the parking lot, his hand went limp in hers. "I don't know why we have to go."

He looked back toward the girls, who were now hugging, then lifted his eyes to her. "I'm glad you don't look like that. You're fucking classy."

Her mind raced in a thousand directions.

"Did you say goodbye to your band?" she asked. They should have probably done that.

"Pff, I don't need to say goodbye to anyone. Let's go." He returned the grip of her hand, now a participating member of their grand escape from the scene he had caused.

With her free hand, Amelia reached into her purse for the keys. The steel cut into her finger as she pressed it tight. She had to think. Art was too far gone to be of any help. There was a bitter taste in her mouth, and not from the coke. So much for being a team.

The apartment would be a twenty minute drive.

Did she finish her last drink?

No.

No, she left her Jack and Coke-the-Cola on the table when she was doing coke-the-powder with Evan. She only had one drink, albeit a double, but that was hours ago. She was focused. She could drive. She swallowed her insecurity, needing to stop thinking about it and just do it.

In her white car with hearts outlined on the window, she sat in the driver's seat. Art slid into the seat next to her. He connected his phone and blasted the music.

"Put on your seat belt," she said when the car was running.

"You and your obsession with seat belts." He rolled his eyes.

When she heard the click, she exited the parking lot. Glancing in the rearview to see Logan kissing the girl that Art had berated, she left her curiosity there. She had to focus if they were going to get home safely.

At a deserted four-way intersection, her fingers rapidly tapped against the steering wheel, waiting for the light to glow green.

Art beat to the rhythm of the music on his thighs, head banging forward, brown hair flying as if he were still on the stage.

Pressing him out of her mind, she avoided her peripheral vision.

On the freeway, Art moved from using his thighs as drums to slamming his hands against the dashboard. As the music intensified, he leaned his body forward and gave a second performance.

The cruise control was set to three miles above the speed limit. Exactly at the speed limit would have been too unnatural. There were only a few other cars on the road. If a police car drove by, every car would be noticed. Blending in was paramount.

As the exit sign for Art's apartment appeared, her shoulders relaxed.

She slowed to take the exit curve, then stopped at the stop sign.

One, two, three.

Her foot tapped the gas again.

A new song started, softer lyrics wafting through the car. Art's singing was low.

As she drove past the Ralph's, his eyes bore into her. She glanced at him, back at the road, then back to him, as he serenaded.

"Sometimes I lie

'Cause all I want to do is impress you."

The street sign indicated they were three blocks away.

Passion carried his voice as he sang louder, desperately.

"Which is why I know you'll leave."

She swiveled her head to him. She'd leave him? What the fuck does that mean?

He broke eye contact as she caught a shiny black cat darting in the headlights.

"FUCK, AMELIA, LOOK OUT!"

Amelia swerved, missing the pet. Gripping the wheel tighter, she tried to straighten the wheel. Every movement was heightened. As she overcorrected the wheel, her foot panicked on the gas pedal.

A high-screeching sound pierced the night as the car skidded along the asphalt.

The car slammed into the light post. Her body lurched forward, then smacked against the leather seat as the seatbelt tightened, restraining her.

Her loudly beating heart was the only assurance she had of her mortality.

Panting, her eyes slid to Art. Terror was etched on his face. He blinked it away and neutralized his reaction, an even better actor than she was.

Oh, I'm sorrrrry blared from the car speakers.

Amelia slammed the heel of her hand on the volume button, silencing the music. Her chest rose and fell. Each breath brought with it the soreness from where the seatbelt had saved her.

"Princess, I am-" Art started.

"Shut the fuck up." Her voice was even.

She had to think. One of them had to be capable of thinking.

With another breath, she closed her eyes and counted. When she opened them again, she made the move. Out of the car, she cased the vehicle.

Her headlight was shattered, with pieces scattered across the ground. Running her thumb over the light, she felt the scratches on her perfect graduation present.

She pressed her fingers to her temple and reviewed her options.

It was risky to drive the rest of the way- a missing light would draw attention. It was worse to leave it. A broken car on the side of the road? Someone would notice and report it to the police if they hadn't already. She scanned the darkened apartments towering above the crime scene. There was no right decision, only the best choice of the wrong ones.

"Fuck, fuck, fuck, fuck, fuck," she muttered.

Art put a hand on her shoulder, and she rolled away from his touch. She needed to focus, not let him distract her. "We need to go."

He ran his hand through his hair, tangled with sweat. For a moment, he opened his mouth in protest, then closed it.

When they were back in the car, Amelia reversed and straightened it. The one remaining headlight partially lit the road to the apartment.

The next time either of them spoke, they were in his room. Her body was tense, reverberating from both the high of the drug and of the wreck.

"Do you care if I do one more bump?" Art's voice was low. "I need to feel something else." He looked at her, as if expecting understanding.

She shook her head in disbelief. He must have taken the movement to mean no, as in she didn't care.

Pulling out the ziplock, he scooped a bump of cocaine with his house key and inhaled the drug. The weight in her chest was heavy, as she struggled to understand what had happened and where the night was going.

His head rolled back, and his chest fell. A smile gently pulled at his mouth. A single tear fell from his eye. She knew the face. He had successfully escaped reality.

She couldn't do it. She didn't want to escape reality anymore. She wanted to be back to herself again.

So she remained as she was. Alone in a heartbreak she couldn't accept.

CHAPTER THIRTY-TWO

Amelia and Art stayed up most of the night. As badly as she wanted to sleep off the experience and have a break from the horror of what she would do with the car, the last line of cocaine with Evan did her in. With the upper drug, she couldn't sleep. It was too much. Truthfully, Amelia was not sure what an acceptable amount of cocaine was, but surely it was less than they had inhaled.

After his extra bump of cocaine, it became the Art show as they lay there.

"After I graduated, my mom wanted me to join the military, like Bryan. She said I couldn't live there anymore. My sister, Aurora, would need the extra space for her baby. I can't believe she's going to be a mom. I really didn't want to join the military. I wanted to play the drums. I found the band online, and I figured I could move out here. Sleep on the beach if I needed to. That's when I got Max's message. It was like divine intervention. I didn't even tell my mom I was moving. I used the money from my grandma to rent a U-Haul to get the drums out here in the middle of the night. I knew she would be disappointed that I wasn't in the military. But you can't bring a drum set on deployment. I sort of thought I was a runaway until you told me at the lifeguard tower that you saw me as free."

Another day, she would have lapped up every word, ingraining his history as if it were her own. She wasn't even sure she was listening to most of what he said as her mind kept turning. He was a drug dealer. She crashed her car because of him. She did cocaine, which was the line she said she would never cross when she met him.

But she had never loved anyone this way. Reconciling all of it was becoming impossible, a dizzying carousel of thoughts. She longed for the simplicity of being tucked underneath her pink quilted bed as her parents' light flicked off.

She had had everything. Yet, as she turned on her side and the air mattress hissed underneath her weight, she had chosen Art, which also meant that she had chosen drugs. It was an adventure, but it was anxiety-ridden and body-destroying, and tonight? Tonight, it was too much.

She didn't know when or how she had fallen asleep, but she was awakened to a pounding at the door. She wiped the trail of saliva from her chin, the only tell that she had slept at all.

"What?" Art moaned with agitation, an arm stretched over his face.

Max opened the door a crack and poked his head through. "We're having an apartment meeting in ten minutes."

"Yep." Art said, eyes closed. Amelia wasn't sure if he even heard Max.

Her head was fuzzy. She slumped off the bed and placed a hand against the wall to steady herself. One slow, weighted step at a time, she made her way to the boys' shared bathroom. Her eyes averted her gaze from her reflection, where Mirror Amelia lived. She reached for the blue-grey hand towel that didn't match the shower towels, and that probably hadn't been washed in weeks.

Turning on the faucet, she washed away the remaining makeup from last night and dried her skin. She was exhausted. Physically and emotionally. Her mind was a xylophone; a mallet knocking into every fucking piece, around and around.

Back in Art's room, he had fallen back to sleep. She dressed in a pair of jean shorts she had forgotten there over the summer and a band shirt featuring an angry deer.

Amelia shook him awake. "Please, can we get this over with?"

He squinted his eyes open. Her face must have communicated her disdain as he groaned again and rolled off the bed.

Five minutes later, they sat thigh to thigh on the couch, each chugging from a plastic water bottle.

"Guys. We have to work this out," Max said from the center of the living room.

Madisson sat in the recliner chair, eyes narrowed. Art was leaning forward, elbows resting on his legs, head hanging low. Amelia was pouting, arms crossed, as she leaned against the couch. She wanted this to be over so she could go home, pop Tylenol, and indulge in a proper shower.

When nobody spoke, Max circled the living room.

"Here's how I see it." He turned to her. "Amelia, you need to apologize to Madisson for how you treated her. That was seriously uncool." Then his eyes found Madisson, his voice softer. "Madisson - you have to let Art and Amelia work out their shit on their own. It has nothing to do with you." He looked at Art and folded his arms, tapping against his bicep. "I, uh, want to apologize to you. I shouldn't have missed your show, man."

"Thank you," Art said bitterly.

Max relaxed his arms and sighed. "Art, you gotta stop dealing. It's getting too sketchy."

Amelia uncrossed her arms, let out a breath, and shifted to

Madisson. "I was completely in the wrong to speak to you the way I did. I didn't know about Art."

Amelia glanced at Art. "You're going to be done with that, right?"

Art hesitated. "After I move what I have, I'll be done," he compromised.

Amelia gave a short nod, but she wasn't sure she believed him.

Madisson rolled her eyes and muttered, "He's not going to be done."

Madisson was probably right and had more confidence to call it like it was than she did.

"If I said I will, I will," Art said firmly, his agitation rising. Probably more from the come down than the attack on his character. Amelia rested her thumb against her lips.

"Okay, Art is going to be done," Max affirmed.

"Okay, then I'll let it go," Madisson said tightly, shifting in the recliner.

They all looked around at each other again.

"Great! We need group bonding, and I came up with the thing." Max smiled widely. "Shrooms."

CHAPTER THIRTY-THREE

A few days later, Amelia picked up her car from the dealership. A quick-talking service advisor with salt-and-pepper hair handed her the keys. He beamed as he told her that he had thrown in a free car wash because of her family's long history with the dealership, fixed the bumper in record time, and recommended that she consider upgrading to a new vehicle soon. She ignored everything he said, thanked him, then forged her mother's signature on the bill. If her dad ever saw it, he would assume Lauren had authorized it. No one would trace her to the crime.

Amelia beeped the keys and located her pristine white car. She reached the driver's side door, and the dozens of tiny hearts that Art had traced into the window were gone. On her drive to the apartment, she had a dreaded feeling that things would not get better with the magic mushrooms.

———

ON THE COUCH, she stared at the mushroom-filled jar on the living room table. Some were plump, others scrawny. Long stems, short stems. All different shades of dirt red. Her stomach grumbled, rejecting the idea of her consuming them.

Art sat beside her. "It's going to be great."

"I don't think I like hallucinogenics," she replied.

She had flat-out rejected the idea at the roommate meeting, and Max asked her to think about it more before he dismissed them.

Art tried again, his voice softer as his eyes met hers. "You don't have to do anything you don't want to, but I promise shrooms are different. And I won't be doing them with you. I'll be your babysitter. Here with you every step of the way to make sure you are safe and having a good time!" He spoke with such enthusiasm, she wished she could match it.

Babysitting was a stipulation outlined at the meeting. Madisson and Amelia would rebuild their relationship through their magic mushroom trip, and the boys would take care of the girls. The summer was coming to a close, and Madisson would be starting school in a week. They all wanted to be on good terms.

Amelia rested her legs across Art's lap. He circled his finger along her skin. Between his confidence and finger along her thigh, he had a habit of corroding her barriers and fogging her mind.

"I've been down this road twice now. I didn't like the salvia. The acid trip was even worse." Amelia reminded Art. Then added, "Why do you care so much?"

He sighed. "Because this one, I think you're really going to like. It's different, it's natural."

Natural, like the pot she also hated.

She didn't hide her exasperation. "Okay, but this is the last one I try." She looked apprehensively at the glass jar on the table.

"That's good since I don't currently have access to ayahuasca," he joked.

Her eyes shifted to him, unamused. "How long will it last?"

"Probably six or so hours."

She groaned. "I had planned to go to the gym tonight."

"We'll walk around a bunch. Skip it." He leaned in closer to her and kissed her neck. The goosebumps rising on her skin betrayed her.

"Fine." She swung her legs off of him.

Art reached for the jar and portioned out the doses. It was hard to tell what an even amount was with their different shapes. He quirked an eyebrow in contemplation as he divided them between Madisson and Amelia.

Max stood with his arms folded. His tongue flipped his lip ring, and he gave a subtle nod of approval.

Madisson took a bite of the mushroom cap, and her face twisted. "This is disgusting."

Holding it by the top, Amelia took a bite from the stem. She washed it down with a gulp of water to combat the bitter taste. It was disgusting, but she was glad she wasn't smoking or snorting anything.

"We could always brew it into a tea?" Max suggested.

"Takes too long," Art decided for them. Max side-eyed him, but didn't push it.

Madisson ate a second mushroom from her assortment. Amelia found a similarly sized one. They took turns matching mushrooms until they finished.

When Madisson excused herself to the bathroom, Art winked at Amelia. She tilted her head in confusion. Max was in the kitchen, back turned to them. Art plucked a fat mushroom from the jar and pushed it in front of her. She didn't move. He put his hands together in a prayer, his mouth downturned.

"Why," she mouthed.

"Because you're going to love it." His voice was soft.

"How do you know?" Her voice wavered.

"Because I know you."

He did. Better than her parents. Better than anyone outside of Madisson.

"It's going to be different than acid?" She pushed down the anxiety building in her chest.

"Completely. It'll be a good trip. I'll be by your side the whole time. We can do whatever you want." He leaned closer to her.

She sighed and took the shroom from the table. She chomped quickly as her mouth contorted in repulsion, then stuck her tongue out at him, proof that she had finished them.

"I love you," he reminded.

"I love you back," she said with an edge.

Forty-five minutes later, Madisson and Amelia sat on the floor, humming along to the electronic music Max had put on, waiting for the shrooms to digest. Max and Art were on the couch, half focused on a video game while passing the fifth of vodka between them. They were laughing, but Amelia had no idea what about. Her eyes were droopy.

"Ready?" Max asked Madisson as he wiped the vodka off his lip with the back of his hand.

"Yes," she said with a half-baked smile.

Amelia stood slowly and pushed her hands in the front pocket of her blue UCLA sweatshirt. She could tell the shrooms had grown from her stomach up and into her mind, like a sunflower rising to meet the sun. Contentment and curiosity replaced the resentment of mushrooms. Maybe Art was right. Perhaps this trip would be better. As long as there were no squirrels.

Max flung open the door, ready for a mission. Art missed the step off the doorstep, but played off the movement. She thought they had been drinking evenly, but if there were an opportunity for more, Art would find it. She may have been spoiled, but he was excessive in his own ways.

Clutching his black backpack, dusted from her hike, Art led the girls behind Max. Halfway down the block, Madisson made eye contact with Amelia, nodding ahead at Art's saunter, and then made a dramatic interpretation, arms swinging wildly and hips swaying with each step.

At the precise imitation, Amelia laughed, hunched at her hips, hands on her thighs, tears spilling from her eyes. *This*, this pure delight, was what Art had been trying to tell her. After weeks of being at odds with Madisson, this lightness would heal them.

The boys glanced back, then returned to their conversation. They each carried a water bottle, presumably filled with more vodka.

Amelia's head swirled as they strolled, wanting to cement every beautiful image. It was similar to the acid, but softer. Instead of the chemical drug's intensity, with its sharp colors, this world was pastel. She was a character in a pop-up book. Each block felt like an entirely new page. The bushes and trees were two-dimensional, like an old school Mario game. As if she could push them over and move on to the next scene.

Madisson paused to tuck a flower behind Amelia's ear, and her heart fluttered at the gesture. Madisson was the type of friend everyone should have. Amelia leaned down and plucked a budding dandelion, swirling with banana yellows and corals. She brushed Madisson's dark hair back and slipped the flower behind her ear.

They held each other's gaze and smiled. Madisson brushed her knuckles against Amelia's cheek. She didn't say anything, but she didn't have to. Amelia understood she had been forgiven.

Walking toward the beach, the pop-up page flipped. They passed a green stretch of park with clusters of people. A group of guys threw a Frisbee and dove after it. Kids played tag, and their laughter filled the space. A couple cuddled against a tree stump. This was where Amelia belonged. She could feel it in her bones.

"Boys!" she called ahead. Max and Art pivoted toward her.

"Can we sit here?" She smiled.

The four formed a circle in the lawn, beneath an apricot sun and against the sage-green grass. A breeze brushed against Amelia's arm. She closed her eyes, inhaling the sweet smell of summer.

A black ant crawled over the zipper of Art's backpack.

Where was it going? Why was it by itself? Was it lonely? An adventurer like herself?

Madisson screeched, flinging her arm across his backpack and ending the tiny bug's life.

A cold sorrow filled Amelia, like a midnight in the desert. Tears streamed down her face.

"I didn't mean to upset you!" Madisson wrapped Amelia in her arms and smoothed down her hair.

Amelia couldn't explain the reaction, couldn't even think about it. The anguish over the ant's death was unshakable.

"You're making a scene. Let's go," Art growled.

He stood up and brushed off his jeans. Slinging his backpack over his shoulder, he took an unflinching swig from the water bottle.

Madisson pressed her cheek to Amelia's. "I'm really sorry."

Amelia gave a nod, and Madisson unleashed her grip. They followed the boys, who were already on their way. She swiped at her tears. It was just an ant. Her reaction was unwarranted. Despite the logic, another tear fell.

At the park's opening was a man in a tie-dye with long grey hair and rectangular glasses. A red and green parrot perched on his shoulder, talons gripping his shirt. Three children, about six years old, surrounded him.

"Oh yeah, Tico loves children." His voice was gruff through his beard.

Madisson froze. Tico squawked, wings flapping, then tucked them back into its side. Its sleek beak pointed upward. She inched toward the man and the children. Her hand started to raise to the bird before Max intercepted. Putting his arm around her, he forced her outstretched hand to her side. He maneuvered her in the other direction. An attempt to prevent a second girl-friend meltdown in five minutes.

When they reached where the pavement met the sand, a blanket of happiness wrapped around Amelia. She forgot the ant and the bird in the bliss of the beach. It was a different happiness from the loud ecstasy where she was crazed in elation. On shrooms, it was a quiet comfort, like fuzzy slippers by the warmth of an evening fire.

"Can we put our shoes in your backpack?" Madisson asked Art.

"Sure." He unzipped the backpack and reached for their shoes. Madisson slipped off her Vans and handed them to him.

"You're so nice," Amelia said, handing him her sandals. There was a whimsical charm in his kindness.

She took a few steps onto the sand and clenched her toes, feeling the warm grains between them.

"We had sex here once." She looked up at Art.

"I could never forget." He gave a wicked grin, as if replaying the memory.

He chugged the last of the water bottle, then crushed the plastic in his hand and threw it towards a trash can. He turned around, and the bottle missed the bin's opening. Turtles crossed her mind. Happy swimming turtles. With Art's blatant disregard for plastics getting into the oceans, the turtles probably wouldn't like him.

She could have put the bottle in the trash can, finished what he started, but the group was walking away. The task was daunting, and she turned her back to the plastic. Her shoulders slumped as she followed the group. The turtles probably hated her, too.

Madisson paused for Amelia to catch up. She extended her hand, and Amelia took it. With Madisson's hand in hers, the emotional pendulum swung again. Turtles were long gone, as the girls danced around shells, careful not to crush them. The magic of the mushrooms returned.

"Let's go!" Maddison burst toward the sea, hand still gripping Amelia's.

They laughed in delusion as they raced toward the open ocean. At the shoreline, they broke apart. Amelia drifted into the wet sand, her toes sinking in and water grazing the top of her foot. Lifting her arms, she shimmied her heels back and forth until the sand covered them. Life couldn't get better. Each ray of sunshine shimmered against her.

Madisson's eyes went wide. "Amelia. You have to know how amazing you are. You're my best friend in the whole wide world. You're beautiful and have this confidence about you. I never want to fight with you again. It's the fucking *worst* fighting with you."

Amelia put her hands on Madisson's cheeks and stared into her swirling cinnamon brown eyes. "I love you so much. I'll never have a different best friend."

They wrapped their arms around each other, the water caressing their ankles until the guys approached.

Max shook his empty water bottle at them. "We're gonna go get a refill."

"I don't want to go," Amelia whined. The receding wave left her feet sinking deeper as she and Madisson parted.

"Good thing you're not my responsibility." His words were short, arms crossed in agitation.

"Max!" Madisson scolded.

He'd passed the drunk line and was teetering toward destruction. More alcohol was not what he needed. But as she was not his responsibility, he was not hers. She closed her eyes as her chest fell. She did not want to be anywhere near Max when he became unhinged.

"Babe, we're going," Max said.

Madisson looked between the two. Amelia had a flicker of hope that she would stay.

"We'll be back soon, right?" Madisson asked.

The hope extinguished.

"Yeah, we will be right back." Max smirked, putting an arm around Madisson, and they turned.

Amelia peered at Art, who had stayed quiet during the exchange. She didn't want to ask him to stay. She wanted him to know to stay. But she was starting to feel that his love for any sort of altered state outweighed his love for her.

He scratched the back of his neck.

"I finished my drink. Come with me, Princess." He reached for her hands.

She pulled away and hung her head.

"I want to be here," she said to the sand.

A seashell in the light sparkled pink, then purple. Being anywhere else felt wrong.

"Will you be okay here for like five minutes? Maybe ten?" he asked.

She didn't want him to go for any duration of time. She wanted to collect seashell shards together and talk about their cotton-candy colors and twisted shapes. She wanted to have lively discussions about chirping dolphins and messy-haired mermaids, and people-watch. She wanted him to babysit her, care for her, as he had promised.

"You're going to go?" she asked.

His eyes flicked to where Madisson and Max had gone, then back to her.

"I'll be fast," he promised.

She dipped her head, and he must have taken it as acceptance. With a kiss goodbye, he jogged away.

Over his shoulder, he called, "Don't fucking leave this area, and for the love of God, do NOT get in that water."

Then he was gone.

CHAPTER THIRTY-FOUR

Amelia did end up wandering. Not in defiance; she forgot she wasn't supposed to. She left the crashing waves and sat at the end of a line of umbrellas and pop-up tents. Her fingers sifted through sand that sprinkled on her thighs and warmed her skin.

Two boys with shaggy hair built a sandcastle. It glimmered, and the sky opened up above it, shining as a spotlight on their creation. They dug a full moat. It reminded her of summers spent with Georgina in the Florida Keys.

"Are you okay?" A shadow came over her.

A woman with curly blonde hair and a sunflower dress stood above. Amelia's eyes found the boys again. They had stopped scooping sand and were looking at her.

"Yeah, this is probably weird. I'll go," Amelia admitted. The words came out slow and unnatural. Muscle memory brought her to her feet. She wasn't sure how she remembered how to stand.

She headed for the sidewalk and chalked it up to divine intervention when she spotted her friends across the street at a tiki bar. Tables were spread across the patio, with blue light rimming the thatched overhang.

Max was yelling at a stocky guy in a backward baseball cap, his fists clenched. Amelia couldn't make out the words. She took a seat on a wall of rocks on her side of the street. Max pulled back his arm and punched the guy, who stumbled backward and gripped the table. It was like watching a movie. She remained seated in curiosity.

Madisson shrieked. A police officer walking by sprang into action, shoving Max's chest against the wall and kicking his feet apart. Handcuffs snapped around his wrists.

Amelia's eyes scanned the events as they unfolded, but the rest of her body remained tense. If she were a statue, no one would notice her. The last thing a girl on shrooms needed was a cop's attention.

Art dragged his fingers through his dark hair. Madisson crumpled against the wall a few feet from Max. With her head in her hands, her small frame shook uncontrollably.

Amelia's chest tightened. She wanted to go to Madisson and comfort her. She wrung her hands in apprehension.

Fear won. In addition to the police, crossing the street was monumental. She had a dark feeling that if she stepped onto the road, she would be run over in an instant, like a disappointing game of *Frogger*.

She turned around on the wall to face the beach. She couldn't look at them anymore. It was too sad.

On the edge, she took deep breaths, then swung her legs.

Out, back, out, back.

The blue ocean glimmered, full of opportunity and light.

Joy ribboned through her, and her friends became a distant memory.

Someone sat beside her.

"I thought I lost you. I was so scared," Art said.

"You said you would be right back." Her words were thin.

"I know, I tried, but Max got into a fight. It was crazy. We went in for one drink, and Madisson was outside since she didn't have a fake ID. When we came out, this clown was talking to her. I mean, between you and me, Madisson doesn't necessarily tell people off. She will let them flirt with her, and she doesn't think anything is wrong with that. But I think there kind of is, you know? That's why I love you. I trust you a million percent. You would never let another guy even think he has a chance with you."

Amelia didn't acknowledge his stream of consciousness. He could have talked for days, and she would have floated through it. His voice was swept up in the tides. When they were together, there was nowhere else she wanted to be. But soon, it would end. She would be going off to UCLA. Things would be different.

"What's happening inside your head, Amelia?" He gave up the monologue.

"This moment," she said, reaching over to his hand, tears welling up. "This is special. Being at the beach, being with you. This may be the last special thing."

"What do you mean?" His eyebrows drew together.

She took a deep breath and tried to form the words. "All the special things in my life may be over after this. I don't know what will happen when I move, and even today, when I turn back around, Max will be in a cop car, and Madisson will be a mess. Right now, in front of us, could be the last special thing."

Art pressed his fingers to his temple, a sigh through his lips.

She wanted him to view the world her way. Pointing to the sky, she said, "There's the double rainbow over there."

Gesturing to the cliffs, she asked, "Do you see how those sparkle?"

Arms wide open. "The rays of the sun are dancing on me. How incredible is that?"

Staring deep into his eyes, blue and promising as the ocean, she explained with sincerity, "All this is special, and I've never even noticed it before. When I turn back around, all of this will be gone!"

"You haven't ever *seen* it before," he corrected. "The rocks are covered in bird shit. There aren't any rainbows. The sunshine is fucking blinding, but it's not dancing."

So, her version wasn't exactly real, but what was real anyway? In the world in front of her, there were rainbows, sparkles, and sun rays, and she desperately wanted to cling to that version of her life. She didn't want to turn around.

But he did. Art, prone to chaos, twisted around. He sighed. She sighed back. They were back to being a boat and a train, like the acid trip.

After a heavy silence, he said, "I'm going to check on Max."

Pushing himself up from the ledge, he left her. Sadness flooded her, but it would be worse to follow him. Pastel raindrops dripped off the double rainbow, crying into the infinite sea.

Time passed, but she couldn't keep track of how much. Her stomach rumbled, a growing mix of angst that she was alone, and that she hadn't eaten since a croissant on her way to Art's that morning. She pulled out her phone. He answered on the first ring.

"Amelia?" he asked.

"Weston?"

"Are you okay?"

"I think I'm hungry."

"Where are you?"

She searched for a street sign and read off the name to him.

"You want me to bring you food?" he asked.

"Yes. That would be great."

"Are you sure you're okay?"

"Yeah. I'm okay."

"Don't move."

She hung up the phone and waited, her heels kicking against the rock wall. There were advantages to not knowing the time. She'd always been a late person. But if people don't think about time, they wouldn't ever know when she was late. They would just be happy she was there. Shouldn't everyone be glad to be together? Why does it matter what time people arrive? Time was a social construct. She remembered hearing about it somewhere, maybe in another life.

When Weston's hand cupped her shoulder, her heart beat quickened. It had been so long since she had seen him. He brushed off the sand on the ledge, then took a seat beside her and handed her a cranberry oatmeal muffin, her favorite. She unwrapped it and took a bite, then gazed back at the water, grateful to share the experience with someone.

"Amelia?" he asked, drawing her attention. His lips were straight, hair a bit longer than when she had seen him last. Even with sunglasses covering his eyes, something wasn't right.

"What's wrong?" she asked. He'd been trying to spend time together forever. He should have been as happy as she was.

"Where have you been?" His eyes fell to his shorts. "What are you doing here alone?"

He surveyed the area, as if searching for something danger-ous. There was no danger. She was just a girl sitting on rocks watching a rainbow cry.

"I'm sitting at the beach." She reached over and took off Weston's sunglasses to confirm her suspicions. His eyes darted with panic, as she anticipated.

He pulled back, as if her gesture was too intimate.

"It's okay," she assured him. "I wanted to see your face. You have a beautiful face. I'm sorry if I didn't tell you that before."

She put the sunglasses back on, covering the eyes that she once stared into, and said, 'I love you.' It was a silly thing to say at the time. She meant it then, but that was in the past before she knew the love of sex on the beach, hearts drawn on the windows, surprise nachos, and watching the person you love doing what they love on stage.

Letting out a breath of air, she took another bite. She missed Art. She couldn't help it.

"Art was here."

"Where the fuck is Art now?" he snapped.

"I'm not too sure." She rubbed her lips together.

He paused, really taking her in. Then asked softly, "What are you on?"

"Shrooms." She lowered her eyes and scratched her nails along the rock.

"How long have you been like this?" His tone dipped in concern.

Perhaps in another world, it would have also made her sad – to be disappointing him at every turn. But in this world, it was hysterical. Mr. Put Together with her while she was on drugs and unhinged.

"What a question! I have no idea!" She cackled.

People acting crazy at this beach town were not uncommon. Weston shifted. While other people may not have been troubled by a druggie laughing on the beach, she figured that it concerned him that *she* was the druggie at the beach.

Her laughter evaporated. She wasn't a druggie. *Was she?* How many drugs made you a druggie? Was it the amount? The variety? The length of time?

"We should go," Weston said carefully to her. "We need to get you somewhere safe."

When she stood, he assessed her again and scrunched his face. "I can't bring you home."

He looked around for an alternative solution. It was surprising that he was still concerned about her. It was off-kilter. Between possibly being a druggie and Weston still having a protective capacity for her, she wanted to think of something else. But she didn't know what. All the special things were ending. Just as she had warned Art about. Her heart flinched, then an idea clicked.

"Take me to Art and Max's. Maybe they'll be there." She surveyed the area. "Although maybe they're still here?"

"Were you with anyone else?" Weston prodded.

"Madisson!" Amelia clapped. They could do this. They could find safety together.

"Have you tried calling her?"

Amelia's face fell. "No."

She hadn't called Madisson because the last time she saw Madisson, she was a pile of limbs outside of a bar. But that could have been hours ago.

Weston walked a few feet away and dialed. The rainbow in the sky paled.

Weston hung up the call and returned to her. "Where are your shoes?"

Her feet were caked with sand, and the back of her heels were bruised from where she had repeatedly kicked the rock while swinging her legs. There was a subtle throb in her left foot. She cradled it to find the source of the pain.

"What the fuck," Weston whispered as he gingerly removed a shard of glass from the arch.

She met his eyes, feeling a greater pain in her chest for Weston than in her foot. He wrapped his arms around her, and his body trembled.

"I'm sorry," he choked.

"For what?" Amelia asked.

"You wouldn't be here if it weren't for me," he whispered into her hair.

"You didn't bring me to the beach!"

He was absurd, and she was back to crazed laughter.

Weston didn't falter. "I should have told you I loved you before. I should have known it then, and I never would have lost you. I'll regret losing you for the rest of my life."

As a few rogue tears slipped down his face, her chest clutched tighter. Her laughter dissolved, and she kissed him. It wasn't passionate; it was meant to comfort him.

But as she pulled away, guilt swelled. She had to get back to Art. Her thoughts blurred after the kiss, protecting her from things she would surely regret.

CHAPTER THIRTY-FIVE

The entire car ride had been wiped from her memory as they approached the apartment with its door wide open. Madisson paced inside with Art's hand gesturing toward her.

"Look, there is nothing you can do. It's public intoxication. They'll release him when he sobers up. Tomorrow at the latest."

Madisson closed the space between them and put a finger to his chest. "You guys were supposed to watch *us*, and *you* got wasted! What the fuck is *wrong* with *you*?"

Weston cleared his throat, and Madisson and Art twisted toward them.

"Thank you for bringing Amelia back here," Madisson said, stepping back from Art and embracing Weston.

"Happy to." He said the words to Madisson, but his gaze hung on Art in disgust.

Amelia took in the scene. Art wasn't happy to see her, but she wasn't sure why.

Madisson walked to Amelia, then rubbed her hands along her arms. "How are you?"

"Good. It's a pretty strange day, though," she admitted.

Madisson's hands remained on Amelia, her smile fixed, but her tone didn't match her face as she glared at Art. "Why is she still like this?"

Art hesitated, licking his lips before he spoke. "She took the mushrooms on an empty stomach. She's been taking my Adderall pretty regularly."

Amelia hadn't realized that he had known. He had taught her that food could affect the absorption of the drugs, which is why she didn't eat the day of the rave. The same must have been true with the mushrooms. But there was something else.

"You also gave me an extra mushroom when Madisson was in the bathroom," Amelia reminded.

Art whipped his head toward her. His eyes bore into hers.

"What?" Amelia asked.

She had never made Art angry before. First, Weston cried, and now Art was mad. What would be next? She was the one on shrooms, yet everyone else was acting strange.

Art shoved his hands in his pockets. "So, I gave her more. I wanted her to have a good time."

"You wanted her to have a *good* time? How about taking care of *her* like *you* said you would!"

"Your over-enunciation is going to get you in the back of the cop car like your boyfriend," Art snarled.

"Are you fucking kidding me?" Madisson asked, her chest rising. Her black hair was messy, and her eyes were bloodshot from crying. She looked half rabid and entirely pissed off.

"Let her chill," Weston interrupted. He picked up the remote and turned on Netflix. He chose one of Amelia's favorite rom-coms and guided her to sit on the couch, taking the spot next to her.

"Can I have water?" Amelia asked Weston. There was a scratch in her throat, and her stomach was still unsettled.

Weston stared at Art to fulfill the request. His eyes shifted to

Amelia, then he ducked into the kitchen. Weston shook his head in repulsion, and Madisson returned the sentiment.

Amelia held her hands in her lap. She couldn't tell who was right or wrong.

Art returned and handed Amelia a water with a lemon wedge. "I'm going on a walk."

It was probably a good idea—it was too tense. Amelia didn't say anything as he left.

When the door closed, Weston put his arm around her, and she leaned into him. Madisson went into Max's room and returned with his pipe and weed. As she lit the marijuana, Amelia noticed her hands trembling. She wanted to hold Madisson's hand, but she was at peace against Weston's chest. She didn't want to risk losing another good feeling. The good feelings had been fleeting.

After Madisson blew out the smoke, she offered it to Weston. He moved around Amelia and took a hit.

"Want any?" he asked her.

She shook her head and admitted, "I don't like marijuana."

"Since when?"

"Honestly, I don't think I ever did."

A dull silence spread across them as she returned her attention to the film. Madisson curled up like a cat in the reclining chair and was softly snoring after a few minutes.

When the movie was almost over, and the colors on the screen were the correct shade, Art returned. There were no more rainbows. The ashtray on the living room table did not sparkle.

"Can we talk?" Art asked her, looking disapprovingly at Weston's arm around her.

"I don't think that's a good idea," Weston ventured.

"I'll be back," Amelia assured Weston.

His arm dropped, but his face remained hardened.

She followed Art outside the complex. The sky had grown grey, and the exterior apartment lights glowed a yellow hue. Their shadows extended on the sidewalk.

"Why did you call him?" Art asked.

Her mouth fell. "Why did you leave me?"

He tapped his foot, then ran his fingers back and forth across his forehead—a manic look in his eyes.

"I'm sorry, Madisson was freaking out. I had to get her out of there. Of course, I didn't know she would be a complete bitch. I figured I would walk her back here and then go and get you."

She folded her arms. "Don't call her a bitch. You got drunk, Max got arrested, and you left me on shrooms by myself."

He paced in front of her. "Listen, I know I fucked up. I get that. Sometimes I do the absolute wrong fucking thing. I didn't mean to leave you. I didn't think we would get so drunk. I freaked the fuck out when I saw the cops, and Madisson was tripping. You would never forgive me if something happened to her. You wouldn't." He stopped, holding her gaze.

She averted her eyes.

He picked up his stride, quicker like a caged animal. "I'm sorry. I know I'm a piece of shit. I know it. I promise I'll make it up to you."

He stopped in front of her, his voice laced with desperation. "Whatever you want! I won't ever drink again if that made you happy."

Her bare feet tingled in the cold. She really needed to get her shoes back from him.

Her voice cut through the night. "For a while today, everything was special. I understood why you wanted me to have this experience. To do it differently from the acid, where we had separate trips. I get that this way, I could've explained to you what was happening to me, and you could have understood because you weren't on drugs yourself. But then you ruined it.

You left. You didn't try to understand me and what I was experiencing." Her body sagged. "I get you have remorse about the day, but I want to go home."

"You want Weston to take you home," he spat the words out as he stopped his pacing.

"You know it's not like that." Her chest fell. She may have compared them, but it was never a competition. She had chosen him from the moment she met him, all summer long. She loved him.

"Fucking go then. I'll see you later." He flung his arm out, granting her permission to leave.

Everything about the conversation was off. He had never once been intimidated by her relationship with Weston or hostile toward her. He was typically quick to back off when she pushed back. Standing firm, shoving her away from him, wasn't Art.

She repeated to Art what Weston had asked her hours ago. "What are you on?"

"Are you serious right now?" His words were sharp.

She didn't know she was serious until his words hit her.

"You're on something." She brought her hand to the crease of her eye and rubbed it. When did the saga of bad decisions ever end?

While he tapped his fingers quickly against his pants, his face remained as stone.

"You left me to do coke?" Her mouth parted, desperate for another answer. To be told she had it all wrong.

He didn't respond immediately. Despite his terrible decisions, he clung to the one good thing he had going for him—he wouldn't lie to her. As if being honest made him a good guy.

A chorus of crickets chirped as she waited for confirmation.

Instead, he said, "Listen, go be with fucking Weston. You want to be with that guy so much, go."

The words cut. At the realization that hurting her was his intention, the dagger turned deeper.

"I don't want to be with Weston. I thought I wanted to be with you." Her voice strained.

"Oh, and one bad day, and now you don't want to be with me anymore." His voice was loud, almost as a joke.

He stepped closer. Inches from her, he towered above her. She couldn't breathe, and her hand trembled. She wasn't scared of the Art she had come to know and love, but this version of him. She pulled back.

His body slacked in response. "Amelia," he whimpered.

She put her hand up, eyes glistening. "I need to go home."

She turned, expecting to hear the echo of his footsteps behind her. When she didn't, she stopped. Over her shoulder, he was gone.

Maybe that was why Lauren told her that you never look back. What if you do and realize you're alone?

Back inside the apartment, Weston was watching the credits roll. Madisson would stay in the chair until Max came home. The best-case scenario was that Madisson and Art would ignore each other until then.

"Can you take me home?" Amelia asked.

"Of course," Weston said. She could have sworn a smile crept up on his face, and thorny vines entangled her chest. There was no winner. Weston was a good guy, but any victory he took was at a cost to her.

Predictably, when they arrived at her house, Weston asked if she wanted him to stay, passing the offer off as a concerned friend. Part of that was genuine. Part of it was selfish.

Letting Weston into her house would be letting him into her bed. She could already imagine it starting as nothing, and she would be explicit about that. But then his arm would brush against hers, and she would be too tired to push back as he wrapped her in close. She would excuse it all. They wouldn't technically cross any lines, and being held after such a long day would be sweet relief. She could play the scene in her head before it even happened.

Even though she didn't want to be alone, even as Art hurt her, she didn't want to make any more regrettable decisions. She had already accumulated a lifetime of regret.

"I just want to sleep," she said.

His eyes found the sky, then dropped to her. He put his arms around her and kissed her on the cheek. "You'll be okay?"

"Yes," she falsely promised. She was being torn apart at the seams. Nothing was okay anymore.

"Goodnight, Amelia." His voice was low.

She made her way to the backyard, feeling his eyes on her until she walked through the ivy gate. In the midnight sky, she glanced up at her parents' dim window. They had stopped staying up for her.

CHAPTER THIRTY-SIX

Amelia spent the next three days doing whatever she could to distract herself from the last conversation with Art.

On the first day, she flushed the Adderall pills. Then she went to Pilates and pushed through the pain. Even without the edge of the prescription drug, Lauren still used Amelia as an example on a shoulder bridge. Walking out on shaky legs, trying to catch her breath, she knew getting rid of the prescription drug had been the right thing.

She didn't hear from Art that day, but Madisson called. Max had been released from jail first thing in the morning. His parents bailed him out and talked down the assault and battery charges, as well as the public intoxication charges. He was set to go before the judge, but things were looking promising.

On the second day, she scheduled a nail appointment and opted for a classic French manicure. Her technician, Amy, asked about UCLA and told her how much she would miss her. She busted her ass at boot camp class in the evening and kept to herself. Art texted a few times, but she didn't know what to say. Weston called twice and then texted asking if she was okay. She responded to Weston, saying she was and thanking him, but didn't keep the conversation going.

On the third day, Art texted her seventeen times. Some were worried, others were angry, and many were declarations of love. She asked Madisson about him, and she shared uneasily that Art hadn't been home much. Amelia wasn't sure what that meant, as he hadn't been with her either. Weston texted three more times, and she left them unanswered.

Madisson and Reyna's joint "Going Away to College" party was two days away, and she needed to talk to Art before then. She still didn't know what to say. He had chosen drugs over her and left her alone on shrooms. Doubted her love for him.

As she had changed over the summer, so had he. She wasn't sure how to get back to normal. What normal even was for them. It was exhilarating, encompassing, but there was also a lot that she wasn't proud of. Their world wouldn't work when she was in college, studying and following her dreams.

The slider opening to her room opened, and Lauren walked in.

"We are having a family dinner tonight." Her voice was firm.

"Sounds good." It had been over a month since their last dinner.

Lauren paused at her casual acceptance. "So we will see you at 6:30."

"Yep, I'll be there."

Lauren looked around the room, as if expecting to find something amiss. "Well, okay then." She turned and left.

Her phone vibrated.

ART

> Amelia please talk to me. I'm sorry. I will do whatever you want. I'm lucky to have you and I know that. Please please respond. I love you.

She let out a breath. It was a conversation for after dinner.

Amelia dressed for the occasion. She wore a long brown skirt with a slight slit, crossover sandals, and a blush blouse. Even with makeup, her hazel eyes dulled. Instead of a summer adventure giving her a spark, it drained her. She brushed her blonde hair back and went to the main house.

A step inside, she could smell Lauren's pot roast. As she entered the dining room, she found Weston sitting at the table, and she slowed.

"Glad you could join us?" she asked, perplexed.

Her father answered, "We asked Weston to join us tonight. We have something we need to discuss."

Her eyebrows furrowed at the formality of the statement. She took a seat. Dinner was set with white linen napkins and iced water in crystal glasses. The air felt colder, and dread seeped into her chest. Something was wrong.

"Is Georgina okay?" Amelia asked.

Her father leaned back and evaluated her. "You have no idea why you're here?"

Her eyes flashed to Weston. His eyes were trained down at the slab of meat in front of him.

"Weston," she commanded.

"I told them about Saturday," he murmured. He had at least had the decency to look embarrassed.

Her skin crawled. How much about Saturday? She brought the cup of water to her lips, prolonging a response. She waited for someone else to speak rather than incriminate herself. A minute or two passed before her mom had had enough of the silence.

"The shrooms, the drinking, being alone!" Lauren shouted. The words were like glass breaking. Her mother never yelled, certainly, never in front of a guest.

Amelia pushed her feet into the floor, steadying herself. Weston told them everything.

"So what?" she finally retorted with a shrug. She didn't know what else to say. It was true. It was a good strategic decision to have Weston join; she would give them that. Without him sitting across from her, able to corroborate the story, she might have tried to twist her way out of it.

James' eyes bore into hers. "So you're done. You're done seeing this boy."

Weston's lips twitched.

"This is what you wanted all along," Amelia said to Weston.

He leaned forward to answer, but James cut in. "This is not about Weston. He's here, so you take accountability. You're going to school in three weeks, and we'll consider this all behind us." He picked up his steak knife and cut into the slab of meat.

"He's coming with me."

Lauren choked on her water. "What?"

"We're getting a place together in LA. I was going to tell you, and now you know." She picked up her fork and dropped her eyes.

Amelia didn't know if that was entirely true anymore, but she wouldn't leave the conversation being told what to do. It was her life. She could make her own decisions.

"Absolutely not," Lauren said.

There was a painful silence in the stalemate. Amelia took a bite of broccoli, feigning confidence as she chewed.

It was her father who broke the tension. "You'll defer a year. Go abroad now," he mused.

"What do you mean?"

UCLA was everything she wanted. She couldn't put the dreams she had been working towards her whole life on pause. She needed to be in L.A.

Her dad shrugged. "Go meet Georgina in Italy and figure out your next steps. I'm sure we can work out a deferral."

Weston shifted in his chair and dragged his fork across his meat, but had yet to take a bite.

"I'm not going to do that," she said quietly.

"You will." James ended the conversation.

She met her parents' eyes, tears prickling in rage. She wouldn't do it. They never cared about her dreams. Of course, it was easier to ship her off to Europe and not deal with her. Amelia pushed back her chair, purposely screeching it against the wooden floor.

"I said I'm not going." She left the house, letting the over-sized door slam behind her.

It creaked open, and footsteps followed in the night. Her car sat in the driveway. She could go somewhere. Get the hell out of town.

She walked past it. She had nowhere to go and hated the thought of it. Hated that her parents knew about her experi-mental drug use. Hated that she considered Weston a friend, and he went to her mom. She let him in, let him help her, and he betrayed her. Her blood was boiling.

"Amelia, wait!" Weston's voice was filled with anguish.

She spun in fury. "How could you do this?"

"He's not good for you." He reached towards her. Stepping back, she let his hand drop to his side. Regret covered his face, but she couldn't decipher which part he regretted. For what he did now? Or the breakup all those months ago?

"You had me." She breathed to still her rapid heartbeat. "You said it–you should have loved me when I loved you. It's too late."

He let out an agonized groan. "How many times do I have to apologize? Stop pushing me away. I've paid the price. I've watched you all summer with him. Come back to me where you belong."

Maybe he meant it to be a comforting phrase, but at the word belong, he lost any remaining ground. She belonged to no one. Not him. Not Art. Not her parents.

She shook her head, refusing to accept anything he had to offer her.

"You can't tell me that kiss meant nothing," he tried again.

"I was on fucking DRUGS, Weston." Her fingers splayed in frustration. "As you so *kindly* pointed out to my parents tonight."

"Then why did you tell me you wished things were different on the car ride back to his place?" Weston said with a pained expression.

Amelia faltered. Had she said that?

"I don't know," she replied. She could have meant it a dozen ways. She did wish she had been a better friend to Weston this summer, as he had been to her after her breakup.

Weston shook his head in exasperation. "I'm not sorry I told them. I didn't know what else to do. I can't go away to MIT and leave you here with him when I can't protect you. I know you still love me. Love doesn't go away like that."

"I don't love you." Her voice broke. The words would hurt him even though they were true.

He looked up at the streetlights, at the stars even higher above.

"What changed?" Weston asked.

"He changed me."

"That is such bullshit."

"I'm a different person now."

"You're the same fucking person! I know you!"

They fell into their pattern of trading sentences without resolution.

"This is how we are going to leave things after all we have been through? Two years of us?" Weston's words were pleading.

"You never even cared until you got jealous." Amelia crossed her arms.

"I have always taken care of you- when you got drunk on graduation night, when you needed help getting into UCLA. Me! I've always protected you, and you've never appreciated me."

"You went to my fucking parents! I trusted you, and you ruined everything. For what?"

Amelia understood his need to have her back was desperation cloaked in the guise of protection. But this would be the end of it. They would never be friends again. Her trust in him was destroyed.

She stopped talking; there was nothing new to say.

"You should go," she said.

"That's what you want?"

"That's what I want." She sighed. "Good luck in Cambridge."

"Whatever, Amelia. Good luck to you. You're going to need it more than me."

He turned and stalked off toward his house.

She had broken his heart as he had once broken hers. Instead of vindication, it felt like an assassination.

CHAPTER THIRTY-SEVEN

Amelia stood on the stoop of Art and Max's apartment and knocked, which she hadn't done in months. It felt weirdly formal, but she wasn't here to see her boyfriend.

Max opened the door and greeted her, "Amelia!" He pulled her into a big hug as if that were normal for them. "I'm sorry about everything. I'm such an idiot," he said, releasing her.

"It's not your fault." She eyed Madisson behind them, who shrugged.

"Of course it is, I got drunk. I caused the whole situation to derail."

"No, really, Max. It wasn't your fault," Amelia said. "Art was responsible for me. He got drunk and left me. Then he went out and did a bunch of coke."

"I feel bad you're even with him, if I didn't bring him here..." Max ran a hand over his freshly shaved head.

Amelia had many reasons to dislike Max, but not one of them had to do with Art.

"These were all of my decisions. You can be sorry to Madisson for -"

"I am," he cut off. "She knows I am." He gazed at Madisson with remorseful eyes.

Madisson nodded in confirmation.

"Then that's the only apology that matters to me."

"Well, I'm going to take a walk and give you guys privacy," Max said. He crossed to where Madisson was, gave her a quick kiss, then left the girls alone.

When the door shut, and he couldn't hear, Amelia asked, "He seems different?"

"Yeah, we had a long talk. I won't be here as much when I start school. He can't be doing things like that. His decisions impact me." Madisson rested her hand on her palm, her eyes weary.

Amelia took a seat cross-legged on the couch, facing Madisson.

"How are you feeling?" Madisson asked. She hadn't pried when Amelia asked to tell her when Art was gone so that she could come over in person.

Amelia sighed. "Well, there are more layers now."

"What do you mean?" Madisson leaned forward on the recliner.

"Weston told my parents about our trip."

"What part?" Her face scrunched.

"All of it." Amelia tried to smile, but the weight of the dinner pressed against her chest.

Madisson's face dropped. "No fucking way." She shook her head in disbelief. "What did you say?"

"I'm moving to L.A. with Art."

Her face soured. "Are you really doing that?"

"I don't know. This is becoming a lot. When is enough, enough?"

"Yeah, I get that." Madisson gazed out the window.

"They told me I could spend a year in Europe," Amelia smirked.

"They fucking would." Madisson howled with laughter and turned her attention back to Amelia.

"I don't know what to do." Her life had been laid out for her. It was the first time she deviated, and she was lost.

"Can I be honest with you?" Madisson said. "Without you freaking out on me again," she said pointedly.

"Yes, let me have it," Amelia conceded. She was still embarrassed about the way she had yelled at Madisson after their L.A. trip.

"He's fucking bad news. He's charming, he has his moments, but he's lost. You can't fix him. Going to L.A," she trailed off. "You know that would not help him. Honestly, I'm saying this to you in our friendship bubble. I think Max will start looking for another roommate. There's been sketchy people over, and it's not good."

It wasn't surprising, but the revelation was heavy. He knew everything about her life, but he had shielded her from his dealings. Whether to protect her or to protect himself from her leaving him, she couldn't be sure.

"Do you think I'm lost?" Amelia felt it, but reality had been blurring for months.

Madisson paused, weighing her response.

"Tell me." Amelia's words came out soft.

"If you go to Europe, I think you will be. UCLA is everything. Don't give up your dream for this dude."

She was right.

"I'm going to have to see him." Amelia added, "Before your party tomorrow."

"Do what you need to. You know I support you."

"Do you know where he went?" She glanced around the apartment. "Or when he's coming back?"

Madisson shook her head.

"Okay, I'm going to go then. I haven't figured out how to do this yet," she admitted.

"Whatever you do, you have me," Madisson promised.

Amelia left the apartment in a hurricane of emotions. She wished she didn't love him. Logically, she would break up with him right then. Call him and tell him that she was through with him putting her in these unforgivable situations. The problem was, he would talk his way out of it.

She drove home listening to the Twin Flames playlist he made, wondering how they had fallen so far, so fast.

CHAPTER THIRTY-EIGHT

Amelia responded to Art the next day, ahead of Maddison's party. She ran her fingers across the options hanging in her closet, wanting to look devastatingly good. She wanted him to know exactly what he was losing due to all his bad choices and how they had affected her.

AMELIA

Headed to town now. Can you meet?

ART

Yes!!!! Gotta get Sky from work some vodka since she doesn't have a fake. Meet me at the liquor store?

AMELIA

Yes

Twenty minutes later, she pulled the BMW to the curb. Art sauntered out with a handle of Skyy vodka, and she was relieved he wasn't exiting at a running pace. He opened the door and leaned over for a kiss before settling in. Reaching into his jacket pocket, he pulled out a pack of Reese's, handing it to her.

"Got you these." He smiled.

"Bought or stole?" she asked, taking them. A pack of Reeses wasn't enough to warrant a run if he paid for the vodka.

"Does it matter?" He gave a nervous chuckle.

He was criminally thoughtful, and she had trouble untangling the two.

He connected his phone. "I've been playing this on repeat, waiting for when I saw you."

Blink-182's "I Miss You" drifted through the speakers.

"I miss you, and I'm so sorrrrry," he drawled in a serenade.

Her lips involuntarily twitched upward. She didn't know how the hell to have these sweet moments with him now when she would be breaking his heart later.

He rested his hand on her thigh, and a warmth crept up her body. She'd been sure that she would break up with him when she saw him. But, he softened her at every corner: the candy, the singing, the heat of his touch.

"I missed you so much." His eyes were clear and apologetic, but it wouldn't last.

It never did.

She was a mess of emotions. Replaying the dinner with her parents and the crushing weight of their repulsion of her choices. Then there was Weston. It felt fucking cruel to be the one digging the dagger into someone's heart. Now, Weston was gone, and while she thought she would be relieved, she was hollow. He deserved it, but he was also right. Art was bad for her.

"You look beautiful." Art's voice seeped in.

"Thank you." The words came out small as her nerves faltered.

He tapped his fingers on her thigh aimlessly, the drummer tick impossible to suppress.

"Should we go somewhere to talk?" he suggested.

She could do it. Rip off the band-aid. Pulling up to a dead

end on a street near the beach, she turned off the car. The horizon was empty, the faint sound of waves in the distance.

Her heart thumped. She was exhausted by excuses and empty promises. Dark hair framed his face and those turquoise blue eyes; he was still the most beautiful thing she'd ever had.

His fingers stopped tapping, and he held her gaze. He reached over the center console, his fingers crawling up her skirt. She didn't stop him, all her nerves lost as he studied her reaction. He leaned closer, and the burning desire fogged her mind. As his fingers touched her underwear, desperate longing rippled throughout her.

It happened quickly. Too quick to do anything but give in. The passion was a glow stick snapping. It cracked wide open, and once it glowed, there was no way to turn it off. Her love and desire for him drowned out logic.

She crossed over the center console. On Art's lap, straddling him, her fingers pushed through his long, dark hair, and his breath against her skin, raising millions of goosebumps. He shifted underneath her to unzip his pants, and she pulled off her black lace panties, tossing them to the floor.

He grabbed her hips, pulling her onto him. He let out a deep breath and brushed a loose curl back. She kissed him hard. Full of passion and anger and all the other emotions she could never hold on to. His energy shifted from sweet to an electric force. All the air had been sucked out of the car. It was the two of them. Art and Amelia. The way she craved.

She pressed her palm against the cold window to steady herself as they moved together. Even after they were done, they kissed until they were breathless. When they disconnected, and Amelia was back in her seat, Art reached down and handed her the panties.

"Next time, skip these altogether." He grinned devilishly, but there wouldn't be a next time.

The heat was now replaced with guilt. It changed nothing. The sex wasn't what was wrong with them. It had never been. Just the same, it wasn't enough to fix everything else. She pushed the shame away. There would be plenty of time to feel it after she had broken up with him.

She pulled her underwear up, then started the ignition. Her eyes were trained on the road as she navigated toward the apartment.

"You know I love you, right?" There was a nervousness to his tone that hadn't existed minutes ago when he was inside of her.

"Yes." She turned at the stop sign.

"No matter what happens, I need you to know I love you."

She glanced at him. "We'll talk about it later, okay?"

He closed his lips in submission and nodded.

She parallel parked a block from the apartment. "I'll meet you inside, okay?" she asked.

He hesitated.

She gave a practiced smile. "Have to freshen up."

He kissed her forehead, then walked toward the apartment, gripping the bottle of vodka.

It was the sweet kiss that played with her heart. She could chalk up the last-minute rendezvous to the undeniable chemistry. But it was the way his lips pressed against her temple, asking nothing in return, that unleashed the butterflies in her stomach. Those butterflies were harder to kill.

CHAPTER THIRTY-NINE

Top 40 music overflowed from the apartment into the complex, reminiscent of the Fourth of July party. Inside, red and gold streamers hung from the ceiling, and balloons littered the floor. Jake, the Honey Cat singer, was upside down doing a keg stand in the kitchen, with Max holding his legs. When Max helped him upright, Jake raised his fists triumphantly, and people around clapped and cheered.

She surveyed the apartment for Art or Madisson, but the place was packed. There were classmates she hadn't seen since graduation in June, neighbors in the complex she recognized but hadn't spoken to, and people she couldn't place at all.

"Hey girl, I heard L.A. was a blast!" Reyna said, wrapping Amelia in a hug and tilting her in her arms.

"Yeah," Amelia said quizzically, releasing her. Madisson must not have told her about how things ended. But that was Madisson, putting their friendship above any drama. "Are you excited for school?"

"So excited!" The smell of tequila wafted from Reyna's lips.

"I'm excited for you." She was glad Madisson had a friend at school.

Popping over to them, Madisson squealed, "You're here!" and wrapped Amelia in a hug.

"Sorry, I didn't help decorate." Amelia eyed the banners with Reyna and Madisson's names coated in glitter.

"Honestly, I wouldn't have wanted you here with him anyway," Madisson said as she laughed low.

Reyna blinked a couple of times, then gave a lazy smile. "I think I'm going to sit down."

"Let me know if you need anything." Madisson squeezed Reyna's hand. Reyna nodded and headed for the couch.

"I'm going to break up with him tonight," Amelia said in a hushed voice.

"That's the right thing to do," Madisson whispered back. "In the meantime, have a drink with me? We have Madisson Mojitios!"

"I'll take six," Amelia joked.

They made their way through the throngs of guests into an empty corner of the kitchen. Madisson's version of the mojito lacked the mint leaf and was scooped from a punch bowl, but Amelia would have taken anything— a little something to take the edge off before her impending conversation.

"Oh, another guest! Let me say hello." Madisson beelined to a girl they had graduated with.

Amelia lingered in the kitchen. She drank half her cup, then refilled it. At Art's height, it was strange she hadn't seen him yet.

She was headed for the living room when the high school linebacker intercepted her.

"Hey, I haven't seen you in forever!" he said.

"Not since graduation night," she smiled politely back, her eyes scanning past him.

"Is Weston here?" he tried to follow her eyesight.

"No, he's already on his way to MIT."

"So you're free then?" He leaned his block-shaped head closer to her.

"What?" She pulled back. It was strange that no one from high school knew Art existed, yet they stood in his apartment. "I've got to go," she said, pushing past him.

Art's Skyy bottle was on the living room table, half of it gone. Proof he had slipped by her.

Her eyes fell to Evan and Logan, the guitarists from Honey Cat, leaning against the wall next to the window. They would know where Art was. She made her way over to them, shoving around a large man.

"Where's Art?" she asked, skipping the pleasantries.

They exchanged a look.

"What?" she asked.

"I don't think Art wants to be found right now," Evan said, taking a sip of his beer.

"What the fuck is that supposed to mean?" she asked.

Logan looked past her.

"Logan?" she asked.

Evan and Amelia both stared at him.

"Listen, he was with some blonde chick outside, but that was like half an hour ago," Logan answered. "You're not going to do anything crazy, right?"

Crazy? Oh, she could be crazy.

"Is he cheating on me?" she spat.

"This isn't our place," Evan said with a belittling smirk.

"What the fuck, Evan?" Logan asked. He turned to Amelia, "He's not cheating. It's uh." His voice dropped. "Heroin."

The air knocked her lungs. Art had never done heroin. Not unless he lied about it on their first date or did it sometime between then and now.

She searched for a clue. Their conversation earlier was

weird. She reached to recall exactly what he had said. *No matter what happens, I need you to know I love you.*

She should have known there was more to it than their fight. There was always more to it.

She pivoted on her heels, throat tight. She had to find him.

Outside, there were clusters of people. Panic, tangled with the alcohol, heated in her chest. She spun in circles.

Groups of men, groups of women, groups intermixed. But no Art.

She stormed back inside, brushing by Max.

"Hey, hey." He grabbed her arm. "What's going on?"

"I can't find Art," she said. "Can I have this?" She grabbed Max's drink without waiting for permission and took a swig.

She laughed bitterly at the memory that the taste drummed up. "Fucking Fireball." She handed it back to him. Panic pounded in her head.

"Amelia." Max said, a layer of concern in his voice.

"What?" Amelia snapped. She needed to find Art.

Max ran his tongue over his lip ring.

She paused. "If you know something you have to tell me." Her voice cracked. All of these people were willing to cover for Art when they should have helped her find him.

Max inclined his head towards Art's room.

It was obvious, but he was *never* in there. She marched over and turned the doorknob.

It was locked.

Pounding her fist against the wood, she yelled, "Get out!"

She waited, straining to hear against the beat of the party.

When it didn't open, she continued to slam her fists against the door.

Fucking mojitos and cinnamon whiskey. Fucking Art.

The door remained closed, and anger dissolved into sadness.

Sliding her back against the door, she pressed her cheek to the cool wood.

"Art, please?" Her words were weak.

There was no response, and so she sat, half-heartedly knocking her fist against the barrier between them.

Her tears had dried by the time the door creaked open.

Amelia scrambled to her feet. Art exited first with a skinny blonde trailing behind him. Even without an introduction, she knew her. Sky. He had to get the fucking Skyy Vodka cause his work friend Sky couldn't get it her damn self. The memory came back to haunt her.

She couldn't breathe. She had to get out of the apartment. Shoving past people, she exited the apartment and into the courtyard.

"I'm sorry," he tried, trailing a few steps behind her.

"Heroin?" She pivoted to face him. She couldn't even feel the chill of the night, heat rising in her chest.

His eyes darted around the people in the courtyard. His voice was low. "I'm not going to lie to you."

"Not lying," she took a deep breath, "doesn't mean you're being honest. None of this is honest."

She stared in animosity into the eyes of the boy who told her two months ago, 'fuck no to needles.'

Shaking her head, she regretted the alcohol. It was impossible to think straight, her eyes watering.

"Show me where," she demanded.

"Why does it matter?" He stood straighter.

She didn't answer him.

He rolled up the sleeves of his black zip-up jacket. His wrist and forearm were bruised. Proof of where he poisoned himself with this drug that was never supposed to be an option. Her toes curled, thinking about him in his room, shooting up. While she was searching for him, he wasn't thinking of her at all.

First came the weed. That was supposed to be it. But then there was also the salvia, which was fine because it was also legal. The ecstasy was pure bliss. Nothing bad ever happened on ecstasy. Of course, everyone should try a real hallucinogen trip at least once. Or more than once, right? But that was the line. Except they snorted the lines of cocaine during Art's show. But this? Needles, it was never needles. They talked about this. They were firm about this one. How quickly it snowballed.

She pressed her fingertips against her forehead. The world was spinning, and the ache in her head had grown to an incessant pound.

Art's voice broke. "Amelia, I fucking hate my job. It's pathetic. I'm pathetic for being there. I'm a musician. I want to fucking play music- and I'm so good at it. Fuck, I have nothing except the music. I'm not sure I even have any real friends outside of you. Maybe Bryan and Max. But you're the best thing that ever happened to me. There is more shit from my past that I can't talk about. But I want to be with you. I want you to know everything."

Sky danced into the courtyard. Her lips were a light, lifeless pink. She wore a flowy dress that showed her bony shoulders and floated between groups.

Amelia saw red. There was no sympathy for Art, but less for her. Amelia narrowed her eyes at the girl who brought the heroin. Sky was oblivious, dancing around to another group.

"Amelia," Art choked. His face was streaked with tears.

Why did this drug make Sky dance and Art cry? Why did he always get fucked up and then end up crying to her with another godforsaken monologue?

Art stepped closer, still blubbering. He buried his head into her shoulder, and she let him. Stroking his hair back, she contemplated. How the fuck had this become her life?

Her body and heart were frozen. There was no point trying

to reason with Art. No point in trying to break up with him. For all she knew, on heroin, he would walk straight into the Pacific Ocean.

"Come inside with me," she finally said.

When she turned, he followed her, zombie-like, back inside.

The party had thinned. The music was lower as people huddled around on the floor. Evan and Logan shared a blunt on the side of the room. Amelia didn't see Madisson or Reyna, but the door to Max's room was closed. The three might have traded the party for the solitude.

Amelia pulled a blue quilt from Art's room and brought it to the couch. She didn't want to be in the room where the heroin was or inflate the stupid air mattress.

Art sat beside her on the couch, his head in his hands as he sniffled.

"Lie down," she instructed, rubbing his back.

He listened. He always listened to her after. If only he could learn to listen to her before he went and fucked things up.

She pulled the blanket over them and cradled his head in her lap, brushing back his tangled hair until he dozed off. If he were asleep, he wouldn't be any trouble. The party slowed around them, and the noise gradually faded.

When everyone had left, she situated herself behind him. Folding her arms around his stomach, she leaned her cheek against the warmth of his back. Her tears dampen his shirt. Knowing it would be the last time she held him broke her chest wide open.

Maybe this love was like a drug itself: all-encompassing, fleeting, and destructive.

CHAPTER FORTY

A groan slipped through Amelia's lips as her eyes squinted open. Art's back was against her chest, pressing her into the couch. There was a subtle throb in her head, warning of the hangover to come.

All of the horrible memories from the night before came flooding back. Gripping the back of the couch, she slid herself out from behind Art without waking him.

His chest rose and fell, and his dark hair pressed against his ears. His peaceful moments and his chaotic fuckups were impossible to balance. She spent the whole summer pretending that the chaos didn't frighten her, that love absolved all his misgivings.

She tore her eyes away, tugging off the Honey Cat bracelet she had worn for two months straight, and leaving it on the table. She could no longer be his day one fan.

Amelia walked along the beach. The cold morning sand was welcome against her rough feet. The wound from the glass in her foot was slowly healing. At the edge of the salty water, there was a wave of relief. The ocean washed over her toes and nipped at her ankles. The tears against her cheeks were cold and salty, too. There was a quote she remembered. The cure for anything is salt water: sweat, tears, or the sea.

She listened to the waves' cadence as they ebbed and flowed. This would not be the last special thing. She had so much to look forward to. The waves would recede, but they would always wash out again. Circumstances would change, but she would have herself. She was the special thing, creating a beautiful life wherever she went.

Amelia had spent so much time at the beach this summer, yet this was her first morning visit. It was as if dawn had arrived to greet her next chapter. She savored her last visit of the summer to the sea, keeping her toes in the water until they were numb. Then she retraced her steps.

She passed by the businesses that were not yet open for the day. Thought of the unknowing participants in her people-watching game with Art. The people she passed when she was on drugs. The people who saw Max get arrested while Madisson fell apart.

Amelia was steady as she drove home. Art had shown her a new kind of love. He had seen her in a way that no one else had. He never had to get to know her; the connection was ingrained. She had wanted a summer of adventure, and he gave her everything she wanted. The problem was that he gave her the things she didn't want, too.

————

Back in her granny flat, Amelia packed the necessities into her two Burberry suitcases. She strode into the main house, leaving the suitcases at the bottom of the spiraled staircase. Upstairs, at the second door on the right, she knocked twice.

Lauren opened the door a minute later, rubbing her eyes.

"I'm ready to go," Amelia said. Her voice was soft and unsure.

"Where?" Lauren squinted. She ran a hand through her frizzy blonde hair.

"Europe. I'm packed."

She opened both her eyes and took Amelia in. "We'll have you booked in a few days. Are you okay?"

James appeared over his wife's shoulder in a plaid pajama set. He gave Amelia a once-over.

"No, she will leave now," he said. "She's ready."

There was an unspoken understanding. If she did not get on a plane now, something, or rather, someone, might change her mind.

"I'll find the flights. Let your sister know you're coming," James instructed.

"Shall we sit and have a cup of coffee?" Lauren asked with a yawn.

Amelia nodded and led the way down to the kitchen.

Lauren started up the espresso machine as Amelia dropped onto the stool at the counter.

"What happened?" Lauren asked over the sound of beans grinding.

"Art's got some issues that are too big for me."

Amelia braced herself for a snide comment. Instead, Lauren set a coffee cup in front of her and leaned across the counter. "I've done my best to keep things as easy as possible for you-"

"I know, Mom. I fucked it up," Amelia groaned.

"No." Lauren waited for Amelia to meet her eyes. "I do that because I know the world is unfair and life will have its storms. I want to make everything I can easy for you, because life will be hard enough on its own."

"You're not mad?" Amelia asked.

Lauren chuckled. "I'm not happy," she emphasized. "But no,

I'm not mad. You came home. You made the right decision. I've been here all along to help you. You just have to let me."

Amelia took a sip of her coffee and repeated her mom's words. She had made the right decision.

The trip took longer than it would have if she had adequately planned. The route made no sense, and it required four flights when it could have been completed in two. She slept on the plane, nursing her hangover from 30,000 feet in the air. She was stuck in a window seat in the middle of the plane instead of business class, but she was okay.

On her layover, she turned her phone off airplane mode, and the barrage of texts from Art came through.

ART

Where are you? Why is the bracelet here?

Amelia your phone is going to voicemail

What does this mean?

I am SO SORRY!!!! I know I fucked up. Please just talk to me.

I promise I won't ever touch anything like that again. I know it was a mistake. I can't explain why I did it but I never thought I would lose you.

You're my twin flame. I love you sooooooo much. Please just talk to me.

Madisson says you're in Italy???? She won't tell me anything else. Please say something.

Oh if you're on the plane you probably don't have service. Just call me after.

Her thumbs hovered over the keyboard, a pounding in her chest. Even from thousands of miles away, she knew she was breaking his heart, and by doing that, she was breaking her own. The pain felt on both sides of their twin flame love.

AMELIA

I love you, but I can't do this anymore. I'm so
sorry.

His response came immediately.

ART

Amelia no. I will never love anyone again. You're
the one for me. I will do whatever it takes to get
you back.

The message bubble started again, and she blocked his
number.

She couldn't let him keep going. He was so good at bringing
her back to him, and she couldn't let him do it anymore.

It was time to rebuild all that she had let be broken.

CHAPTER FORTY-ONE

Amelia tore off a piece of an everything croissant and buttered it. The day was light blue, with thin clouds stretching across the Italian sky. She and Georgina sat at a bistro table on a cobbled street. Italian and English voices blended in the background.

"So was Italy everything you thought it would be?" Georgina asked, taking a sip out of a tiny espresso cup.

"Could have used full-size cups of coffee."

Georgina laughed. "I guess it's time for us to both get back to the real world."

After spending three weeks together, they would be heading back to move Amelia into UCLA and for Georgina to figure out her postgraduate life.

"Are you seeing anyone when we get back?" Georgina ventured carefully.

"Madisson will be over to help me pack. Weston's already in Cambridge, but I emailed him an apology. I was really harsh over dinner." He'd been quick to respond and planned a lunch over Thanksgiving break at Lillian's Cafe, their favorite. She was glad to have another chance at their friendship.

Georgina reached over and tore a piece off Amelia's croissant. She chewed and waited for her to continue.

Amelia's lips gathered in the corner. "No, I will not be seeing Art."

Madisson had relayed that Max kicked him out after the heroin. Art moved in with the Honey Cat singer, Jake.

Between the beginning of summer and the end, her love for Art smudged the line between right and wrong. Things had become clear with the distance. She didn't have to make the best out of the bad decisions. She could make the right ones.

"Then let's get you to UCLA."

Nerves fluttered in her stomach as she stood on the edge of her dream, but, for the most part, she was confident. Clouds danced in the sky, and her Italian manicure glittered in the reflection of the sun. With a deep breath, she understood. This would be the next special thing.

ACKNOWLEDGMENTS

The readers, thank you so much for picking up this first book of mine. It was a wild ride, and I hope you enjoyed every acceleration, high, and drop. If you loved this book, it would mean the world if you reviewed it and recommended it to a friend.

My husband, for letting me live in the fictional world and for being the epitome of a partner and a father, and for sharing your big brain and letting me bounce my word choices off of you. I love you.

My parents, who encouraged me to write this story. I never felt any judgment, only pride, and it's because of your support that I had the confidence to put this story to paper and share it with the world.

Claire, for being with me every step of the way. Thank you for helping me navigate the storytelling and the business side. Thank you for every walk in ten degrees where we talked through marketing, plot points, and the grand vision of interconnected stand-alones. You have been the closest person to me in this process, and it has meant the world to me.

Tami, the first person I trusted with the first six chapters. You validated that my writing and the story, with a bit of refinement, would be a good book. Thank you for a lifetime of honesty.

Layla, for helping me with initial edits and character building. Then again, for being my sounding board for the cover design, and finally for moderating the launch of this book. You're the best.

Lala, for creating the perfect band logo and being an overall inspiration.

To my fabulous beta readers: Kelly, Claire, Megan, Layla, and Amber. Each of you brought something unique to help shape Amelia's journey. I am forever grateful.

Jhandi, for encouraging me to indie-publish this masterpiece. I wasn't certain what I wanted to do, and your belief that I could not only do this as an indie but do it better than trying to be traditionally published was everything.

Meg Rosenthal, I feel so lucky to have found you as my editor. You believed in Amelia and Art's story and the vision. From your genius guidance and constant hype girling, this book is the very best it can be.

Hot Girls Who Write, the community that has shaped my writing journey. You have been the biggest cheerleaders, resource sharers, and inspirations.

The baristas at CDA Coffee Company, for letting me linger in the back while writing, and for being people I look forward to seeing. Special shoutout to Molly, Taylor, and Tay!

ABOUT THE AUTHOR

Alyssa K. Burns is a journalist and author. She earned her Bachelor of Arts in Communication from California State University, East Bay, and her Master of Business Administration from California State University, San Marcos. An elder emo, iced coffee enthusiast, and wife and mother, Alyssa enjoys dancing in the kitchen and creating messy fiction.

AlyssaKBurns.com

www.ingramcontent.com/pod-product-compliance
Lightning Source LLC
Chambersburg PA
CBHW050030120726
47903CB00006B/1976